Keeper of My Soul

Keeper of My Soul

Keshia Dawn

www.urbanchristianonline.net

Urban Books, LLC
97 N18th Street
Wyandanch, NY 11798

ISBN 13: 978-1-60162-665-3
ISBN 10: 1-60162-665-7

First Mass Market Printing June 2014
First Trade Paperback Printing January 2011
Printed in the United States of America

10 9 8 7 6 5 4 3 2 1

Distributed by Kensington Publishing Corp.
Submit Wholesale Orders to:
Kensington Publishing Corp.
C/O Penguin Group (USA) Inc.
Attention: Order Processing
405 Murray Hill Parkway
East Rutherford, NJ 07073-2316
Phone: 1-800-526-0275
Fax: 1-800-227-9604

Keeper of My Soul

Keshia Dawn

Other Books by Keshia Dawn

By the Grace of God
His Grace, His Mercy

Stories Appearing in Anthologies

"Stroke of Purpose" (*The Triumph of My Soul*)
"Baby Boy" (*Bended Knees*)

Follow Keshia Dawn:

www.KeshiaDawnWrites.com
Facebook: KeshiaDawn
Twitter: THEKeshiaDawn

Dedication

To book clubs and Christian fiction readers
everywhere!

Thank you for the e-mails and the continuous
words of encouragement.

This one is for you. Enjoy.

Prologue

The sky split down the middle, pouring rain from the seams as he pulled out of his driveway. Headed toward the highway in order to leave Houston, the nonstop rain seemed to follow Keithe for the entirety of the four-hour drive into Dallas. The gray clouds that followed seemed to promise no let up anytime soon.

For the past twenty-four hours, Keithe had had an ongoing battle within himself to find the courage to do what was right. Against doctor's orders, Keithe fought for the gumption to get into one of his vehicles, his Porsche, and start on his journey that would finally set him free. Each time, it was Michelle and the love he had for her that halted his steps. But today was different. She had finally pushed him to his limits.

Michelle, his wife of fifteen years, had betrayed him in ways that he couldn't believe someone would do. With all the cheating, the lying, and manipulating she had done, through all of that turmoil, he had made up his mind to stand right by her side, regardless. Not just because she was a socialite, a respected judge in the community, but because he had made vows to her that he had actually taken to heart. After fifteen years of a rocky-road marriage, it all seemed to be in vain.

Driving, Keithe replayed the scene in his head of the last moments of what he was sure to be the end of his marriage. Reaching over to the passenger's seat, Keithe dug around in his medicine bag. Retrieving his daily seizure medication he'd been taking for the last five years, Keithe hoped his meds were able to calm the jitters, ward off the onset of a seizure he felt deep in his body. No matter what, he had to go.

He couldn't think of another way the entire scenario could have gone. He wondered if he should have just spent the rest of his life ducking and dodging, blinding himself about his wife's mishaps, as she had, but he knew he couldn't. Years had already gone by without him really considering himself, thanks to his ever-loving wife and her ability to persuade him with her gift for gab. The years full of denial that had passed were long enough to make him feel as if he'd wasted an eternity.

Not one time had he messed up, and if he had, she would have shot him down, making him believe his correspondence with another to be the ultimate marriage betrayal. But no, he stayed. And what did he get in return? The scene that had taken place in front of his home earlier that morning.

Screaming at the top of her lungs while standing on their wet and cold lawn, Michelle had made it known that she wouldn't forgive him if he left the house.

"Whatever," he had roared back, allowing the then drizzling rain to seep onto his bald head. Standing toe-to-toe with his wife in front of their million-dollar home, Keithe felt daggers in his back as he turned to continue a wide-legged stride toward his prized vehicle: his Porsche. Just because she loathed the car he had bought himself for his fortieth birthday, he made sure he loved it.

Just when he'd thought he was in the clear to leave for his route to work, once more, and relieve himself from the rain that had started to sprint from the full clouds, the fists she had balled to her sides were put to use. Michelle, almost fifty-five years old, used her physically fit ability to run and jump on her husband's back, landing punches anywhere they would stay. Keithe, like many times before, had to pry and push her off his body and restrain her from doing any more damage. He didn't care for another argument or another fight. Enough was enough.

"Enough, Michelle," Keithe had let slip through his lips without the parting of his capped and pearly white teeth. Looking down at his wife, who had landed violently on the wet ground, Keithe fought the urge to help her up and make it all better. Her hatred had finally reached into his heart and furnished him a rite of passage to give her a taste of her own medicine.

The demands of who, why, when, and where were way too much for him to get into, especially when he'd gotten information that let him know Michelle definitely hadn't been who she had claimed to be. For all the questions she had for him, he had once had the same for her. There had been fifteen years' worth of unanswered questions as to why he wasn't enough for her, or why she wouldn't love him the way he loved her. Today had changed everything.

"Michelle, you've brought more men to our bed than I care to imagine. Should I remind you?" He had taken a step forward with his foot landing in a grassy, muddy puddle. With splats of residue landing on her silky apparel, Michelle struggled to rise from her wet seat and rid herself of Keithe's presence.

What Keshia Dawn's writing peers have to say . . .

"There are dozens of young talented authors on the scene, but few have the talent, charisma, and potential as Keshia. I am confident that she will be a consistent force to be reckoned with in this literary game for years to come."
—Brian W. Smith, bestselling author of the novels
   Beater;
   Nina's Got A Secret;
   and *Mama's Lies-Daddy's Pain*

"Keshia Dawn is able to do more than write. She is able to tell a story; whether short or novel length, Ms. Dawn brings life into every page."
—Elissa Gabrielle, literary entrepreneur and publisher with Peace In The Storm Publishing Company

"From *His Grace, His Mercy* to *Keeper of My Soul*, Christian Fiction Author Keshia Dawn is definitely on a purposeful mission of sharing God's word through powerful fiction prose!"
—Fon James, author, life coach, and speaker

Acknowledgments

Thank you is what I continue to say to God for His ability to show Himself through my writing. For my personal growth, I'm in awe of what God can do. And in being obedient to His word, He has released books from me that have been ministry for others. Thank you, God, for your son Jesus.

My family has been continuously by my side through my writing, sometimes giving me ideas and inspiration to spin out words like a spider's web. Elder Donald and Fannie P. Sauls (the P is for priceless), I'm grateful for you and thank you for being good to my Chayse. She loves her Pawpaw and Nana! My sister, Fanasha, you are a rock wrapped in all the love you are now sharing with Baby Kayden. Thank you for making me an auntie, and finally bringing a son into Daddy's life. You are a great wife and mother. Oh, and sister! Continue to allow God to point you in the direction He would have you to go, love you bunches. Li'l sister, Angel, I pray God's blessings as you start off your twenties with a bang. Stay with God throughout your college years and roll into adulthood with God's manual tucked tight. Can't wait to see how God is going to move in you. Love you bunches.

Baby Chayse, who is so not a baby anymore, you have definitely been here before. You remind me so much of me, and that's a good thing, LOL. You inspire me to be all I can be (even past age thirty) so that I can show by example how you can do and be anything you set your mind to. President maybe?

Too many family and friends to name, but you all know who you are! Especially everyone who celebrated *His Grace, His Mercy* with me at Brooklyns in Dallas. Love you, guys!

The literary world can be full of friends (I don't worry about the foes). Through that, loyalty is not lost. Fon James for continuing to be the best literary buddy an author friend can have. Being a life coach looks good on you! Thank you for allowing God to speak "realness" into my life. Let's keep 'er going!

I'm ever thankful for Urban Christian and their approach to stand out in a world where so many are lost. Christian fiction is not just entertainment, but it's a ministry that surpasses drama. It's an example of how to deal with issues with God leading. Joylynn, thank you for staying the course and pushing us authors to seek God for the words that will become permanent. Blessings.

I hope *Keeper of My Soul* blesses you. If so, drop me a line and let me know. If not, drop me a line and let me know. It's all in love.

Blessings,
Keshia Dawn
www.KeshiaDawnWrites.com

When he had reached for his wallet, Keithe's shoulders eased of the tension, but it was replaced by heartbreak. The faxed paperwork, which was folded enough times to make a home for itself, was his weapon. Michelle's eyes landing on the paper caused enough embarrassment to make her turn and hurry back toward their home.

The piece of crinkled paper that lay in his wallet housed creases of his disbelief. More than twenty times in the few hours since he'd owned the results, Keithe had opened and refolded the test results his doctor had faxed over to him after he'd given him the details over the phone. The results told of his wife's latest tryst. The latest scum must have been his clone twin, because from where he was standing, Keithe had inherited the same residue: an inherited pile of gonorrhea he was sure Michelle forgot to tell him about.

Deciding to keep the paperwork would come in handy for a time such as this. If he couldn't forget, he surely didn't want his wife to forget how she had given him a disease that someone else had let her borrow.

"Crazy self!" Cutting his verbal fight short, Keithe then headed toward his car, making sure she didn't come back at him before he made it to his black-on-black Porsche.

When he pulled out of their driveway, Keithe was soaking wet, with fresh scars on his arms and hands on top of the ones that had barely healed. He could see Michelle standing under the threshold of the entrance door with her arms folded across her chest. In her damaged silk champagne-colored outfit, she stood without tears, but with a glare that once burned holes right through to his heart.

"That's right, get out of here," is what he thought she might have said if he hadn't sped off so quickly. Instead, her longest finger was the wave that sent him gliding over the puddles on their street.

Keithe made his way to the office but his mind just wandered back to his homelife. Half the day had passed before he realized his body was there but his mind was still on the other side of town. He left with no real sought out plan. He just knew he had to get away.

The forced, almost four-hour drive allowed him to think back on his life and how he had spent it. Wasted. Yes, he was the number-one sought-after attorney, living in the lap of luxury, but he was just as depressed as a homeless person would be. Instead of being penniless, he had no happiness.

Coasting on the highway, re-familiarizing himself with Dallas's surroundings, Keithe retrieved his BlackBerry from his holster. Scrolling to a text that he had gotten hours ago, he was glad he'd gotten the information, because he hadn't a clue exactly where he would land while in Dallas. Nighttime had greeted him as he proceeded into the live city, and just as they had been along the route there, the thunderstorms were treacherous. Nevertheless, it wouldn't stop Keithe's quest to go into the part of town he felt he should have already been familiar with. Tapping the brakes, Keithe slowed his vehicle. He hoped the rain would let up just a bit in order for him to make out the name of the apartments he needed to venture to.

Easing along the almost flooded streets of North Dallas, his heart suddenly ached as he thought about the situation at hand. He prayed for acceptance and wished he had made up in his mind a day earlier, a year earlier, for that matter. All he ever wanted to do was live right and be right, wanting to have a family and be the husband and father God had wanted him to be: the same type of man his father had been to him and his mother. But it never happened, and with Michelle, it never would.

"Found it," Keithe announced to himself as he inched his way into the upscale apartment complex. Excited about the possibility of resting without argument, Keithe drove further into the crowded complex.

With pressure added to the gas pedal from his size-fourteen Cole Haan shoe, Keithe looked down toward his gadget-filled console in search for the defrost mechanism. One push turned the contraption on. Just before Keithe placed his eyes back on the narrow pathway, he searched once again for the button to lower the force of the breeze. Studying the space a little longer than he should have, Keithe raised his eyes to see the windshield clearing, but not before his vehicle made contact with something other than the road.

"Oh my God!" was all Keithe had enough time to shout before hitting the brakes. The hard braking forced his face into the windshield, but even with the short daze and blood trickling down his face, Keithe was concerned with the object he'd hit.

With the rain clobbering his sporty ride, he struggled to remove his six foot frame from the car to check the seriousness of the accident. It was dark and rainy, and the image of a human, maybe even an animal, was what came to mind first. As Keithe made his way to the front bumper, he found nothing. The dark of night and the rain meshed; Keithe, without thought, got on his hands and knees to see what had gotten stuck under his vehicle.

It only took a tenth of a second for Keithe to find his breath that had lodged itself in his chest. Saturated with rain, but no longer feeling any effects, he pulled himself up as fast as he could.

"Oh my God," his voice rang out, the second time in less than ten minutes. "Oh, God, oh, God, oh, God," he cried out as he made his way back into his car and reversed. "Somebody help me!" Before he could gain energy to start his search for help, the pressure built up from a seizure in waiting caused him to black out while his body jumped against the steering wheel.

CHAPTER 1

Stoney

"Stoney, g'on out yonder and get me a switch from that tree. I'm fed up wit'cha, girl." Grandma Susie was ready to make a promise of her threats. "G'on now."

Walking as slowly as her bony legs would tote her through the screen door, Stoney hesitated as she teetered under the threshold. "But I didn't even do nothing," the seven-year-old mumbled under her breath. "I just don't want no medicine, that's all."

"Wha'cha say, gal?" Grandma Susie positioned her big hands on either side of the rocking chair's armrests, hoping to show Stoney that there was no playing. "Don't make me come out there and get it myself."

Once her bare feet landed on the porch, Stoney looked back at her grandmother and snatched her head back around as fast as she could. Knowing her grandmother couldn't see her facial expression, Stoney stuck out her tongue and wrapped it in the corner of her mouth, which was her only comeback.

This would be the third whooping she'd gotten in one week, all because she didn't want to take medication that Grandma Susie said she didn't have a choice but to take. Grandma Susie said, "If I gotta take some medicine, so do you." Every time Stoney drank the bottled purple stuff, she didn't like the way it made her eyes look at things. She'd heard Grandma Susie tell her old lady friends that giving Stoney medicine was the best way to get her to sleep, hushed up, or to sit down somewhere. As far as Stoney was concerned, she didn't want to do any of the above.

Finally moving forward in Grandma Susie's mission for her to get self-destruction ammo, Stoney stood in front of the only thing besides medicine that she hated: the switch tree.

With the house she lived in with Grandma Susie behind her, Stoney looked to her left and watched her friends scatter off on the hidden trail. To her right was the alley that would take her toward town. Peeping over her shoulder, Stoney took off toward the alley, hoping her plan to run away led her right into the arms of her mother: someone she had never laid eyes on.

"So are you down? Hello? Earth to Stoney." Vicky snapped repeatedly in her coworker's face.

"Uh, huh? Oh, girl." Stoney sat up straight at her desk. Lost in the recap of her youth, Stoney broke loose from thoughts of one of her runaway attempts.

"No can do, Vicky the Vixen," Stoney joked around with her coworker and friend who had been pressuring her all afternoon to have cocktails after work. Remembering that she held a tablet of medication in her left hand, Stoney reached for her bottled water to wash down the pale capsule. "When are you going to give up? If I don't boogie, you know I don't guzzle." Stoney stared at her friend before her frequent eye flutter took over. When Vicky's own eyes began to water while looking at Stoney's repeated eye jerking, Stoney paid no mind, and continued her reasoning on why happy hour was out. "Drinking is for the birds. Plus, hanging around you already has me acting thrown off. What you trying to do, get me locked up?"

"Uh-uh. Chunked is more like it. I feel ya, though." Vicky shared a laugh with her younger counterpart. "You're doing the right thing." Easing seriousness into the conversation, a short and vibrant Victoria really did admire Stoney for being young and making God the head of her life. Totally.

Knowing Stoney had been raised by her grandmother, Vicky could argue with some of the old-fogy ideas that her young friend had about individuals and the world itself, but she respected the twenty-one-year-old for at least giving her life to God and sticking with it. She just wished Stoney would take her advice and lose the coffee-colored stockings and sandals.

"Girl, keep doing what you doing," Vicky halfway chanted. "By the time I was your age, I had twenty-one painted on my forehead and all I wanted was for the bartender to keep mixing and pouring. No small talk please." She hunched her broad shoulders and turned her face, giving an Academy Award example of her story. When she saw Stoney give her a questioning start, Vicky announced, "Oh, that was months before I knew I was pregnant. By the time I was twenty-five, I had sobered up and was pregnant with my third child." Vicky let out a weakened sigh, thinking that in her thirty years she had experienced a lifetime.

Getting up from her desk, Stoney shook her head about Vicky's comment. "You are a mess," Stoney said in her nasally tone. "Anyway. I have choir rehearsal and I'm teaching a new song tonight," she shared as she filed away patient charts for the doctor she worked for.

"Brother Mike is letting us borrow space in his home since new bleachers are being put in the choir's stand. You know he got that *bad* house everybody been talking about. I sho' can't miss tonight. You sure you don't want to come?" Stoney sang to her girlfriend. "I keep telling you he got the sweets for you."

"Hmm. That's nice," Vicky responded, and then silenced herself. Vicky had had a major crush on Brother Mike since she started going to Bethel Sanctuary five years earlier. Recently she had made her move, jumped the gun, and acted on her feelings before knowing all she needed to know about Brother Mike. There was no way she would let on to Stoney, who was still considered fairly new to the church, that she had been all up and through Brother Mike's new home. And she surely wasn't going to let on that the fling they had had flung. He may have been sweet, but on her, she figured, he wasn't.

"Girl, well, let me run and meet up with the girls. You know li'l Risha Coleman from church charging me by the hour now for keeping my kids." With the "no she ain't" expression on Stoney's face, Vicky knew she couldn't believe it either. "Yeah, girl. I know. Okay. Well, I'm out of here. I'll see you at church on Sunday if I don't see you tomorrow."

"Cool. See ya." Stoney gave her friend a quick hug and waved her out of the office. Glad that she was finally close to someone who was more like a big sister than just a friend, Stoney allowed her smile to linger longer than usual.

Not used to having any female friends back home, Stoney thought about what Grandma Susie would say if she'd known that Stoney had let someone in her personal life. That was just something people shouldn't do, as Grandma Susie always said. *"People just nosey and want to be in your business."*

"Aw, Grandma Susie." Stoney snickered to herself upon reminiscing on her grandmother's words. "Vicky is different. I finally got a friend."

When she first moved to Dallas, Stoney became one of the smartest female students at the most expensive private university in town. That's where she met Vicky, who had given her the heads-up about an open position at the optometrist's office. Their initial meeting at a scholarship banquet ignited a quick friendship.

A student herself, Vicky had defied odds like no other, getting a two-year degree and fighting tooth and nail to get accepted into the prestigious school. She had set out to prove that having three kids out of wedlock didn't automatically label her doomed. "Just don't try it," was always her retort, once she tooted her horn about breaking the odds of statistics. Finishing up her interning at the doctor's office, it wouldn't be long before Vicky had her own white jacket with her name embroidered on it.

Along with providing a job, Vicky befriended Stoney even more when she invited her to church. Since then, a year earlier, Stoney had been attending Bethel and had even joined the choir. No sooner than that, she had been voted the choir's assistant director, right under Brother Mike.

Now at the age of twenty-one and two years after her grandmother passed away, Grandma Susie's death had left Stoney alone in a town where their family came in the form of her grandmother's friends. Being alone until she moved to Dallas, Stoney had to grow up quickly and make decisions for herself. She hadn't even thought about packing and moving in with friends, who she knew could turn into foes overnight. She just kept her job as a cashier at the Brookshires in Greenville, Texas, and paid bills as they came in. With the small planked house long since paid off, Stoney didn't have to worry about the roof over her head. If it weren't for her move to Dallas, no doubt she'd have resided in the house she grew up in.

Raised under her grandmother's lax care, Stoney learned at a young age to pay bills, cook, and clean a house, along with saving for a rainy day. On top of that, her grandmother inadvertently instilled in her the importance of an education, and drilled in even more how important it was to plan for the future. The only thing she didn't teach her was how to heal from the past.

Over the years growing up in her grandmother's care, it was a rare occasion when Stoney could bring up her biological mother or ask questions pertaining to why she wasn't being raised by this mystery woman. On one of those good days, Stoney could hear Grandma Susie say, "Your mama loved you, but I guess the timing wasn't right. She was angry about lots of stuff." But if she caught her grandma on a hot, fan-in-the-window type of day, the conversation was always, "She just selfish. Always was and always will be." And for asking, Grandma Susie would lay into Stoney, telling her, "Stop being so disrespectful. You act like you ungrateful I took ya in or something." With all of that, Stoney never knew when she would get the truth. But it was all too late now. Passing away in her sleep at age eighty, her grandmother didn't have a chance to give her history to go on so that her future wouldn't be repeated. That was her main reason for the move to Dallas: to find her own past.

Being born and raised in Greenville, Texas, for most folk, meant that all roads led to the closest big city. That was only one of the reasons Stoney followed suit. With the leftover money from the insurance policy, Stoney found herself an efficiency right smack dab in the middle of Dallas and called it home. Her other reason for moving to Dallas was that she planned to scout out her birth mother. Being that she only had a picture to go on, she had to go back to the drawing board on more than one occasion. Nevertheless, the one thing she wasn't going to do was give up hope.

Finished earlier than she thought she would be, Stoney scribbled something on a prescription pad and rushed out of the office. Standing in the hallway, waiting for the elevator to arrive, Stoney wished it would arrive sooner than later. One of the young doctors always made it his duty to try to escort her out of the building to her car. Besides being embarrassed about driving her grandmother's older-than-thou Ford Escort, Stoney hated that Dr. Connor flirted with her every chance he could.

The chime of the elevator's arrival sounded off. As soon as her heels touched the glossed wood of the compact room, Stoney repeatedly pushed the "close" button.

"Hold the elevator, please," Dr. Connor yelled.

"Dang it," Stoney grunted. Sweeping her bangs off of her rectangular eyeglasses and giving them their signature push up off of her nose, Stoney stood up straight and tried to look as serious as possible. Vicky had told her that to get someone out of her face, someone she was not at all interested in, looking serious would always do the trick. But to Stoney, Dr. Connor was in a league all his own.

"Hi there, Stoney," a lean and toffee-colored Dr. Connor spoke as he entered the elevator. With his white jacket draped across his arm, he stood not too far away from Stoney.

"Hi, Dr. Connor." Stoney kept it short while trying to keep the sweet out of it. Seeing him, she suddenly regretted taking her khaki jacket off so soon. Her new off-white camisole she had chosen to wear under her jacket left her cleavage screaming for cover. When Dr. Connor pushed the button for the first floor, Stoney was relieved. Exhaling, she then pushed "G" for the garage, and silently thanked God she wouldn't have to be bothered with his advances today.

Right as the elevator started to move downward and Stoney thought she was home free, Dr. Connor, being the overachiever he was, the good doctor, changed his mind.

"Oh, you're parked in the garage today? I'll just ride down with you," he offered without question.

"No!" Stoney yelled before she knew the venom that had come out of her mouth. She lowered her voice. "I mean, you don't have to do that."

"Nonsense. I can just take the stairs back up," he suggested.

It wasn't that he was a bad-looking man, or that he came off as a stalker. It was just the mere thought of what Grandma Susie had told her about his kind.

"Folks who got it easy will see a young gal like you and think they can do what they want to. If ya smart, you'd getcha all the education you can and then take a pick of the man you want. Don't be no man's flunkie."

With those words embedded in her heart, Stoney only knew what her grandma had told her. As far as she knew, it was the truth. Some may have continued to call her country, and that was all right by her. One thing she didn't want to be called was dumb. Better safe than sorry was all she knew to be.

"Got any plans for the weekend?" he asked as the doors opened. Single with no children, the twenty-nine-year-old Dr. Connor had taken a liking to the well-developed and smart (now twenty-one-year-old) college student.

"You know me, just church and hanging with other young people at the church." She thought if she often referred to herself as a young lady rather than a woman, he'd back off. So far he hadn't bought into it.

She could wear all the skirts—long ones, short ones, pleated ones, or A-line ones—it wouldn't matter. Stoney couldn't hide the body that made her age appear to be on the other side of twenty-five rather than next door to twenty. Cornbread fed took a new meaning with Stoney.

After the elevator's doors opened, Stoney took off walking at a faster pace to Old Crusty, while Dr. Connor reminded Stoney of an earlier conversation.

"You know, you really should consider the surgery. If your eyes are giving you problems like they are and your eye prescription is as fluctuating as it is, it seems to be necessary," he recommended in his expertise. Taking her keys from her hands, Dr. Connor did Stoney the unwanted favor of unlocking her door. "Plus it's free. You can't get any better than that. That's one of the perks of working for doctors: free health insurance."

With her inability to control her blinking for the moment, Stoney gave a gentle, polite smile that housed full lips. Nodding in agreement instead of reminding him that she didn't have anyone to care for her after the surgery, Stoney eased her body closer to her old standby car.

"You have beautiful eyes, Stoney, and I'd like to see them more often without your glasses."

Her uncontrolled and rapid blinking had been a reaction from medications she'd started taking as a teenager. Not bothering to mention it to him, Stoney tried not to acknowledge him at any level. Retracting her keys from his hand once he'd unlocked the door, Stoney moved closer toward the driver's door. After easing inside, and with the door shut, she threw him a fake wave and blew out the breath she'd been holding in. Through gritted teeth Stoney blew out steamed breath.

Making her entrance onto the smooth-flowing Central Expressway, Stoney drove while reminiscing about her new life. She hadn't dated at all while being in Dallas. As a matter of fact, she had never dated. Grandma Susie had made sure of that.

In high school, when young girls were painting toes, doing hair, getting ears pierced, and eager to turn sixteen—the age their parents were dreading but at which they had agreed to allow them to have boyfriends—Stoney wasn't able to participate. Grandma Susie had made it very clear that Jesus, church, and school were all the boyfriends Stoney needed.

For the last year since Stoney had made Dallas her home, she hadn't found anyone who interested her, nor was she really looking. Grandma Susie may have been dead, but her spirit still lived very much in Stoney's thoughts.

As she drove, tears ran down Stoney's face as she allowed her mind to focus on being motherless and not knowing who would remind her when it was okay to date, kiss, or marry. If there was anything she hated, it was not knowing.

Driving in the big city, each chance she got Stoney glanced at the picture she had taped on her dashboard. Inadvertently it allowed her to wallow in self-pity. Stoney told herself that keeping the only picture she had of her mother was for the just-in-case moments. Just in case she ran across someone she thought could be her mother, Stoney wanted the proof close by.

It hurt in a different spot in her heart, not having a mother around and not knowing if she was dead or alive. At times she felt that if she knew her mother was dead, seeing a grave or something, it would bring closure to her burdened heart.

All Grandma Susie could tell Stoney about her mother was that the woman had dropped

Stoney off within two weeks of her birth. She had brought Stoney to Greenville from Lord knew where, with the best baby clothing, the most expensive baby furniture, and Pampers galore. Stoney's mother didn't leave a birth certificate, social security card, or anything that would link them. It was even up to Grandma Susie to name her as she had. When asked about her name years later, Grandma said exactly what Stoney had figured: *"Ya mama had such a stony heart, girl, I couldn't see ya being named anything else."*

Only God had slowed down the process of the pain of not having a mother or a father. But being alone in a city where girls frequently shopped the malls with their mothers, Stoney's heart often pained as if she were a kid again.

Staring one last time at the picture of her mother, MaeShell, Stoney parked her car in front of Brother Mike's mini-mansion. When she got out of her vehicle, Stoney dusted invisible particles onto the ground, knowing he would give her a once-over. It made her laugh how attentive Brother Mike was about her hair, clothing, or anything having to do with fashion. Always saying how he liked "his girls" to look nice, Stoney thought he'd make someone a good husband one day, and couldn't for the life of her understand why Vicky was so against being friends with him.

After adding her khaki jacket back to complete her Anne Klein outfit, the very one that Brother Mike had picked out when he accompanied her on a shopping trip, Stoney retrieved her songbook folder and purse, and headed toward the door.

It wasn't until she had reached the front door and looked back that she realized she must have been the first to arrive, being that no other cars were parked out front. Wanting to reverse her steps and sit in the car until someone else drove up, Brother Mike, one of her new best friends, opened the door with a smile.

"Hey, Stoney. Come on in. Ugh." He threw his hands up to his mouth. "Is that a ponytail, or better yet, *was* it?" He escorted her through the threshold and locked the door behind them. Knowing that Brother Mike had never made a move on her, and was more like a brother than friend, Stoney tried her best to relax, but couldn't stop thinking how Grandma Susie had told her about putting herself in certain predicaments. Without realizing he had asked how she was doing, Stoney asked, "Am I the first to arrive?"

"Um, yeah." By the way Stoney's brow furrowed, and the way she had been clutching her belongings, Brother Mike could tell she was a bit uptight. Having had plenty conversations with

Stoney, he knew that Stoney held her guard up high, and he respected that, especially since she seemed to be in the world all alone. "Look, I'm going to go finish putting the finishing touches on the appetizers and beverages. If you don't mind, make yourself at home, and please answer the door if anyone shows up." Not waiting for a response from a dazed Stoney, Brother Mike pushed up the sleeves of his button-down, crisp canary yellow Ralph Lauren shirt, and headed toward his kitchen area.

Taking minor steps around the front part of a home almost the size of their medium-sized church, Stoney didn't know where to begin. It seemed as though the windows made up the majority of the house, but not in an awkward way. Peering out one of the windows a distance away, she could see the sparkle of a ground pool through the wood blinds. Hot as the early May's day was, and with having no working air conditioner in her car, Stoney wondered how the water would feel against her warm skin. As soon as she thought about swimming, she then remembered a swimsuit would have to be worn in order to do so.

"Don't worry, I'm not even thinking about it," she spoke confidently, as if she were talking to someone in the very room with her. Grandma Susie, to be exact.

In the living area, Stoney walked a short distance to a curio housing family photos. Unlike Grandma Susie's house, where she had pictures covering the majority of the walls with nails and tacks, Brother Mike had the type of taste that Stoney hoped to be able to one day afford. Taking a glance at the walls and seeing no photos tacked on, Stoney remembered when she moved out of Grandma Susie's house. In order to have it rented, she had no choice but to take extra money off the deposit for the sake of all the holes punched through the paint. When she thought about her own place, her studio apartment, Stoney realized that she hadn't thought about complementing her space with art, pictures, or anything, for the fear of messing up her apartment complex's property. Stoney made a mental note to ask Brother Mike to help her with that portion of her life as well.

"You need anything?" Brother Mike called out from behind a wall. Not knowing which direction he had disappeared to, Stoney responded with uncertainty.

"Ah, yeah. A cup of water, please," she replied.

Through the glass, there were pictures of him and his fraternity brothers that were displayed in the medium brown elevated curio. Other photos of the choir members and different conferences they had attended over the years were crowded in as well. Stoney even recognized herself in some of the newer photos. As she glanced at another photo of Brother Mike and who seemed to be a friend, she wondered if he was another frat brother, and out of nowhere wondered if the nameless fellow was single. Thinking he was a handsome something, Stoney's eyes glistened as she wondered if Brother Mike would even introduce her to someone special.

"Oh my goodness, Stoney." She scolded herself by slapping her mouth with her open hand. Feeling guilty about thinking that very thought, Stoney blinked her eyes shut and said a quick sinner's prayer. "Lord, forgive me for my sinful eye and my sinful thought. Amen."

As she kneeled down to focus on other photos, her lingering question about the guy's attached status was soon answered as she saw the same guy in a wedding photo with his bride.

My dear Jesus, I was pining for a married man, she prayed to herself, for fear of Brother Mike hearing about her disgusting sin.

That alone didn't stop Stoney from staring at the photo the best she could with it being housed behind glass. Overlooking her weakness, Stoney needed a closer look, especially at his wife since her face looked vaguely familiar. Just as she was about to open the curio, Brother Mike walked in with most of the choir members trailing him. Too wrapped up in her own hunt, Stoney never heard the chiming of the doorbell.

With her stare evident, Brother Mike welcomed a question from Stoney, once he trailed his eyes to where Stoney's gaze had been focused.

"You know him?" he asked with his chin almost landing on his chest. He handed her the water she had asked for.

Quickly standing erect from her crouched position, Stoney didn't dare try to pretend she wasn't interested. "Uh, no. She . . . Um, is he one of your friends?"

"Yeah. That's my frat brother. He lives in Houston, though. You know that's where I'm from, right? H-Town," Brother Mike barked as he put his curved hands around his mouth to make his chant louder. Everyone laughed.

"That's his, um, wife." He smiled and patted Stoney's shoulder as he started walking to where the others had gathered. "The wicked witch of the south if I shall say." He looked back at Stoney with an even bigger smile.

Looking more at the picture of Keithe, but not forgetting his bride, Stoney chose to hold the rest of her questions in until after she and Mike were alone.

CHAPTER 2

Keithe

He stood in one place the majority of the night while his wife made rounds kissing up and making herself seen throughout the party. If there was one thing he was tired of, it was being an arm piece, escort, and a friend with benefits.

Keithe was mad at himself, again, for even considering chaperoning his wife at another one of her shindigs that didn't do anything for him. For the ten times he'd go out on the town with her, she would accompany him to church only once. But still he tried to be the decent and caring husband.

Although they were in the same profession, Keithe couldn't care less about being on the social scene. Being a lawyer was all he had ever wanted to be ever since he could remember. It wasn't for the high-profile cases that often landed on his desk, nor the television spotlights he became a frequent guest on, but it was for what he could do for people: help them. Unlike his wife, who was, had been, and always would be about herself, Keithe was a sincere individual, whereas Michelle was downright selfish.

It had only been two weeks since he and Michelle had made up for the umpteenth time. Or rather, she had promised, sworn, and loved on him in order for him to forget her latest fiasco. But he had. Now he wished he hadn't.

The rumor he'd been hearing about her having yet another affair, with a judge in the same downtown building, stuck in his stomach as he had eaten lunch one day in a local deli. Just hearing her name released in a paralegal's conversation was sickening enough. Listening further about her being connected with someone she had said was like a son left Keithe hardly able to swallow what he had in his mouth. Throwing the remainder of his lunch away, Keithe decided to leave before more details were shared.

Never in his wildest dreams did he think loving a woman fifteen years his senior would leave him with as much of a headache, and heartache, as a teenager being dumped a week before prom. Still, Keithe tried. Even up until the very moment when all he wanted to do was leave.

After Keithe closed his eyes for a brief moment, let out a breath, and prayed, "Lord, give me the strength," he set his Cherry Coke on the nearest table and made his way to his wife. Standing in the middle of two men who seemed to be hanging on to Michelle's every word, she didn't realize Keithe was in her presence until they made eye contact.

"It's about time we head out, Michelle. It's almost midnight and Sunday school will be here before you know it." He slightly touched her elbow, hoping she would excuse herself from the disrespectful hounds. He really couldn't blame them, though, with the beauty his middle-aged wife possessed. Like most people, he wouldn't be surprised at all if they didn't even know Michelle was married. Sorta like the whole R. Kelly divorce. Married? Who knew?

With the muscles relaxed in her face, the naughty-by-nature, middle-aged woman shot Keithe a ferocious glare. "I'm not ready, *dear*." Twirling around, allowing her husband to continue his chat with her backside, Michelle stuffed her sparkling clutch under her opposite arm while trying to pull up her strapless, sequined dress. Not spilling an ounce of her liquor of choice, Michelle downed a shot, threw her head back, and pretended to talk about her profession.

"But we already made plans for church, Michelle." He closed in to her ear. Figuring he would have to pull out all the stops before she did, Keithe switched to her other two-carat-filled ear and whispered, "Remember the deal. Church." All he received in return was a hard and stale huff.

He figured Michelle felt empowered since she had been in the driver's seat for the night. Soon enough, if she didn't follow his lead, she'd see just how much he really cared.

For the last ten years Michelle had been acting more on a mother level than his wife. The respect that was missing from her as his spouse was worrying his own forty-year-old psyche, making his graying specks more evident, which resulted in his cutting his mane. Loving Michelle was breaking his heart and that too was becoming more noticeable.

At age twenty-five, Keithe had thought the world of Michelle when he first laid eyes on her as she spoke at one of his law school lectures. From the day at brunch when Keithe was brave enough to ask her out, he had been a wide-nosed, eager, and young graduating law student, believing the dreams Michelle had spoken to him.

After a few months of courting and her wining and dining him, Keithe believed Michelle really

cared for him. When she started speaking about
the circles she could involve him in, the more
he fell for her. No doubt at all, if it weren't for
Michelle pulling strings for him, he wouldn't be
where he was career wise.

Just as Michelle snatched her elbow away,
Keithe silently counted backward from ten and
walked away. The last thing he wanted was a
scene, which for Michelle was always a great
drunken adventure.

"That's it," Keithe mumbled under tightened
lips. Hard steps led him toward the exit. Only
once did he stop, and that was when he arrived in
front of the valet's booth. Standing and waiting,
Keithe silently scolded himself about not hiring a
driver for the evening. He hadn't partially because
Michelle had begged him to just let her drive
them.

For the last five years, he'd been under a
doctor's order: no driving. His stressful marriage
and career had taken a toll on his body, produc-
ing violent grand mal seizures that came out of
left field. Tonight he didn't care. It would just be
the chance he'd have to take.

When he turned around to kill time, still waiting for Michelle's Jaguar to arrive, he caught his
sour reflection in the glassed pane.

Decked out in his owned, never rented, tuxedo, Keithe couldn't understand what it was about him that wasn't enough for Michelle. Beyond being a dark chocolate kind of handsome, and having deep, chiseled eyes that were only for her, Keithe was a respectful and loving husband. Head over heels in love with Michelle, Keithe had never wanted to stray as she had. He'd never wanted to make her hurt as she had made him time and time again. Even when Keithe wanted children and knew that being a father was a blessing beyond compare but she didn't, he still loved her through it all.

God-fearing, a praying man who seemed to be what all the women on the talk shows said they wanted was exactly what Keithe was. Sunday after Sunday, sitting as a deacon in the front pew, he had to fight off women and their advances. Anywhere he went, for that matter. Even at a gathering at his wife's expense.

"Hope you're having a good evening," Chasity, the young, white court reporter who worked out of Michelle's courtroom, spoke toward his reflection, then to him. "Are you leaving? Is the judge on her way down?" She checked to see if she had a few moments to push up on him, as she frequently did.

"Yes, I'm leaving." He took a step forward to add space between the two. Peering around her as she took the same amount of steps he did, still looking out for the judge, Chasity wasn't giving up that easily.

With a quick look down at her plummeting bust line, Chasity spoke to Keithe, hoping that he caught her drift. "Hmm. Well, I'm waiting for a cab, but if the judge is not going with you, maybe I can catch a quick ride. If you know what I mean." Her eyes told her truth.

Squeezing his own eyes shut, Keithe, for a brief moment, thought what it would be like to actually take Chasity up on her offer. Or any woman who had called, texted, or boldly walked up to him, offering her services. Shaking his thoughts clear, Keithe believed, "As a man thinketh in his heart, so is he."

Taking the key from the valet driver, Keithe added another tip to the driver on top of the one he'd given when he and Michelle first arrived. Without so much as a slight glance, Keithe got into the leather-interior car and sped toward his home.

On the ride away from the live and bright downtown Houston's nightlife, a world he didn't care to be a part of, Keithe wondered why he still cared. Better yet, why he still tried. His wife wasn't a team player, and she definitely wasn't planning on switching her Patrón for Communion anytime soon. But then again, he knew this, and if he were being honest with himself, he had known it from their very beginning.

At age twenty-five, when he married the then forty-year-old Michelle, he had been on the same level as she had. He partied, tossed them back, and hung out late with her. But through it all he still made it to church service; he still made time for the Lord. *Then* it didn't matter that she had stayed home from church and never made promises to attend. But now he was forty and more than just saved. He had a relationship with God and wanted to share that experience with his wife. Something that Michelle obviously wasn't trying to do.

Pulling to the back of their gorgeously landscaped stucco house with a four-car garage in the rear, Keithe shut off the engine and just sat. "Thank you for the ride home, Jesus." He openly thanked God for allowing him to make it home safely. "Jesus, take the wheel." He just couldn't help but do the reenactment of the very funny Mr. Brown from Tyler Perry's movies. "Oowee." He stretched to get out of the driver's side.

He already knew the devil's hell Michelle would bring when she got home, and almost opted to undo his bow tie and sleep in the car. The thought of them arguing almost made him crank the car once more and go to the nearest five-star hotel. Instead, he thought about all the hard work he did on a daily basis to try to make his marriage work. He knew he had as much right to their bed as she did. Her ignorance would just have to go ignored as far as he was concerned.

As soon as he made his way into their abode with the lofty ceiling, Keithe did exactly as he felt. Instead of doing what Michelle would have recommended, taking clothes off in the bedroom only, Keithe undressed as he made his way through the winding house. Shoes here, pants there, shirt elsewhere. When it was all said and done, Keithe only had his socks on to show evidence of his no longer caring what Michelle thought.

By the time his head hit his favorite pillow, the only rhythm in the marriage bed was that of his pounding headache. The BC powder, a crushed aspirin concoction, was the only thing that helped him doze to sleep. Twelve-thirty was the time the loyal and dependable husband fell asleep. Without any sound of an alarm, two twenty-eight in the morning was the time he awoke to his wife's drunken stupor.

"How dare you! How dare you leave *me*. In my own car! Do you know how humiliating that was for me?" Michelle barged into their master suite and turned on every light within her reach.

Her energy level never letting up, she raced around to where Keithe had been in deep sleep and snatched the 1000-thread-count sheet from his body.

"Did you hear me, Keithe?" she slurred from her drunken lips. "Keithe, are you listening to me?" She stood over his head. "Not to mention, sir, you aren't supposed to be driving. What, you want to kill yourself on my watch?"

"Michelle, leave me alone," Keithe managed to get out with one stale and heavy breath. "I have to get up and be at church early." Thinking for only a millisecond, Keithe didn't give her a second thought as he pulled his goose-down pillow over his head to ward off the light.

"I don't give a—" Right as Michelle was about to make an obscene gesture toward the house of God, Keithe flew from the bed with only his boxers on, and stood in her face.

"I don't have the time or the energy for this or you. But you, you better watch your mouth when you talk about something that means so much to me." He tried his best to be civil.

"More than me, right?" Michelle already knew the answer, but wanted him to say it. "I said, more than me?" she asked as her husband grabbed his pillow and walked away from her.

Stopping to make himself clear to his disrespectful, yet breathtakingly beautiful, wife, Keithe fought the urge to hold her once more.

"Yes. Much more than you, Michelle. Now if you'll excuse me."

CHAPTER 3

Michelle

Michelle was no longer sleeping off her drunken trance, but still couldn't bring herself to get out of the comfortable and curve-catching silk queen-sized bed. When she glanced at the open space on her husband's side of the bed, she figured Keithe had long ago dressed and called his driver to take him to church. Then she abruptly remembered that he had removed himself from their shared quarters after the entrance she had made. Screaming at the top of her lungs hadn't guaranteed herself or Keithe a good night's rest. At first thinking maybe he would sleep the day through, knowing her husband all too well, Michelle knew he would att-end church regardless.

Looking over at the decorative and antique wall clock, she saw that a quarter to twelve was the time. That alone meant that Keithe wouldn't be home for another two hours or so. Unless he went to brunch with his church friends, Michelle could account for her husband's whereabouts. Silly as it sounded, Michelle thought maybe that was the problem: him being too good to be true. Sucking her teeth, Michelle couldn't believe her marriage had turned out to be a bland, dull, and uneventful inconvenience.

Some days she didn't know if it was just Keithe or if it was the fact that he was such a holy roller. If she had known he would turn out to be so into God, she would have rethought the path in marrying him. Then again, she couldn't tell the future. All she had known was that the young man she had encountered loved being around her, and wanted and needed her. Now things were different.

It wasn't like she didn't believe in God. Michelle prayed and had even tried the "God thing" before. She just didn't dwell on the hope that some man she didn't know could possibly help her through all of her woes. If that were the case, why so many years ago did she have so much heartache? Why didn't He make her crooked paths straight as He seemed to do for everyone else? Loving men had always seemed to have a damaging effect on her, and loving Him, God, didn't seem to differ. So by the time Keithe came into her life, Michelle figured she'd go for someone she could train.

She had moved from Dallas to Houston, and started a new life where no one knew her or would question her about her life's circumstances. Doing lectures at colleges throughout Houston's metropolitan area, at age forty, she spotted Keithe's eye for her and didn't deny the attraction she, too, had for him.

A brief courtship led to the nuptials she'd always felt were way overdue for her. With the previous love of her life, Marcus Jeffries, Michelle felt her chances were swept away once he rekindled with a high school love, Gracie Gregory. Being bitter over that only led her to one day fall in love with a friend of his. Ultimately, what she thought she and Ky had didn't last either. But then again, all the issues seemed to fall in her lap. With the entire ruckus she had caused both men, she knew why she had to revamp, leave Dallas, and start fresh. That was what she thought she had then found with Keithe: a new, fresh beginning.

In the early stages of their marriage, life was good. He with his dark skin and height of a NBA point guard complemented her "pretty girl" appeal. Never once cutting her hair, Dark & Lovely creased her hairline then as it did now.

Easing out of bed, Michelle walked over to the mantle that graced their fireplace in their room, and stared at their wedding photo. Deep down

Michelle knew that Keithe was a great man and a hard worker, and that he really did love her. All the issues their marriage had inherited had no doubt come from her.

"What is your problem?" she asked her own photo. "You're not getting any younger, woman. Why are you still trying to push him away, knowing he is not going anywhere?" she questioned herself. But she knew the answer. There was no trust. She never really had any, and if she didn't make any real effort, she never would trust a soul.

That was just it. For ten of the fifteen years they'd been married, Keithe had stood by and let her get away with the ridiculous antics that she'd brought into their marriage. Cheating on him, lying to him, arguing, and even fighting him had become her way of affection.

At first he'd argued back, and even found himself physically pushing her harder than he wanted to, but he made a complete change. He turned 180 degrees and started going to church more, praying more, and reading the Bible more. There was something deep within her that wanted the same thing, but she just wouldn't let go of the stubborn ignorance that lodged itself in her. It was the same ignorance she had held for her own mother. When people didn't or couldn't do things in the fashion

Michelle saw fit, she closed down and veered the way she wanted.

With her latest 'do matted to her scalp, Michelle made her way into the hallway, en route to find some sort of breakfast. Before she could make it past her bedroom door, a yellow sticky note caught her eye. As the note was plastered to the floor, Michelle had to hold on to the door's frame to steady herself as she reached for it.

"Huh?" was all she could muster, and she had to make herself read Keithe's writing out loud to believe it for herself.

Going to Dallas for a quick getaway. Don't know when I'll be back.

It was all she could read before the churning of her stomach's alcoholic content made her turn around and head for the bedroom's private bathroom. With her head submerged into the toilet bowl, all Michelle could think about was the boldness of Keithe to pull such a stunt. Even with the tight grip she always claimed to have on Keithe, Michelle could see him pulling away from her. Never having to be on the other side, the side that Keithe stayed on, Michelle could hardly take not knowing what was going on in her husband's head.

She made it back into their bedroom and dialed the town car's phone. Michelle was even more in shock when the driver let her know that Keithe wasn't with him.

"Did you drop him somewhere?" she asked.

"No, ma'am. He cancelled Sunday service today and said that he was driving himself into Dallas." He gave her all the details that had been given to him.

Without even a thanks flown in the driver's direction, Michelle disconnected the call and sat on the side of the bed.

Like a ton of bricks falling from a decaying building, Michelle felt her world, once again, falling down around her. It was just like times before: same game, different man.

CHAPTER 4

Keithe

Once more, Keithe gave his praises to God for His traveling mercies. Pulling into the parking lot of Bethel Baptist, the calm and respectful gentleman glanced at his image in his rearview mirror. Doing so, without hesitation his thoughts went right back to Michelle. He was always asking why she grabbed for the rearview mirror when the driver's side visor was made for glances, and there he was doing the same thing. With a slight chuckle, his heart warmed as he thought of how he loved her so.

It was as if he could predict her next moves, and he wished she'd switch up her game at least some. A predictable man could just about always be disappointing. Running a cool hand over his bald head, Keithe knew by the days passing that he would have to either accept Michelle for who she was and take it as that, or leave her on a permanent basis, not just for a trip to Dallas as he had now done.

Getting out of the car, Keithe opened the back door of his Range Rover and retrieved his suit jacket. He had made it into Dallas around eight in the morning and gotten a room. No doubt his frat brother would coerce him into staying with him, but for at least an hour or so he had been in need of a place to rest his eyes. After he slept extra hard on the Marriott pillows, Keithe gathered his luggage and headed toward the church he always visited while in Dallas.

Right on time, he fell in line with the other parishioners gliding toward the doors of Bethel Baptist. Though he couldn't call out any names, faces he had known from prior years' visits recognized him as well and they said their hellos.

"Good morning, welcome to Bethel Baptist. Do you need a program, envelope, visitor's card?" a male usher offered Keithe as he walked through the threshold.

"Morning. Program and envelope, please. I'll pass on the visitor's card." Keithe nodded and accepted the colorful items the seasoned usher gave him. "Thanks."

Never one to need attention or be the center of it, Keithe slid his tall and lean body into the pew that housed fewer people. Standing from his quick sit, Keithe halfway raised his chocolate and pin-striped sapphire suit jacket from his seat. With a quick nod to his left, Keithe let out a "Morning," toward a woman who was more than giving him the eye.

With the bow of his head, Keithe took a moment before getting involved in the church activities, and whispered a prayer.

"Lord, once again thank you for traveling mercies. I pray that you remove self and dwell in my heart so that I may hear what thus says The Lord. Amen."

Peering around the church, Keithe didn't bother when he didn't immediately land his eyes on his frat brother, Mike. Knowing his friend was the lead choir director, Mike's place was, always had been, and always would be behind the organ.

"Good morning, Bethel." A busty woman who looked to be one of the mothers of the church assumed her duty of bringing attention to the front of the medium-sized room, while standing behind a podium that couldn't start to hide her rounded hips. "I said, good morning, church," she said again, wanting to get a better response, while her canary-colored hat bounced on her head.

"Good morning," Keithe said along with the members and other visitors who had all made their way into Sunday morning's service.

"We are now going to ask the praise team to come to the front and lead us in this morning's worship service. Let us give them a hand praise as they make their way up. Amen?" the buxom woman forced from the crowd.

"Amen," Keithe returned with raised eyebrows as he finally laid down the program that had been cramped in his hand.

"Good morning, church! If the Lord has blessed you, woke you up this morning, and has given you another chance to right the wrongs you've made, stand on your feet and help us praise Him!" a young lady Keithe had never seen at the church before yelled into the microphone. "I know I might be young, but I want to take it back old school this morning, saints. If you know it, sing it with me." She prepared the congregation before she sang, "Have you tried Jesus? He's all right." She gave the question and answered in song.

With the blessed sound of the young lady's voice filling the sanctuary, Keithe, like others around him, stood and embraced the entrance of the Holy Spirit in his heart. Tapping the linoleum floor with his feet (which were covered in $500-plus shoes), Keithe swayed back and forth between the sounds of the spirited jubilee.

"He's all right," Keithe sang back, enjoying himself in the Lord. For the moment, Keithe enriched himself in a place where no harm could be done to his heart, his feelings wouldn't be mangled, and his life was secure. When he went a step further and closed his eyes and raised his hands, Keithe made up his mind to praise his way through his circumstances.

In the midst of another four songs sung by the praise team, the fullness of the Lord came in and swept throughout the church. Before the Word had even gotten a chance to be taught in the morning service, people were already renewed in their souls.

One testimony was asked to be given, and, like racehorses, a man, and a woman with a ferocious feathered hot pink hat, battled to be first pick.

The lady won the spot. "Goodness and mercy have guided my way this morning. If it had not been"—she swayed her hands in front of her body, pausing for the effect—"for the Lord on my side, saints, where would I be?

"I give honor to the pastor and the first lady and all to whom honor is due. You all know I travel quite a ways to come to the church on a regular basis. Over highways and byways. Well, this morning an eighteen wheeler almost took the lives of me and my daughter. Being that there were only two lanes, I was in the left-hand lane, making my way around the truck. I know all about blind spots and how to drive around big trucks, being that my daddy is a big rig driver. I make it my purpose in getting away from being on the side of the truck." She threw out the explanation.

"But right as I got middle ways, the truck started to come over on my side. Remember I said I was on the left-hand side of a two-lane highway?" She looked around the church. "Well, most of that time, there was a guardrail there." She stopped for a short praise of "Hallelujah!" After four hard stomps to the church's carpeted aisle, she continued.

"Well, he came over on my side of the road, and all I had time enough to do was call on the name of Jesus. Just as I swerved off of the road, the guardrail was gone, and I was able to land in the grassy median. Hallelujah." She stopped to think of what could have been, might have been, if it had not been for being covered by the blood.

"I just want to thank the Lord for seeing me and my baby through, because you all could have gotten a bad report on this morning, but I know who Jesus is!" Mike finally made his way to the organ and gave the keys a hard hold. "He is a way maker." The deep tune penetrated. "A bad report shaker." Mike's fingers danced across the keyboard, bringing others to their feet, clapping along with the tune.

After the lady was able to dance in the spirit for a minute or two, she finally settled with a serene composure. "He can bring you out of anything! You all pray for my strength as I continue to grow in the will and the direction God so chooses for my life."

With the entire church band's ensemble collaborating, the praise going forth left people on their feet, praising the Lord right along with the sister with the testimony. Not in a rush to settle God's praise, hand clapping and foot stomping made a tune.

Keithe loved the praise going forth and joined right in until Mike cooled the organ keys down. Before long, the senior pastor of the church made his way to the pulpit, following protocol. Announcements, tithes, offerings, and A and B selections rendered from the choir readied the sermon for the day.

Trying his best to stay focused on the oration that Bethel's senior pastor began, Keithe fought to get his mind focused on the scripture at hand, but couldn't help glancing at the young woman who must have had the same problem as he had, as she was squinting over her glasses.

Although still true to his feelings for his wife, Keithe couldn't help but wonder who the young lady was who kept stealing glances at him from the front of the church. Ever since she had sat down from directing the choir, her full eyes had been one of the main attractions for him. Shaking his head, hoping that it would clear his mind so he could receive more of the Word, Keithe stared down at his Bible, searching for the passage.

"Scoot over," Keithe heard from a familiar voice just as he was about to re-read the scripture for clarification. Moving a foot over, Keithe rolled his eyes at Mike. "'Sup, dude? Why you didn't tell ya boy you were coming through?" Brother Mike whispered.

"I see *he* still talking in third person," Keithe joked around, whispering back at his friend as they did a silent brotherly handshake. "Aren't you supposed to be at the organ? Sounds like your pastor's getting ready to gun it."

Throwing a wave toward the pulpit, Mike rolled his eyes. "Anyway. Yeah, I just wanted to see what was up. You cool? What you doing here?"

"I'm chill. We'll talk about it after church. I'll be here for a few days." Keithe knew it was only because of his seizures, and doctor's recommendation, that he had the flexibility to take time off from work. He was allowed a lighter workload once his illness started getting the best of him.

With all of the ruckus he'd been going through with Michelle, there was no better time to relax than the present.

"That's what's up. We were just talking about you Friday night, looking over my pictures at the house," Mike nonchalantly said while peering around the church. "So this is how it feels to sit out here with you people. Hmm."

"Dude! Shut up." Keithe knew his friend to be outspoken and more than arrogant. It was always true what others said about the two: opposites attract. "Who else was talking about me?"

"Huh, oh. Stoney," Mike said as he pointed in her direction. Just as Mike looked up toward the front and laid eyes on her, Stoney was giving him the evil eye. "Oh snap, let me get back up there." Just as he was about to get up, Mike made sure Keithe would be staying with him. "You know I got you, right?"

"You know it," Keithe agreed as he slammed his knuckles toward his friend's awaiting fist.

Scooting back in his original spot, Keithe closed his Bible, and his eyes roamed toward the front of the church once more. Bypassing the pastor, who had been in full swing, Keithe's gaze landed right back at the lady he had been mesmerized with since service first started.

"Stoney," Keithe barely mumbled as he intertwined his fingers and placed them in his lap.

CHAPTER 5

Stoney

It took everything within Stoney to stay on beat at the beginning of service. While leading praise and worship, it wasn't until she was halfway through giving God praise that her eyes landed on him, far off in the back of the church. It was an unmistakable gut feeling that told Stoney what her mind wondered. *Is that him?* It was the raw realization that the photo she had become acquainted with at Brother Mike's home had become her reality. Nudging her sister in Christ, who was a part of praise and worship also, Stoney had her take over with the rest of the songs.

She couldn't believe it. She didn't know if God was working on her behalf or if it was a trick of the enemy. What Stoney did know was that she dared not give the enemy any victory. It had only been two days prior when her eyes had landed on him at Brother Mike's home. The face she had seen then had stayed in her mind the entire time they were at choir practice, and she had even dreamed about him that night. And the next night, for that matter. And, low and behold, here he was in Sunday morning's worship. Keithe, whatever his last name was, was at her church.

For a split second she almost forgot that his picture wasn't the only one that was in the photo. Halfheartedly wanting to see the wife in the physical as well, to get a closer look at the possible competition, Stoney didn't bother making her request for her presence known to the Lord. Sitting in the bleachers, Stoney twisted and turned and even stretched her neck to see if he had been accompanied by her, his wife. When there was no sight of Keithe's spouse, Stoney knew she had to pray extra hard.

Lord, you are going to have to help me through this. If this is a trick from the enemy, keep me, dear Lord, from his presence, Stoney prayed silently as she walked from the choir's stand after service.

After service, Stoney thought it was best for her to get as far away from the church as possible. Rounding the banister, she headed toward the exit.

"Stoney, don't even try it," Brother Mike called out to her.

Jumping from her name being called, Stoney stopped in her tracks.

Turning as slowly as possible, she put in a quick extra plea to the Lord for help. "Please, Lord, please, Lord, plea . . ." Opening her eyes and pushing her glasses back in place, Stoney held her lips closed tight.

"Girl, where are you running off to?" Brother Mike asked as he stepped closer to the shy twenty-one-year-old, leaving his guest behind. "I thought we were going to do brunch, lunch, or just eat a bunch of food?" Laughing at his own corny remark, Mike bypassed anything Stoney was thinking to come up with to say. "Anyway, girl, come on. Leave your car here and ride with me." He turned, almost bumping into Keithe.

"Oh. Keithe, I almost forgot you. This is Stoney, my assistant, more like a little sister. Stoney, this is Keithe, more like a brother . . . a long-lost brother who only comes to town when something is going wrong." Mike crunched his eyebrows toward Keithe, who was shyly scratching at his eyebrow. "Anyway, y'all come on."

"Nice to meet you, Stoney." Keithe spoke in a confident tone.

"Hi," was all Stoney could mutter as she found the floor with her pupils. The butterflies in her stomach must have launched toward her eyes.

Batting her eyes as if she were taking advantage of a flirtatious moment, Stoney, in her pointy Nicole pumps, led the way.

When she took off behind Mike, and bypassed Keithe, Stoney's eyes landed on Keithe holding out his hand. Figuring him to be the gentleman he seemed to be, Stoney thought she would just scream. When she felt his hand on the small of her back, she thought she'd just die.

Stopping in her tracks, Stoney held tight to her New International Version Bible and made her plea, which she knew wouldn't be easy to pull off with Mike. He never let her down on any level, and she hated to disappoint him, but today she had no choice.

"You know what? I think I'm going to pass. Really." Stoney took a step to the side in order for Keithe to make his way closer to her and Mike.

"What? Oh goodness. What is it? Because of Keithe?" Mike asked as if Keithe hadn't been standing there. "Girl, you better come on now. Keithe ain't nobody." He made a crazed "you know what I mean" face toward his friend, who just shook his head.

Halfway humiliated, and hoping her lighter-than-caramel complexion didn't give her away by turning a shade of red, Stoney squinted and looked over her glasses. Fumbling with the belt on the front of her wrap dress, Stoney thought of something to come up with.

"No. Not at all. I'm just going to go ahead and head home and study some more. I still need to digest . . . I mean, yeah, um. I had plans to study in order to be ready for my test this week. Finals are coming up." Staring down at her path to walk away, Stoney knew that Mike would lay into her thick later on, but for the time being, she didn't care. She just needed to get as far away from Keithe as she knew how to.

When no one moved, said a word, or even acted as though they would budge, Stoney took that as a sign to get moving.

"Uh-uh. You are for real, aren't you?" Brother Mike called out with one hand on his muscled hip. "Stoney, why would you break our routine? You know we do brunch every Sunday." He crossed his arms in front of his heaving chest hidden behind his off-white summer blazer.

Taking a step closer to the two, Keithe felt out of place. He even wondered if he should have kept his hotel room for his brief stay. "Look, if it's me, if I've intruded, please forgive me." He then turned his attention to Mike. "If you give me your key, I'll go ahead and head to your house so you guys can do your thing. I don't mean any harm, Stoney." Keithe turned back to Stoney with a weak, but bright, smile.

"You drove?" Mike broke the monotony with a worried question. When Keithe nodded, Mike said, "What's up with that? It better be on doctor's orders, too, man." Keeping in contact mainly through e-mails and text messages, Mike knew all too well Keithe's prescription for driving: don't.

He said my name. Stoney bit her bottom lip, still stuck on the fact that Keithe acknowledged her by name. Not wanting the visitor to feel inadequate, or as though she was Miss Prude of the Year, Stoney rethought her entire approach.

Stoney thought going to brunch with the two could actually be beneficial for her, especially when she really wanted—no, needed—to know more about Keithe. But she couldn't go. He was her first crush ever and she had no clue how to act in front of him.

"Oh. No, please." She paused. "It's fine. You're fine," she addressed a ready-to-depart Keithe. "I'd just rather you all go along and catch up. I really, really have lots of stuff to do, Mike." She hoped her friend would get the picture and forgive her this one time.

"You sure?" Keithe asked, raising his eyebrows to add depth to his question.

"I'm sure," Stoney answered as she turned toward the church's exit.

"Whatever you say," Mike mumbled, and resumed his walk in the opposite direction.

Hesitating in his own departure behind Mike, Keithe extended his hand toward Stoney. "It was nice meeting you, Stoney."

"Likewise," she oozed from her cotton-candy-glossed lips, and turned back toward Keithe. Placing her hand in Keithe's palm, Stoney knew she'd be repenting for thinking the thoughts she had. And for lying. She had no doubt she'd lose a dress size for all the fasting she'd have to partake in.

Picking at the roasted chicken she'd bought from a local chicken shack, Stoney hadn't been able to release her thoughts from Keithe's manly build. While sitting at her two-seat dining table, dazed and rocked, Stoney daydreamed and just wondered. She wondered how she could allow herself to get so caught up with one man in particular . . . and so soon. But deep down, she knew why. The fineness he possessed was deep enough. The thoughts lingering in her mind were more of a fulfillment of sorts.

After her meal, tired from an exciting afternoon, Stoney could do nothing but nap. Waking from the short energizer, Stoney sat in the middle of her bed, looking over schoolbooks with the pages staring back at her. The month of May had finally made its way into Dallas and the spring semester was just about over. Finals were the only things keeping her from enjoying the outside.

She couldn't believe how Keithe had waltzed into her life. There were too many things she'd thought of within the last five hours of leaving the two friends, and she couldn't believe it was all happening in her world.

Stoney had been plagued with thoughts of getting into Keithe's life and luck had just landed in her lap. There was no doubt in her mind that God had opened a door. Believing the Bible, Stoney was stuck on the "what my heart desires" part. Yes, she had fought the instinct that told her that God didn't like ugly. But as Mike had filled her in later that night, Keithe just existed in a marriage; he definitely wasn't living. Now she just needed to know which move to make next.

Right as she snapped her fingers, her cell phone rang.

"Hello?" she stated, still holding her snapped fingers closed. "This is she. Hey, Mike. Wassup, dude?" She looked around for her favorite candy.

"Oh nothing, gal," Mike joked. "Keithe felt bad for you not being able to hang out with me today and wanted to invite you to dinner tomorrow night. Of course, I'm choosing the restaurant since you still stuck on Dairy Queen."

Crossing her legs in the middle of her bed, Stoney popped a stick of licorice in her mouth and bit off a wad. "Raw, das tweet." She talked through a mouthful, doing the silent happy dance. Thinking she could brave the waters the second time around, Stoney was happy for the opportunity to be able to breathe in the same room as Keithe at least one more time.

"What? Girl, stop chewing that licorice and talk to a brother." Mike knew her all too well.

"I said, 'aw, that is sweet.' What time should I be there?"

Hearing his line beep, Brother Mike told Stoney to bring a change of clothes with her and to just come right over to his house after work. Hanging up the phone, Stoney stood in the middle of her bed and did the Funky Chicken.

A knot in her stomach caused her to suddenly kneel in the bed and hold her torso. Ever since she was a little girl, nerves that plagued her caused her to get a sick feeling. The pain that shot around like a loose pellet from a BB gun sent Stoney almost crawling to the restroom for her medication.

Grandma Susie had said it was ulcers from always worrying about not having a mama or daddy. Standing in her tiny restroom with a cup of water, Stoney reached for the bottled medication that still had her Grandma Susie's information on it. Thinking about being in Keithe's presence, Stoney almost forgot about the striking pain until a jolt caused her to kneel once more.

"Uh-oh." Stoney took a peek inside of the large orange bottle and saw the small amount of pills left. "Shoot. I forgot to call in the prescription," Stoney said aloud, popping two of the pills in her mouth. Stoney stood at the mirror, holding her side with her free hand. The pain she often felt was just the courage she needed in order to continue her fraudulent intake of Grandma Susie's medications. Working at a doctor's office gave her the negative confirmation to never wean herself from the daily doses.

She had long since fought and won against her guilty feeling of taking medications specifically ordered for her grandmother. Since it had been Grandma Susie who initially prompted Stoney to take pills in order to make her feel better, the young woman rolled with the punches. She figured her grandmother would want her to take care of herself. One way or the other.

Going back into the bedroom, Stoney found her cell phone lying on the dresser. She pressed the speed dial number that held the drugstore's number. Using the automated service, Stoney spent the next ten minutes refilling all five medications prescribed for her late grandmother.

CHAPTER 6

Michelle

At fifty-plus, Michelle was too grown to wish she were another way. All she knew was to hold the place she held and roll with the punches. To her, there would never be a clear understanding why she had received the hand she was dealt. She just knew to keep her guard up, her heart on loan, and to always be ready to cover her own costs.

With a full day come and gone and day two landing right on her forehead, Michelle couldn't believe she had actually spent two nights in her bed alone, only to awake with the sun beaming down on her head.

"What was the whole point?" she questioned herself about the skylight she had wanted so badly when their home was being built all those years ago. She just had to have it, and now she wished she had listened to her husband and the builders and maybe added it to her bathroom instead of bedroom. The way Michelle felt at the moment, she wished she had left it out all together.

"There has got to be something they can do about that," she muttered, rolling over in the bed in another drunken stupor. She didn't know when, but whenever her body had its energy restored later in the day, Michelle's top priority would definitely be to have someone come out and see what construction would have to be done to get rid of the hideous add-on. Even if she had to hang a sheet from the ceiling, Michelle was adamant about getting that thing covered up. It was either that or stop drinking, and the latter wasn't an option.

Without so much as getting out of the bed, Michelle reached over and picked up the cordless phone from her nightstand. She had told herself that she would give Keithe time to calm down and make his way home, but that was the same day he had left. As soon as she had found the sticky note on the floor, Michelle had gone into a rage and dialed his number, leaving voice mail messages, demanding he pick up immediately.

"How dare you leave town? First you run off and leave me at the party last night and now you leave town! Keithe, you'd better answer this phone, because, baby, it don't take nothing but that much," she had snapped, "to *make* you come home." The threat she had hoped would descend into his heart, manifest, and rush him home was out of the question. There was no call back. So now all she could do was to try once more.

"Keithe, it's been over a day and I haven't heard from you." She ushered her sensitive and drunken voice through the phone. "Honey, I really am worried about you. Please let me know if you are all right. Do you need your driver? You know your doctor's orders, Keithe." With her pleasantries not lasting long, Michelle's catty tone weaseled its way through. "Mike seems to *not* know where you are, when we all know you are right there at his house," she shouted into the phone. Having taken the morning off, out of court, Michelle had nothing better to do than concoct a plan of worry for Mike.

"When you two stop having boys' day out, please return my call." Hanging up, Michelle didn't care that she'd gone back on her word and started again with threats. Like some others, from the moment she had met Keithe's good friend Mike, she had made up her mind that he wouldn't be her cup of tea. He never sat well with her, and as far as she was concerned, he never would.

Finally sitting up in her bed and scooting herself to the edge of the queen-sized mattress, Michelle had no choice but to start her day. Slipping her feet into slippers that were as comfortable as her mattress, Michelle slid into the turquoise and brown bathroom.

Michelle's routine for the past fifteen years of marriage had vanished since Keithe's impromptu vacation. For years, morning after morning, day after day, Michelle would constantly remind her husband to put down the toilet seat. Since the day her husband had disappeared, Michelle had come into her very own sanctuary-styled room in their house and had nothing out of place. Toilet seat down, toothpaste in its rightful place, and face towels still neatly stacked.

"Ugh." The middle-aged socialite walked deeper into the restroom and loudly and violently sat on the toilet's cover, after slamming it shut. Resting her head in her hands, Michelle felt the material of her midnight blue silk scarf and snatched it off of her head. Throwing it to the floor, Michelle didn't want to give in to her feelings.

"Now what?" she said to nothing or no one in particular. With her mind racing, Michelle had already calculated the expenses of the divorce she felt was coming. Obviously it was coming, with Keithe showing how fed up he was by leaving town. Sitting and thinking, Michelle couldn't recall a time when Keithe had gone so far as to not even answer her phone calls. And now with him being in Dallas and around his ever-so-flamboyant friend, Mike, it was only a matter of time.

All because of her socializing. People talked, sometimes too much, about her business. And with that, word seemed to always make its way back to Keithe about her secret lifestyles, and her boyfriends. Like at the party, she couldn't help that she was the center of most people's attention. And if they happened to be males of the species, what could she do about it?

"It ain't like he really don't know anyway." She wanted to make herself believe that Keithe was and always had been okay with her philandering ways. "Ugh. Anyway, what he don't know won't hurt him," Michelle finally verbalized. "At least I'm not mindlessly flaunting around town with a man on my arm like some old bats I know." She really wished she could get herself to believe that her actions didn't affect her marriage.

Easing from the seat and making her way over to the tan and cream tiled shower stall, Michelle reached in with her right arm and turned the water on full blast. For the getaway she needed, Michelle made sure she left the temperature on hot. Placing herself in front of the mirror, Michelle knew it had been awhile since she had had a one-on-one with the woman in the mirror. It was something she always avoided, but for the sake of getting Keithe back under their roof, she psyched herself up. She had to think of something or someone who would bring him home. Even if it had to be the God he served.

"Oh, Michelle. You've done it this time." Reaching and turning the intercom's radio on, Michelle knew it was locked on the AM station Keithe frequently listened to. "What the heck," she announced as she placed her hands on the bathroom counter and just stood. Waiting for something to happen, Michelle just looked in the mirror at her made-to-believe-ageless, yet aging, face.

There was a tingle that rumbled in her gut and Michelle didn't have to think what it was. It was her truth. For the person she was always running from, Michelle knew the person she had become was just that. Someone she had put together.

She tried to do anything and everything she could to be different from others. She wanted to stand out. For that, she was criticized as trying to be too good or better than the rest. As a child raised in a small town where not too many people were striving to get out, Michelle's wants were always more than the home her mother barely made for her.

As soon as she walked the stage at the small town's high school graduation, Michelle ran as fast as she could and far as she could . . . or where her money would take her. She had gotten tired of being her mother's keeper. She no longer wanted to be there just because her mother needed and wanted her to be.

It wasn't long before Michelle realized that she and her mother didn't have what most everyone else had. Their measly things didn't mean anything once Michelle knew for herself that the world had more to offer. From then on, it didn't take long for the two to disagree on mostly everything.

With her father passing away when she was younger, and her mother not having the education or the gain in order to pull their small family further in life, Michelle's anger excelled. Angry about her mother's mission to do nothing but cry over spilled and spoiled milk, Michelle made up her mind what her future would look like.

Dallas was where she landed. In her early twenties, Michelle's real intentions were never to lose herself in school, or drift too far away from family back home. Her dreams kept her going.

To some people, the things she wanted and fought for may have been petty. But for all of the name-brand clothes she wasn't able to buy or wear as a young girl under her mother's strict rules, plus having no money in the bank, Michelle fought to reverse. From the peace of mind of starting over to "Michelle" from "MaeShell," she was nonstop. Leaving the name given to her by her mother, Michelle's goal was to leave everything behind.

While college drove her, scholarships prompted her, and internships to anywhere she wanted were her inspiration. By the time she had completed her undergrad at a university in the Dallas/Fort Worth metropolitan area, Michelle had evolved into a sophisticated mover and shaker. The world she had longed for from what the television shows had offered had finally become hers. Grad school and taking the bar weren't far behind. Once she'd accomplished these, Michelle set her mind for even greater things.

Michelle didn't actually mean to stay away from home, never visiting, or to actually forget her mother. But she knew her mother's friends would look after her and care about her well-being. What she couldn't understand was why her mother's illness had to hinder her. Why her mother's depression had to be her grief as well. Why she had to be a babysitter to her mother. And now, as if her life were teaching her a lesson, she had become a caretaker to her husband and his seizures.

A tear actually making its way onto her cheek caught a powder-free Michelle off guard. Afraid to allow herself to be vulnerable as she had so many times before with men, Michelle was adamant in winning her husband back, without losing who she was or who she had claimed to be. She had waited too long to get a husband, and there was no way she was giving up companionship that easily.

Wiping the fog from the mirror, Michelle swore toward her own reflection. "Keithe, I promise you, I am not going through any unnecessary mess with you." Looking down, Michelle whispered, only halfway believing herself. "I do love you . . . just not enough to lose me." Her voice gained strength.

Falling in love was for the birds, she'd told herself on too many other ventures. She'd stepped out on Keithe, but that was to cover her own feeling of falling in too deep, although she'd never let on to anyone her true feelings. She may have been married, but Keithe was still a man with his own mind. She never wanted to forget that. He could leave her at anytime, and that was all she thought about.

Too many times had she been left by the men she trusted, loved, and believed would be there for her. Too many times had she fallen in love in just enough time to be thrown away by the very man she'd given her heart to. For that, Michelle's skin grew extra tough.

Michelle wouldn't fight against the truth. She loved her husband. But all that letting go and letting God stuff wasn't something she was about to do. Just like she let her mother go, Michelle knew without a doubt, if it boiled down to it, she could do the same with Keithe.

CHAPTER 7

Keithe

Keithe had been in Dallas for two days and he hadn't spoken to Michelle even once. She had called and left messages on his cell as well as on Mike's home voice mail. Nonetheless, he had no enthusiasm for hearing her voice. If divorce was in the files for them, she'd certainly given him a good send-off: a headache that just wouldn't quit.

Lucky for him, he had a dear friend in Mike, and was grateful for the room he'd offered him. Meeting Stoney and being a part of the friendship she and Mike had made Keithe feel needed and wanted at the moment.

"So, what's the deal with Stoney? She seems like a cool kid." Keithe started off the conversation with a hand glide over the top of his stubbly bald head. The trio's Monday evening dinner left them scheduling a follow-up for the next day.

With an eyebrow raised toward the television, Mike's eyes slowly drifted in the direction of Keithe. Knowing all too well the moves Keithe used to make back in their college days, Mike knew for sure the glide placed on his friend's head meant something more.

"Um. Cute kid, huh?" Mike didn't let on his suspicious thoughts. Pulling at his goatee, which was longer than it had to be, Mike pushed himself up by his gold-toed socks and turned to his friend. With his elbows on his knees, Mike looked Keithe right in the face.

"What's up, Keithe? You've been here since Sunday morning and still haven't said why."

"What do you mean, man? I can't just come to visit my friend?" Keithe squinted his brown eyes, which were heavily layered with eyelashes, and acted as though the television program held his attention.

Picking up the remote, Mike clicked the small red button that made the HDTV screen crawl to black. "You know what I mean. Come on now. Your judge, I mean, your wife." They shared a quick laugh. "You know better than anyone, that lady is not about to let you out of her sight." Mike threw the remote on the cushion next to him and sat back.

Still holding on to his laughter, Keithe knew he couldn't keep anything from the sly, and always fly, Brother Mike.

"Yep. You got me there, bro. I don't know. Michelle just pushed me over the edge this time. She, ah . . ." Keithe thought it would be easier to share the embarrassing ordeal with his best friend, but it wasn't. "Man . . ."

"What's up? What's the deal, man?" Mike waited on the opposite sofa for his friend to spill the beans. "What'd she do *this* time?"

Nodding before he let it out, Keithe internally pumped himself up. "She cheated on me, man," he said, and then looked down into his lap, hoping he didn't have to go any further.

Pursing his lips and narrowing his eyes, all Mike needed to do to seal the deal was switch his head to the side and yell out, "Whatchoo talking about, Willis?" But he didn't. Mike quieted his thoughts and wondered what to say. Jerking his neck back, Mike shook his head.

"Go ahead." Keithe threw his non-calloused hands in the air, waiting for his friend's remark. "I told you so. Go ahead and give me all fifteen years' worth of 'I told you so's.'"

Almost choking on the words that replayed in his mind, those very words that his friend had trusted him with, there was no room for jokes in Mike's heart.

"Again? That's all I want to say, man. Again?" Mike had to catch himself from becoming too emotional. But with the new feeling he himself had longed for, a union, Mike couldn't keep his mouth shut. "That's not cool, Keithe. For real, though." He didn't want to allow his anger to surface to the utmost, but Mike couldn't help letting it out. "See, that's what I'm going to have to work on, dawg. That's what I'm talking about right there. Man be wanting to go to the next level, and then what? What's he suppose to do? Sit back and get hurt? Get burned? Not cool at all," Mike chopped.

Third person, Keithe thought. "Right. I mean. But that's just my situation, Mike. You can't label all marriages like mine. But you cool anyway." Keithe stood to stretch his legs, not wanting to get too deep into Mike's business. "Plus there really hadn't been any *real* evidence on the other assumptions." Keithe wanted to set the record straight. "But I did overhear about it this time. And man," he said, starting to pace the floor, "you should have seen her at this gala the other night. Her *colleagues,*" he said loosely, "were all over her." Not paying attention to Mike's change of expression, Keithe was in his own world.

"Your wife is on fiya, man. I'm just saying." Mike looked into his friend's eyes and shrugged.

"Oh, and don't think I'm letting you off the hook about questioning Stoney."

"So what you gonna do *this* time?" Mike asked. Regardless of how his friend tried to maintain the innocence of his wife, Mike, if he were a betting man, would declare Michelle had been made a pro on the cheating scene.

Raising his shoulders into a shrug, Keithe flipped his bottom lip and answered his friend. "I mean, marriage. Divorce? I don't know. I'm tired." He leaned even farther into the sofa's cushions.

"Yeah," Mike barely oozed from his lips.

Knowing he had a plethora of stuff to dish to Mike, Keithe didn't want to linger too long on the conversation that had to do with his erroneous marriage. "It's just another something I'll have to deal with with Michelle. Just pray for me, dude," Keithe asked his friend before he closed his eyes.

Wanting to be there for his friend, Mike knew that, sooner or later, tough love would have to overpower his words. No matter what, he'd have to let Keithe know that Michelle would be the death of him if he didn't get out of that marriage.

CHAPTER 8

Stoney

She arrived right around six o'clock, after work, on Mike's doorstep. Feeling perkier than usual, Stoney was excited to be able to hang out with Mike, and especially with Keithe. She'd called Vicky on her way over to Mike's abode and asked her if she wanted to tag along, but her friend, always finding something else to do, declined.

"Girl, I don't know why you don't want to be in the midst of Mike. He really likes you, Vicky," Stoney tried to persuade her dear friend.

"Chile, Mike ain't stuttin me. I don't know why you don't get it." She wanted so badly to give her opinion about why she and Mike would never be a couple, but thought it best to leave her beliefs to herself. Vicky thought there was something about Stoney being raised in the country that gave her the benefit of the doubt. Being raised in the city herself, Vicky knew how to watch her back as if her life depended upon it.

Hesitating, and not wanting to make her friend angry for no good reason, Stoney ceased the conversation. "Hmm. Oh well, I was just trying to help. Anyhoo. His best friend is down for a couple of days and we are all going to hang out and have dinner." Stoney bit her lip, wanting to share her crush.

"His best friend? A man? Ha." Vicky shook her head while holding her phone between her shoulder and ear. "Humph. I guess."

When Stoney pulled up to the house, she could hear in Vicky's voice that she was holding back something. Not wanting to keep Mike and Keithe waiting, Stoney ended the conversation and hoped her friend would open up to her later on.

"About time," Mike sassed when he opened the door after Stoney initially knocked. Already decked out in his white linen V-neck shirt and fitted jeans, Mike ushered Stoney inside. "Well, come on now. I'm hungry." He flamboyantly let out a comical growl.

Waiting in the wings, decked out in a crisp sky blue button-down shirt with the cuffs turned up, was Keithe. Stoney was thinking how lucky she was to be in the same room with the handsome man.

"Hi, Keithe," Stoney spoke, knowing that her grandmother would have belittled her manners if she hadn't spoken as she entered someone else's home.

"How's it going, Stoney?" Keithe gave her a friendly hug and peck on her cheek. Backing away from the entrance, Keithe made room for Stoney in her arrival.

"What took you so long?" Mike dragged behind Stoney, relieving her of the bags she carried.

Balancing herself better, Stoney continued to walk farther into the house as Mike made his way down the open hall. "Thanks, Mike," Stoney said. "That Dallas traffic, of course." She tried to walk so that her heels announced her presence on the ceramic floor, just as Mike had taught her to do. "And you know I had to sit still in the car after I took my medication. Didn't want to fall out on your lawn." She gave a quick giggle and the batting of her eyes started.

"Are you okay?" Keithe stopped fidgeting with his watch, and questioned Stoney after hearing about her medication.

"Huh?" Stoney was confused. "Yeah. I'm great, why do you ask?" She hadn't a clue that her routine could be labeled unique.

Scratching his temple and letting out a chuckle, Keithe wished he hadn't asked the question after the look Stoney gave him. Wishing Mike had been in the foyer instead of down the hall setting Stoney's things in one of his vacant bedrooms, Keithe went ahead and answered. "Well, you just said you had to take your medication, so I wondered if you were doing okay."

"Oh." Stoney waved off the concern. "I'm fine. Just my daily medication I have to take." She headed to the living area, which housed the curio, the same one where she first received her glimpse of Keithe. "You know, for pains and whatnot. Don't you take some sort of medication?"

"Um." Keithe coughed, took the "I guess I told you" tone from Stoney, and swallowed his embarrassment. "Actually, yes. But besides my seizure medication, no," Keithe gladly answered and silently thanked God for his mercies.

"Hmm." Stoney decided not to respond, but just remembered what her Grandma Susie had told her one day when she tried to get away with not taking any medication.

"Girl, don't be like them folk who try to pretend like ain't nut'n wrong wit'em. Please believe me, here. Everybody got som'in wrong with them. That pain hit 'em hard enough, I bet they take something."

Shaking her head, almost forgetting that Keithe stood close, Stoney let out a, "Right," as if she were answering her grandmother.

"Huh?" Keithe said.

"Oh, huh? Nothing. Nothing at all," Stoney countered, and batted her eyes quickly, making room between the two of them.

"Okay." He decided to leave it alone.

Standing off to the side and in her own little world, Stoney squinted and stared once again at the photo of Keithe and his wife. A closer look at the missus in the photo piqued Stoney's interest, and her eyebrows touched in the middle. Just as her neck grew another inch, Mike peered out of the bedroom and waved Stoney down the hall.

"Snap, snap. Girl, come on now. I know y'all hear my stomach trying to attack y'all from down here."

With laughter spilling out of his two best friends, Mike made his way down the hall to keep Keithe company as Stoney scurried to get dressed. In the process of switching positions with Mike, Stoney, as if a light bulb went off, glanced once more over her shoulder at the photo before she made her departure.

On the car ride into Addison, Stoney opted to sit in the backseat even though Keithe offered her the front seat several times. Sitting in the front or the back really didn't make any difference to her. What was getting to her was the goody-two-shoes act Keithe had tried to portray back when they were at Brother Mike's home. She silently hoped the night would get better. All looks and no brains made for a crush to be crushed.

"So how was work, Stone Cold?" Mike asked.

"It was a fair day. Oh, up until that varmint of a doctor just *had* to walk me to my car, yet again." She rolled her eyes and acted all giddy, like a child in a candy store, as she readied herself for another pill or two.

Sitting on the passenger's side, Keithe maneuvered his back to the window so he could get a good look at Stoney when he spoke to her. "And what's so wrong with that?" When Mike fixed the rearview mirror of his Lexus, all eyes were on Stoney.

"Uh. Okay," she giggled. "Well, Mike knows, but, anyway. This particular doctor always has to make it a point to compliment me about this, compliment me about that. And then heaven forbid if he doesn't get to walk me to my car in the evening." She rolled her eyes into the back of her head. "You'd think I was Princess Tiana of New Orleans and someone was trying to capture me."

"Well." Keithe shrugged. "Maybe you are." He shrugged again. "And someone just might." He turned back and looked out the window at the scenery of Dallas.

When Mike jerked his chin to his chest in an instant, he took his eyes off of the road and glanced at Keithe with a scrunched forehead. When Keithe looked back and mouthed, "What?" Mike just flipped his lip and shook his head. Instead of questioning his friend about the coy moment, Mike just drove.

Blushing, and silently adding brownie points to those he'd lost, Stoney wished to stop there, but knew she needed to make her point to Keithe.

"Hmm. Well, I know better." She was serious. "What does a doctor need to be all up in my face for? He probably thinks I'm some naive little girl and he would try to take advantage of me. I'm no one's flunkie. Nor fool. I'm from the country, but I ain't no duck." Her eyelashes patted the tops of her cheeks.

With that out-of-the-ballpark remark, Keithe had no choice but to turn back around and face Stoney, and Mike wasn't far behind with the tilting of the rearview mirror. With all the undivided attention Keithe was offering Stoney, she didn't know what to think about it.

What she did know was that if he didn't start backing up out of her face, she'd have to place him on the pervert list as well. *Old men are just dirty*, she thought.

Searching deeper in her purse, Stoney rummaged until she found a small Ziploc bag full of medications. Without looking up, Stoney scooted, pushed, and pulled at stacked medicines until she came to the one she was looking for.

"For such a young lady, you sure take a lot of medications," Keithe declared, and looked as if he wanted to take his words back. The way Stoney looked at him made him grab his neck as he turned to face forward. Keithe didn't miss a beat in shutting the visor in front of him, warding off the look Stoney was giving him through the mirror.

When she felt her space was granted, Stoney popped her pills in her mouth and swallowed the cocktail, waterless. The bitterness settling on her tongue, Stoney's eyes flapped like hummingbird wings, as if that would ease the taste. Hoping she didn't have to keep her defenses up, Stoney sat back and rode the rest of the way in silence.

In the middle of their Indian cuisine, Stoney finally settled her nerves and was ready to present herself to Keithe. Braving the waters, Stoney thought there would be no time like the present to make known the flutter in her heart. Although he had gotten under her skin two times in less than two hours, worrying about her medications and not his own business, Stoney was willing to put it all aside so that she could let him in on what she'd realized: she liked Keithe.

But first she thought she'd find out more about his marriage and what it really was, or wasn't. *Breaking up a household is not going to be blood on my hands,* she thought. "I know that's right," she answered herself. Not noticing the two men staring her way, Stoney was all smiles during the meal.

"So tell me more about Houston, Keithe. Sounds as exciting as Dallas is." Stoney sat with her hands in her lap and shoulders hunched, almost touching her ears. "Dallas is the farthest I've ever gone. My mom moved me from here to Greenville when I was just a baby. It took a while, but I'm back to stay. Well, at least until I find my mother."

Keithe took a sip of his raspberry lemonade and then dabbed the corners of his mouth with his cloth napkin. A Houstonian at heart, Keithe was more than happy to brag about his great city. "Well, you know, what can I say? I mean, Dallas is cool, but Houston is cold-blooded." He smiled toward Mike, knowing his friend would counter that.

With a twist of his lips and eyes, Mike said, "Stoney, forgive him. He was born and raised there and will probably die there. You're asking a man who lives for the humidity in Houston. You see he went bald, don't you? You should have seen him trying to wear a curl back in the day. The curl juice used to be zapped up by the time he'd leave home for church in the morning. Looking like a microphone wrapped in the church's choir robe." Mike made himself laugh. With Stoney half laughing, half feeling sorry for Keithe, Mike kept his laugh going for a bit longer.

With Keithe still making piercing eyes at Mike, Stoney found the opportunity to bring up Keithe's wife. "Well, how does your wife like it? Is she from there too?" Hoping his facial expression would give away his true feelings, Stoney sat up straight in her seat.

"Michelle?" Mike asked, before Keithe had a chance to think about the question.

"Yes. Michelle." Stoney furrowed her brow and silently thanked Mike for the confirmation of her competition's name. "Your wife, Michelle," Stoney said, redirecting the question to Keithe, smiling on the inside and the outside.

"Um." Keithe scooted his chair closer in order to rest his elbows on the table. "No. Um, no, Michelle is actually from Dallas," he finally answered. Seeing their waiter approach the table, Keithe leaned to his side, his hand in search of his wallet. With his mind made up, Keithe went to pull his credit card from its holding place.

"Don't you even try it," Mike yelled out.

"No, no. Mike, I got this, man. You are all ready allowing me to stay at your place. Let me do this, man." Keithe patted his chest to reassure his friend. While handing his card over to the awaiting waiter, two pieces of paper fell from his wallet to the floor.

"So." Stoney was ready to continue their conversation about Keithe's wife. Seeing the pieces of paper fall close to her, Stoney bent over to retrieve them for her new friend. Once they were in her hand, she unconsciously turned them right side up, finding one to be a business card from the law firm he worked for. The other was a picture. "Oh." The word slipped from Stoney's lips as she stared deeply at the picture, losing her breath in the process.

With the twinge of familiarity back at Brother Mike's home now up close and personal, Stoney was able to feed her sense from earlier. Now holding a photo of Michelle, Keithe's wife, Stoney's heart raced. Her eyes watered and flapped nonstop.

"Stoney. Hello. Stoney," Mike called out to his protégé, on the verge of snapping his fingers.

When she finally came to, realizing that Mike had called out her name more than once, Stoney looked up, only to see the two men watching her.

"I . . . I'm sorry. Uh. Is this your . . ." Stoney couldn't bring herself to ask it. Still holding the photo, Stoney felt her skin steam. Wanting to hold on to the photo a bit longer, at least until she got back to her car that was parked at Brother Mike's place, Stoney had to fight to keep her breathing intact.

With his hand open, waiting to receive his wife's photo, Keithe held a quizzical gaze toward Stoney. "Uh. Yes, that's my wife. Michelle." Keithe retrieved the photo, and almost smiled as he looked down at the smile his wife gave back.

"Excuse me." Stoney shot tall from her seat. Walking as fast as she could, Stoney didn't stop until she hid herself behind the restroom door. With her back hard to the door, Stoney was tempted to turn and retrace her steps. Wanting to let out all that had built up in her heart within the last few minutes, Stoney's eyes filled with tears as she sank to the restroom floor.

CHAPTER 9

Stoney

Stoney couldn't leave the scene fast enough. As soon as the trio made it back to Mike's house, coffee was out of the question for her. Even after venturing to the restaurant's restroom to gain her composure, she couldn't pull herself together.

"Stoney, you sure you don't want to come in and watch a movie with us?" Mike asked. "It's Tuesday, and you know you don't have nothing on your schedule," he joked.

Trying her best to hold in the cry that had been playing drums on her larynx, Stoney scrambled around in her open purse in search of her car keys. Her red eyes told one story while her voice gave off a lie. "I'm just . . . tired, Mike. Keithe," she choked out, "it was really good meeting you and seeing you again. I . . . I'm going to go."

By the time Mike made his way into the house and rushed to bring her duffle bag out to the car for her, Stoney was halfway down the street.

At the first stop sign she halted at, Stoney pulled her bucket of a car over to the curb. Snatching her seatbelt off, she threw her car in park and leaned her head onto the steering wheel.

"Why, why, why?" She beat the edge of the wheel. "What is going on?" She held up her hand, still leaving her wet face plastered to the center of the car's driving utensil. "I don't get it," she cried out from her broken heart. It was the same heart that seemed to be playing tricks on her.

"You see now, don'cha? I tell you the truth. Stoney, yo' mama don't want you, girl. You think if she did, she'da found ya by now. And look what she done gone and done."

Shaking her head while saying, "That's not right. That's just not right," Stoney fought against what she heard her grandmother's voice telling her. With little energy, Stoney looked at the picture that stayed plastered on her dash. "It just can't be." But her gut told her otherwise.

Right as she had gotten up the nerve and was about to let Keithe know that she more than admired him, her real reason for being in Dallas was brought back to the forefront of her mind. Nothing could be set in stone with a photo, but for some reason, Stoney's gut feeling was telling her more than she could ever believe.

Stoney cried out at the top of her lungs. When she noticed a car pull up to her side, waiting its turn at the stop sign and anticipating a left turn, Stoney felt embarrassed by her carrying on. Jerking her car into drive, Stoney floored the gas pedal.

Before she knew what was happening, a jolt was felt from the outside of her car. Stoney's car had been hit on the backside. It was a mere tap, but enough to dent the back of the vehicle. With tears in her eyes, Stoney didn't dwell on the fact that her shoulder had made contact with the driver's side window. She only screamed for the fear of not knowing what had happened.

"Oh Jesus, oh Jesus, oh Jesus," Stoney muttered without looking over her left shoulder. She attached her foot back to the gas pedal once again. Speeding off down the residential street, Stoney left the scene.

"Now you done went and got my car in a wreck. If you focus on what ya need to focus on, you wouldn't be getting ya self in all this mess. You need to take a pill and go to sleep somewhere, girl."

Wanting to do just that, Stoney looked through the rearview mirror to make sure no one followed her. With the sniffles, she reached inside of her bag with one hand, while holding tight to the steering wheel with the other. Just as she pulled her Ziploc bag from its holding place, Stoney remembered the prescriptions she had called in. Making a quick right, Stoney made her way toward the drugstore.

With her eyes flapping in full swing, Stoney pulled up to the pharmacy's drive-through. After pushing the button and waiting, five seconds couldn't have passed before she pushed the buzzer once again. "What is taking them so long?" She reached outside the car in anticipation of hammering the buzzer once more. "Wh—"

"Yes, ma'am, may I help you?" asked a young lady about Stoney's age. Stoney had a friendly rapport with the lady behind the glass from all the times she'd picked up prescriptions. "Oh, hey there, lady," the smiley faced young woman said, calling Stoney by the pet name she always called her.

Stoney threw a wave at the girl, named Mercy. Knowing she didn't have to make a note of the specific prescription she was picking up, all Stoney wanted was to get her prescriptions and go.

"Are you okay?" Mercy tiptoed to look toward the back of Stoney's car. When she saw smoke soaring from the car's rear, and noticed tears in Stoney's eyes, Mercy really wished she could do something for her.

"Yes. I need to pick up my prescription, please." Stoney sat halfway out of the car, sweating and biting the inside of her mouth. *No small talk today.* Stoney was trying her best to keep her tears at bay until she left the pharmacy.

When Mercy spent more time than usual in front of the computer, Stoney started to get antsy. Looking toward the back of her car, Stoney finally saw the smoke coming from her only means of transportation. Waving toward the large double-paned window, Stoney mouthed her concerns. "It's for Susie Hart. S-u-s-i-e. Hart: H-a—"

"I have it right here." Mercy half smiled at Stoney.

"About time." Stoney didn't hold back her irritation.

"Hmm. Oh. Wait. It's been flagged. It's showing . . . Well, wait one second please." Before Stoney had a chance to object, the young woman left the window.

Stoney pushed her back into the arch of the seat and just sat. She pulled down the visor and started to push imaginary strands of loose hair back into their place. She drilled her thumbs on the steering wheel and just sat. Inhaling deeply, Stoney sucked up her tears and the dripping of her nose.

When she heard, "Ma'am," Stoney turned her torso and gave all of her attention back to the young lady who always made her day.

"Yes." Stoney's fluttering eyes started.

"The pharmacist is going to need you to come inside." Mercy kept an open appearance on her face and hoped her customer would oblige.

"Um. Girl, it's for my grandmother." Stoney hoped it wasn't too late to be cordial. She hoped it would make the getting smoother. "The same prescription I always get. H-a—" Stoney started to spell out the last name again before she was interrupted.

"The spelling isn't the problem. It's saying that this Susie Hart is . . . Well, it's saying that she's deceased. And has been deceased for about two years, is what it says."

"It? Who is it? And by the way . . ." Stoney's nerves got the best of her and she couldn't place Mercy's name quick enough. "What's your name?" Stoney wanted to cop an attitude, not thinking of how she was, and had always been, in the wrong. "Because I don't know what you're talking about." Stoney threw out attitude and rolled her neck. "I just got a refill a week ago, Mercy." Her thinking became clearer.

Just when a response was about to be given, the head pharmacist cut off the girl and spoke with Stoney through the microphone. "Miss Hart. I take it you were getting this medication for your, uh, grandmother?" He took a look at the name on the computer screen.

It wasn't until that very moment that Stoney realized what had slipped her mind. She may have been taking medication as far back as she could remember, but what the medication wasn't was hers. With the ability to call in prescriptions for patients, Stoney had been able to simply call in prescriptions for herself; for Grandma Susie. She would have to switch up. Putting the prescriptions under her grandmother's name had run its course.

"Ah. Yes. Yes, sir. My, uh. My grand . . . grandfather sent me to get it for him. Is there a, ah, a problem?" She pushed up her glasses and waited for the answer, as her eyelashes did the jig behind her updated bifocals. Internally she prayed that the lie would make it through.

When he moved closer to the microphone, Stoney thought she was going to stop breathing. When he asked her to come inside so that he could explain some things, she thought she would take her last breath. Nodding, Stoney quickly put her car in gear and drove forward.

"Lord, ain't no way I can go in there." Stoney knew better. There might have been a delay in her thinking, but she knew nothing good would come from her stepping foot inside of the pharmacy.

Not daring to announce her plan to the universe, for fear of confessing her wrongdoings, Stoney drove out from under the covered drive-through as tears started their descent once more. Almost speeding out of the pharmacy's parking lot, Stoney floored the gas pedal to no avail. The most she could do was coast into the nearest parking space available.

Girl, get a grip. You can always write ya own prescription. Just put it in ya name, honey. You work at the doctor's office.

She had been so certain to cross her Ts and dot her Is and now she'd slipped up and rode the wrong wave for far too long. Still, with tears in her eyes, Stoney thought about the idea. Just as she did at the doctor's office for other patients, surely she could write out a new prescription for herself.

"I don't know why I didn't do that in the first place. Oh, Stoney." Adding a smile to her sadness, Stoney bypassed the thought of sitting in her dead car, and wiggled a small dance in celebration of her next plan.

Picking up a piece of licorice from her purse, Stoney, with the new thought about prescriptions that would be hers, finally let herself ease back into thinking about the situation she'd left: Keithe and his wife.

Stoney was still stuck on the situation. How could a simple crush wind up being more than what she could have ever imagined? The picture she'd held in her hand left her shaken and confused. Wishing she would have blurted out her thoughts with the two friends, Stoney was in such a state of shock and couldn't let what was in her heart be known. How could she let on to Keithe what she was thinking?

With the very thought of ways to get back in Keithe's presence at least one more time, Stoney had a whole new mission. She needed to confirm if the photo she'd held was of a woman who could possibly be her mother.

When she heard the familiar voice crawl into her thoughts, Stoney squinted, and, for once, tried to fight for her sanity. "The Lord is my shepherd," she started from memory.

"He may be your shepherd, but what He ain't is your mama," Stoney heard. *"All that hard work you did to build up your nerve and now what? That would be just a shame if his wife is your mama."* Grandma Susie's voice crept

through. *"Just a shame, I tell you. If that girl is your mama, that means she just went on with her life. If she can leave her own mama and not come back and check on me, what makes you think she cares twice about you?"*

"He lets me rest beside the stilled waters," Stoney continued.

"How in the world ya gon' rest by some water and you don't even have ya medication? The least you can do is go'n and do the prescriptions, just in case."

"He makes me . . ." Stoney tried not to listen. "He makes me lie down . . ." Relaxing her shoulders in defeat, Stoney shed tears when she realized she wasn't strong enough to let go. "Well, just in case," she said.

CHAPTER 10

Mercy

It had been a long day and the worst part wasn't yet over. Mercy still had to make the trip across town to have *the talk* with her mother and father. She didn't know how she'd do it, but what she had to share, Mercy was sure would leave her parents perturbed and disappointed. Nonetheless, it had to be done.

Making her way through the automatic doors, leaving the drugstore after work, Mercy stood for a brief moment reminding herself where she'd parked.

After pointing her keypad in different directions, while pushing the alarm button, Mercy's hunt was over. "Ah." She looked in the direction in which she heard her alarm chirp. During her short walk in the direction of her Volkswagen Beetle, Mercy stopped once her eyes landed on a familiar face. Only able to catch the side view,

Mercy zeroed in on Stoney bobbing her head as if she were talking to someone.

Stepping off of the curb, Mercy didn't think twice when she realized the young woman who frequented the drugstore seemed a bit distressed. Recalling the events that happened close to two hours earlier, Mercy was happy the driver's side window was ajar.

Starting to make her presence known, Mercy realized she didn't really know the young lady's first name. The last year or so it was either, "hey there," "hey lady," or "how are you doing," to start their conversations.

Figuring the patient's and her grandmother's last names may not be the same, Mercy announced her presence by saying, "Hey there, lady." When Stoney didn't budge, Mercy rapped lightly on the shaky window.

Stoney jumped. "Huh? Oh. Oh, hi. I'm sorry. I was just leaving." Stoney fumbled with her car keys that were still in the ignition, hoping the pharmacy worker would leave her alone. Looking around Mercy, Stoney needed to make sure neither the pharmacist nor the police were behind her.

"No. You're okay. I was just leaving work and saw you here." Mercy didn't know how to say it, but she figured the two girls were about the same age. She just decided to be real. "It looks like your car is pretty busted to me. Are you waiting for a ride?"

With no answer, when she saw Stoney slouch back into the driver's seat, Mercy asked, "Are you okay?" Taking a step back away from the car, Mercy didn't want to press the young lady.

Nodding frantically, and then shaking her head, Stoney didn't know what to do to control her emotions. With not having her medications on hand, and the fear of almost being caught trying to get them, along with not having the strength to walk away from the drugs all together, Stoney couldn't keep her tears at bay.

"St . . . Stoney. You can call me Stoney. I . . . I'm gonna be all right," she lied while holding the steering wheel extra hard.

Lord, I know what you're saying, but . . . Not wanting to question God, especially with her own situation she'd put herself in, Mercy did as her heart was told. "Do you want to go to the tea shop and talk about it? I mean, if you don't have anything else to do, that is. Doesn't look as if your car is leaving anytime soon." Seeing the pain in Stoney's eyes, Mercy knew a friend was what Stoney needed. "Of course, you can ride with me and I'll take you home," Mercy reasoned.

Finally peeking through the half-open window, Stoney agreed with a nod.

"Great. I'm parked right over there." Mercy pointed to her cream-colored vehicle. "Get your stuff and come on." Walking toward her car, Mercy quickly dialed her parents' number.

"Hey, Mom?" Mercy greeted her mother, of whom everyone often stated she was the spitting image. She didn't just share facial features with her mother; Mercy had inherited the muscular, lean build her mother naturally owned.

"Hey, Mercy. How are you?" her mother responded.

"I'm fine. It looks as though I'm not going to make it right this minute." She was happy to buy more time away from her parents.

"M-and-M." Her mother called her by her nickname, referencing the colorful way the young girl often dressed. "I told your dad you were coming and now you pull the rug from under us? No fair," she said with a chuckle. "He's going to be gone, but at least try to see if I'm up when you make it in," the overbearing mother thought to ask her only child. "You know I'm nosey, honey."

When she thought of what she had to share with her parents, Mercy let her light, pearly smile wane. "Well, yeah." Mercy didn't want to say more. The news she had to share with her parents wouldn't leave a laugh being shared over dinner.

The plans she and her parents had made for her to take a year off from college had come to an end. With only three months left for her to leave for pharmaceutical school at the University of Houston, the growing abdomen underneath her work jacket would make or break her plans. Nevertheless, Mercy knew it had to be done. But not before she helped someone else in need.

Hearing the spring's light wind beat into the mouthpiece of her daughter's cell phone, Mercy's mother asked, "You still there, honey?"

"Yes, ma'am. Okay. I'm going to let you go, but I'll try to stop in to chat with you before I head to sleep myself." She opened her car door.

"Sounds like a plan. See you then. Oh, Mercy?"

"Yes, ma'am?"

"You received a letter in the mail today. Something from your doctor's office. Did you have an appointment? I wonder if it's an old bill or something."

"Oh. Okay. Thanks. I'll stop in and get it." Mercy narrowed her eyes. Rushing the rest of her words out, Mercy didn't bother to answer her mother's question. Exchanging their love salutation, the two disconnected the call.

CHAPTER 11

"So, was your day that hard?" Mercy questioned Stoney, who was slouched in the booth right in front of her.

Before answering, Stoney took a sip of a flavored tea that Mercy had endorsed as the truth. With another gulp of the savory taste of different leaves, Stoney couldn't help but agree with her about the cooled concoction.

"More than hard. Almost detrimental to my health." Stoney knew she was speaking her own truth, and wondered if Mercy could read between the lines.

"Well . . ." Mercy knew she couldn't sleep on what God had placed in her heart, no matter how she felt about her own situation. "You know God is the ruler over all."

"Yep. I know." Stoney rolled her eyes, not knowing why she had grabbed an attitude once Mercy brought God into the conversation. It was He who had made a way for any and everything having to do with her life.

Noticing the frown Stoney was harboring, Mercy kept on. "Have you given your cares over to Him? I know I have. I mean . . . I'm pregnant." She looked down at her belly. "I'm not married, and I still have to tell my parents about it all." Mercy wanted Stoney to be comfortable with her. The only way she could was by being transparent.

Stoney seemed shocked by the confession. Stretching her upper torso while leaning forward, Stoney tried to get a better look at Mercy's stomach. "Really? I can't even tell."

"That's because I still have this lab jacket on," Mercy said. "It's been my wall of hiding." She chuckled, really wanting to shed her own tears. "I'm barely in my first trimester."

Raising her eyebrows, Mercy could tell what Stoney was thinking. She was shunning her without looking at her own daily barriers.

"We all have our own crosses to bear, but I thank God for allowing me the opportunity to repent to Him and start fresh. I don't even want to go into what the enemy was putting in my mind at first," Mercy confessed.

When she saw Stoney buck her eyes, not believing what she was telling her, Mercy continued. "I'm just real. You'll have to excuse me." She shrugged. "I didn't say I wanted to do it, I said what the devil put in my thinking."

Thinking about her own heartbreak, Stoney suggested, "Real stupid if you ask me. Why waste God's time if you were doing your own thing to begin with?" Stoney shook her head.

With a throw of her head, Mercy shot back, "Oh, and so trying to get your *grandmother's* medication for her is not doing your own thing?" Mercy rested her elbows on the table. "I mean, seriously, what were you going to do, deliver them to the cemetery? Pah-lease."

"No, I . . ." Stoney sat up straight and looked around the small tea shop.

"Exactly," Mercy confirmed. "I know my situation is not pretty, but at least I'm living up to my mistake. I could have listened to the enemy and really done my own thing."

"What about adoption? I wish my mother would have opted for it." Stoney felt comfortable enough to share some of her own experiences.

"Nah. I'm better now. That was just a moment I had. But it was real heavy on me. Plus, it's not just my child, and the dad, I must say, is unique compared to many young men of today." Mercy answered the questions about her and remembered what Stoney had said about her own mother. "So, did you and your mother get into it or something?"

"I guess so." Stoney took one of the last gulps of her tea. "I don't know her, so I figure I must have done something to her at birth." Stoney knew the joke was really pain seeping out. "My grandmother raised me," Stoney said with pain in her heart.

"Oh, is your mother still living?"

"Living?" Stoney answered the question with a question. She thought about the photo and didn't want to make any assumptions, but really couldn't help herself. "Living *la vida loca,* I'm sure," Stoney said without going into details. "Honestly, I don't know. I want to know. I want to know her and meet her and for her to know me." Stoney finally looked into Mercy's eyes. "I just don't know how to get to her. You know, find her." Still stuck on the photo, Stoney made a mental note to get back over to Mike's house sometime soon, only this time with her photo of her mother.

"Why not look for her? Have you tried that?"

Shaking her head, not letting on just how close she thought she might have come to her mother, Stoney waited, wanting to know what Mercy would think of next.

"You should. You should look for your mother, I mean. I could help you if you'd like," Mercy said.

With that, Stoney thought once more about telling Mercy about her encounter, but didn't. Wanting to hear Mercy say it again, Stoney said, "Would you? Really? Oh my goodness. Serious?"

"Serious. I mean, it's almost the summer, and I'd love to help you until I go off to school in the fall. Sure, it'll be fun to see what we come up with." The two displayed their giddy sides.

With a smile to confirm their plans, Stoney couldn't wait to brainstorm with Mercy. With the lead she thought she already had, Stoney was still determined to do her own sideline investigation.

CHAPTER 12

Keithe

On his road trip back to Houston, Keithe took it easy down I-45. All he wanted to do was drive and listen to the sweet sounds of J. Moss and Karen Clark-Sheard.

"(Ooo) How can people live without Him/ How can people pray and doubt Him?"

It was just the song Keithe needed to think about why his wife couldn't get it together. Why couldn't she live for God and why couldn't she just pray and not doubt? Heck, why couldn't she change?

"Because she doesn't want to," Keithe answered himself when he thought about the question he planned on asking God. "Lord, I don't even know what to expect on this trip back home to Houston. This girl . . . no, this *grown* woman can't seem to be faithful, respectful, or decent at that. Am I wrong? Is it me?" He jabbed at his chest while easing onto the highway in his Range Rover.

"Seriously. For real though." He wiggled his knees, as if doing so would get God ready for what he was about to share. "Back in the day, in college, ya boy, yeah." He figured he'd slow it down when he realized his actions back in the day were nothing grand to speak of. "I did my thing. But I married Michelle for your honor and your glory, God. Are you holding me accountable for things of my past? Huh?"

Waiting, but not directly waiting, for an answer, Keithe just drove and listened to his song of choice. When he heard the song fade out, he hit the repeat button on his steering wheel, which made the song start over.

"Ooo," the melody started again.

"Lord, I've kept my promises to Michelle, and I'm going to keep my promises to you. I . . . I just need your help in keeping my mind stayed and focused on you, Lord. I really want to be the head of my household and follow you, Christ, as you followed the church. I want that."

Thinking of Stoney, Keithe knew the butterflies that fluttered in his stomach when he thought of the young girl were serious territory he knew he shouldn't cross.

"Please, Lord, keep my heart pure and my thoughts on you." Not making the verbal confession, Keithe believed that if he didn't bring up what he thought his heart was feeling, he wouldn't have to face the music.

Exhaling, Keithe turned the volume up on his ten-disc CD changer and rode the first wave of the four-hour drive.

His major concern was if he would seek a divorce, or hold on tight and wait for the next big tsunami to make its way into his one-sided marriage. There was no way he was going to play with his own emotions. He knew the truth, but he also felt the pain. All the tsunamis in his marriage were beginning to look the same. The latest one just had a new name.

"I love that woman." He made promises to the space inside of his truck. "I just wished . . ." His words trailed off. There was no one—no one—he could go to and ask for help, advice, or anything when it came to Michelle. No cousins, no siblings, and no parents. Michelle was an only child, and since she had been an orphan, a ward of the state as she had said, there was no family linked anywhere.

He had tried on numerous occasions to ask her if she'd like to dig into her family background to see what they could come up. The last time he'd asked, with the glare he'd received from his wife, Keithe made a mental note not to even try to care as far as her family was concerned.

With the ring of his phone, Keithe smiled once he saw his mother's number appear on the screen.

"Hey, Mrs. Ladybug. How are you doing?" he greeted her.

After a slight chuckle, Keithe's mother said, "Well, that's why I was calling you. I wanted to check on my prince."

"Your prince is fine, Mother. Sorry I didn't get to return your phone call before now."

"Well." She took a breath. "I'm not going to say it is all right, but I understand." Changing her tone, Keithe's mother let him know that she knew what had transpired between him and the woman she had grown to despise.

"I called your home, Keithe Katrell." She used his middle name when she wanted the truth. "What is it that she did this time?" Never one to fake with her son, Ladybug, as she was affectionately known by all who were blessed to be in her circle, had always let it be branded that she didn't envy Keithe's choice in wife. It hadn't always been that way, but the more Michelle did to hurt her son, the less Ladybug was having it.

"Nothing to brag about," he said about all the deeds that were completed by his wife. "It's time for me to make some decision is all." He hoped that would buy him some time in explaining to his mother.

"Hmm. While you're pondering what to do with your wife, do I need your father to renovate the guest home out back?" Ladybug suggested as she looked through her kitchen window. Living in Sugar Land, a suburb of Houston, Ladybug was more than willing to make arrangements for her son.

Really giving the idea some thought, Keithe considered that it would be better to go home and see which direction Michelle was willing to go. "How about I let you know later on in the week, Ma?"

"Gotcha. I love you, son. You're a fabulous son, and any woman, who is a lady," she said without having to curse her distaste for Michelle, "would be grateful to have you. If you're not somebody's love, then you are with the wrong someone, son."

"I hear ya, Ma."

"Good. Make sure you hear me, or I'll see to it that—"

"I gotcha, I gotcha." Keithe tried to soothe the roar in his sixty-five-year-old mother.

"Good, because she's in my league. I can take care of that if need be," Ladybug said with a "sho'nuff" appeal. "Ol' cougar, got my son in an uproar." She veered their two-way conversation toward a one-woman show.

"Love you, Ladybug."

"Love you too, dear. Oh, and don't think I don't know that you dismissed your driver. Son, please be careful. Okay? Did you take your medication?"

"But of course I did. I'm being extra cautious, Mother."

When he clicked the line off, Keithe thought back on the early days he and Michelle shared, back when she'd willed herself to be a wife, and all the wife he needed. But something had switched. No longer interested in playing games with himself, Keithe realized he'd always seen what he wanted to see. The depth of who Michelle was had been seen once Keithe realized who he was and wanted to be.

Just as women had their levels of expectation with men—tall, dark, and handsome—Keithe craved the brown, beautiful, and slightly bowed legs of a woman. Michelle was all the physical he'd wanted. With her intellect amplified beyond his own, Keithe fell head over heels for his wife the moment he met her.

It hit him like a ton of bricks, the same bricks that he had used to build blinders. It was he who had done all the dramatic changing. It was all for the betterment of himself, but still, it wasn't news, but he finally got it.

"Lord have mercy. Just what am I suppose to do now?" he asked when he realized he'd pulled the old switcheroo. All the partying, drinking, and smoking that he'd once participated in got him caught up in a life with a woman who couldn't understand why he had changed. He was the one who went to church, walked to the altar, and meant what he'd spoken to the Lord. Now he saw it: his salvation had become the serpent to his marriage as far as Michelle was concerned.

"You said divorce isn't an option." When the Lord spoke to his heart, Keithe knew he had all the right reasons why he could flee from someone who didn't have his best interest at heart. Michelle had committed adultery, didn't want the same lifestyle as him, and seemed as though she loathed the God he served.

"I really have been playing myself. I've really been trying to make it work. This is crazy, Keithe." He hoped he'd finally hear himself and listen. "Lord, forgive me for abusing myself. I've only wanted to make this marriage work because I gave my vow to you. But, Lord, unless you tell me to stay, it's time for me to cut my losses and move on."

Not a man of many tears, Keithe pulled in his lips and held tight to the tremble, hoping it would quickly disappear. He knew more than just talking about it would help him over this hump. He knew fasting and praying would be his guides into a peaceful heart and mind.

All the riches and material offers only sup-
plied limited peace. The love his wife sparsely
gave him was for the love of the flesh. It would
take Jesus and Jesus alone for Keithe to dwell in
a peaceful nature.

One more time, though not his last, Keithe
pushed the repeat button and waited for the
song to begin.

"Ooo . . ."

CHAPTER 13

Stoney

Three months had passed by and Stoney still had not regained her energy. Since the day she'd had dinner with Mike and Keithe, Stoney had been drained beyond compare. Her emotions had been all over the place. From wanting and longing for her mother, to wanting and longing for her drugs more, and even getting an itch of the love bug, Stoney didn't know what to think and she didn't know what to do with her feelings.

Initially she had gotten to the point where she felt she would have to eventually bury her hopes and her dreams of ever becoming reunited with her mother. That was before her dinner with the two friends. When the interaction had taken place between her and Keithe, Stoney lost momentum to conquer her heart's desire. In the midst of it all, she had to decide to put her crush on hold until she found out more about her bloodline.

The day the choir met over at Mike's house was the initial time the photo of Keithe and his bride stared back at Stoney. Then before the trio departed for their late lunch a few days later, something nudged her thinking. The woman in the photo spoke volumes to Stoney, and secretly her heart had raced, but she thought nothing more of it. Recollection of that moment, mixed with her feelings of the photo Keithe had of his wife, made Stoney's gut jolt. The only thing left for her to do was compare the two pictures side by side. And when she did, everything would ring clear for her. It was called "clarify and verify." If the lone photo that she had in her possession from Grandma Susie was a match, her mission would be halfway solved.

During the choir's mid-week rehearsal, Mike noticed how sluggishly Stoney had been presenting herself, and decided to take her to a late lunch. Since her car was now in the shop, he felt it was his big brother duty to take her where she needed to go. Before their arrival at their favorite eatery, it was only happenstance for him to stop by his place. Making his way into his bedroom, Mike left Stoney to fend for herself. In her waiting, Stoney found an opportunity.

The day at the drugstore when her car was whisked away by the tow truck, the only important thing Stoney had taken from it was the picture. Tucked away in its new home, Stoney eased her hand inside the darkness of her everyday purse. Feeling around for what had become her inspiration, Stoney walked toward the curio as she waited for Mike.

When she looked back, hearing Mike's voice shout out the song they had learned with perfection, Stoney didn't hesitate to clutch the picture in her hand. Bypassing all of the photos she had seen on the last visit, Stoney hurriedly opened the case and knelt.

"My good Lord today." Stoney fell backward and landed on her bottom. As if the wind had been knocked out of her, Stoney panted. Feeling her mouth become dry and her eyes become watery, Stoney shut them both. "My mama," she mouthed with a question in her voice.

Hearing Mike shut his bedroom door and start down the hall, Stoney rushed to get herself together. Just as she stood, shut the curio's door, and placed the photo back in her purse, Mike became visible.

"You ready, Chaka Nun?" Brother Mike referenced what he'd said was a mixture of who Stoney was. Chaka Khan for her raspy voice, and being a nun for her overly heaven-on-earth approach to everything.

"Yeah. I . . . I'm ready," Stoney said. Wishing she had the nerves to share what she felt were her misfortunes with Mike, Stoney just followed suit and trailed behind Mike out of his front door.

When Stoney only drank a glass of sweet tea and refused food, Mike started to worry.

"Stone Cold? You have to eat something, girl. You gon' be skin and bones. Although, that may take some time to accomplish," Mike said with a snicker, referring to her Southern-girl build. "You know, Southern men love the Southern appeal: hips, Stoney, hips." When Stoney's eyes landed on him and looked as though they could burn a hole through his flesh, Mike stopped.

Trying to add his serious side to the conversation with the quickness, Mike asked, "What's the deal, seriously, Stoney?"

Knowing she couldn't tell him about all of her woes—thoughts of Michelle, Keithe's wife, possibly being her mother; her inability to get any prescriptions approved right away—Stoney just shook her head and rolled her eyes. She stared down at her bowl full of salad.

"So . . ." Mike pushed.

Another beat passed before an almost disoriented Stoney agreed to talk. When she shared, "I feel like, I don't know, I'll never connect with my birth mother," she bit the inside of her cheek, hoping not to shed any more tears for the moment. Stoney's heart fluttered when she thought about how close in the world she was and had been to her mother. Especially having had Keithe in her presence.

Mike sat up straight and offered, "Is that what this is about? Your mother? I didn't know you were still, well, really looking for her like that."

With the fresh feelings she still held about her unknown mother, Stoney pulled from some unknown source of energy to explain. "Well, I never really gave up. I just had to wait for the right timing, you know. But now things have changed." She tried to watch her wording. "I was so close."

She'd known Mike long enough to confide in him about a lot of things, but sharing her thoughts on Keithe's wife being her mother was out of the question. There was no way she was willing to take any chance on anyone thinking she was crazy.

"I had enough of that," she thought out loud about people thinking she was crazy.

"Enough of what?" Mike wrinkled his forehead.

"Huh? Oh, never mind," she said, batting her eyes. Never making any lifelong friends while in Greenville, kids her age more or less thought of Stoney as a young old maid. Never able to leave her grandmother's sight for more than going off to church or school, if anyone needed to locate Stoney, on her front porch was where she'd be.

Stoney was taunted by other kids because of what they'd heard their own parents say. It was Stoney who learned firsthand, from the mouths of babes, how depressed her grandmother had been. She had learned that her grandmother's bouts had begun even before she was given to her. By the time Stoney had been placed in her life, Grandma Susie had turned into a bitter old woman.

Tilting his head to one side and halfway closing one eye, Mike tried his best to get Stoney to open up. "Well. Why do you think things have changed now?"

Sick in the stomach is what Stoney felt as she thought about Mike's question. Reminiscing to the day at the restaurant when Keithe made their usual duo team a trio, Stoney shrugged and spoke without thinking. "It just has. Like when Keithe said she . . ." She saw the expression on Mike's face change once she mentioned his friend. "Um, his wife. You know. She didn't want kids. What . . . what if my mom didn't want kids and looking for her would really be wasting my time?"

"Hmm. It may be just something you'll have to go through to find out. You can't compare your situation with Keithe's. Michelle is totally off-kilter. Pit bulls are afraid of that cougar for sure." He badly wanted Stoney to relax. Never seeing her so upset, the dark bags under her eyes told him she had been more worried than he had realized.

The day at the Indian restaurant with Mike and Keithe, Stoney had tried her best to regain her composure in the restroom. When she made her way back to the table where the guys were still chowing, she pumped herself up to share her findings with Keithe. In the minutes she had spent in the three-stall restroom, Stoney had talked herself into mentioning the picture and its resemblance to the one she owned. But first, she thought she'd get more information in order to surprise Keithe. The surprise had been on her.

"So. With you all living in Houston, was she, Michelle, okay raising children in Houston?" Stoney had asked in a shaky voice, wanting to know if she had siblings to get ready for.

With Mike feeling sorry for his best friend, knowing all that he had recently gone through with Michelle, he tried his best to rescue him.

"Naw. Keithe tried to be like me: no kids. But he can't hang, though." The two men had laughed.

When tremors attacked her eyes, Stoney didn't slow down on the questioning. Gripping the cloth napkin that lay in her lap, Stoney wrapped it twice around her hand to the point of her blood flow being slowed down.

"Oh, no kids?" she asked. "What about your wife?"

"Hmm." Keithe bucked his eyes, taken aback by the question. "Oh, no, neither of us had any children outside our marriage. Our marriage was the first for the both of us." Keithe released his thinking further about his wife being a mother. "Wow. I hadn't thought about that in a while." He chuckled. "Michelle with children would be like . . . like Mike with a Chihuahua. And we all know Mike hates dogs."

A sarcastic grin on Mike's face, the mutual friend threw in a fake chuckle for the two. "Ha, ha. Whatever. I'm going to the restroom. Please, please, carry on without me," Mike offered while shifting away from the table.

Plastering a forged smile on her face, Stoney started twisting the napkin, which had already made an impression on her skin. "Wow. Pretty much dislikes children, huh? Well, there would be no chance in her having any babies for you, huh?"

With crumpled eyebrows, Keithe said, "Well, yeah. Plus, she's pretty much out of that range for children now anyway." Keithe didn't mind sharing his wife's older status to Stoney. "My wife is older than me. She was forty when we married fifteen years ago. But"—he threw out his hands—"I loved her that much to sacrifice that part of my life. That's what marriage is about," he said, trying to make himself believe it.

"Loved?" a tense and heartbroken Stoney asked.

"Did I say loved? I meant love. I mean, we've weathered some storms, I won't deny that." A beat passed. "What's up with the long face? It was just a misuse of the word," he tried to joke.

"No, no." Her eyelashes waved rapidly. "It wasn't that." Silencing herself, Stoney had just sat and picked through the rest of her dinner.

Now Stoney was at lunch once again with Mike, and her inklings had been verified. The pictures were more identical than not. As far as Stoney was concerned, it was more than possible that Keithe was married to Stoney's mother.

Pulling out her ratty and faithful Ziploc bag, Stoney quickly swore when she realized the contents were scarce. "Sorry," she apologized when she saw the way Mike looked at her. Without self-denial, Stoney couldn't even blame the way Mike's eyes questioned her.

Only able to get by with sample medications from the doctor's office, those scarce, low-dosage pills didn't give her the get up and go that she needed. Her game plan of writing her own prescriptions wasn't as clever as she had thought it would be. As bold as she had been before, her nerves had gotten the best of her.

"Are you going to be okay?" he asked between sips of his own sweetened drink. "I've never seen you this worked up, Stoney. Actually, you mind if I pray for you?"

Shrugging, before she could oblige and allow her friend to help bring comfort to her, Stoney stood. "I'll be fine. Since my car is in the shop, the doctor's office has scheduled me part-time hours. I'll be able to get some rest. Actually, I need to meet a friend." Stoney glanced at her watch. "She's been helping me look for my mother, and she's supposed to meet me at my apartment soon."

Standing and pushing his chair back, Mike gathered his personal belongings. With the seriousness placed on her face, Mike wanted to get Stoney where she needed to go. "I'll be praying for you, Stone Cold," he said as they walked to his vehicle. With no response one way or the other, the two rode in silence.

With Mike driving toward his friend's apartment, Stoney looked around at the scenery and sighed. A very hot August let Stoney know that summer was still present, but just the thought of fall made her dread the upcoming seasonal change. Sluggish and no longer motivated about anything in life, Stoney had a rough time dealing with the fall season. Grandma Susie had passed away during the breezy season, and from that point on, when the air became thinner and leaves began to fall to the ground, it reminded Stoney of death.

If she had had her own vehicle, there was no way she would have continued having dinners with Keithe in the first place, especially after realizing that the people in both photos were one and the same. She hated that she left Mike hanging, but she couldn't take it anymore. She couldn't share her heart's pain with him and felt that she would only be fooling herself. Stoney realized he had a close connection to her mother and there was nothing she could do about it; it was a connection that she wasn't offered. There were no wrongdoings on his part, but the mere fact that he had access to a world she was locked out of made Stoney grieve.

With her own assumption that pictures don't lie, all Stoney could think about was all of the progress she'd made over the last two years and how it had all started to crash down around her. MaeShell, the name written on the back of the photo she'd retrieved from her grandmother's items, never wanted her.

Reminiscing on the conversation she'd had with Keithe, it seemed Michelle hadn't even acknowledged Stoney to her husband. And if that were the case, it was possible that no one in Michelle's life knew she existed. It was like she was nonexistent all over again. It was very clear that Michelle had gone on with her life as if Stoney had never been born.

It was one thing growing up and not knowing why her mother wasn't in her life, but now, things had changed. The very thought, knowing about Michelle living the high life, played pat-a-cake with Stoney's heart.

It just ain't fair. I guess favor ain't fair after all, Stoney whined in her thoughts.

Stoney had often thought her mother was deceased, or maybe had an illness that prevented her from taking care of her, like Grandma Susie. There were numerous thoughts she wished, anything to not make Michelle be found guilty of actually abandoning her. But now, none of those scenarios could hold true. Michelle just flat out didn't want her. Michelle didn't want Stoney.

The hope of her mother giving her up for adoption and papers being lost had dissipated at top speed. No mother waiting under the tree as those reunited on those television shows would be the image she had recently envisioned. To the world, Michelle or MaeShell was still childless, and, from what Stoney could gather, heartless.

With no great reunion to plan, Stoney knew she had to get her life back in order. Vicky had called too many times to count over the last few days. Since Stoney started working part-time hours, due to her transportation troubles, she wasn't worried about seeing her friend at work. Being that Vicky had graduated back in May, Stoney wouldn't have to worry about running into her at school, either.

"School," Stoney mumbled. She barely made it out of the spring term and had no idea why she even signed up for summer classes. Summer II classes had ended, and she'd only seen the inside of the classrooms a total of two times. Most times she couldn't bring herself to get out of bed. No prescriptions, no family, no mother: Stoney didn't have much hope to really live life.

The only other thing that had kept her going was the friendship she had started and kept with Mercy. When she gave Mercy a one-sided account of how and why she arrived in Dallas, being the overzealous person she was, Mercy decided to give Stoney help in her search, a search that Stoney believed to all ready be complete. Just thinking about having someone to listen to all of her woes added warmth in her heart.

Mercy had become a permanent fixture in Stoney's life. For the past two months they had grown rather close. Stoney had poured out her heart to Mercy about not knowing who her mother or father were, and the inability to locate them. Giving her bits and pieces of information, Stoney never informed Mercy of her chance meeting with Keithe or that she had been as close as possible to her mother. She wanted to buy time and see what all Mercy could actually come up with. With Mercy soon heading off to Houston the next month for school, and only being home every other weekend, Stoney wanted to get as much information about her mother as possible.

It had been months since she found the news of her mother, never mentioning her to Keithe. It had been the same amount of time since she'd been able to get her regular string of prescriptions filled. The only thing she could do for her fix was to steal sample drugs that the pharmaceutical reps dropped off at the doctor's office.

Mike may have been joking, but it was a statement that was overdue. Stoney had indeed lost twenty-five of the 185 pounds she'd held, and in only two months. Her hair was barely holding on to the foamed rollers that she used to style her homemade mushroomed hairdo she wore every once in a while. Church was no longer a priority, and when she did go, she no longer lent her vocals to the choir.

When Mike pulled up to the address of Stoney's friend, she readied herself to see what her new friend had been able to find out about her own mother dearest. Now knowing she was going off of more than an assumption, Stoney was ready to dig deeper into who Michelle really was.

"I hope to see you at the youth choir's annual this weekend," Mike reminded Stoney, hoping she would actually make her way to church.

With just a nod to soothe her friend, Stoney eased her way out of Mike's running vehicle.

CHAPTER 14

Mercy

The time being spent on researching the whereabouts of Stoney's mother had finally spilled over to visiting each other's homes, but now Stoney took advantage of the extra time. Before the end of the week arrived, Stoney went from a part-time worker to being fired with nothing to do, due to her own selfish dealings. Stoney and an almost-four-months-pregnant Mercy had been in full swing, finding all they could find on Stoney's mother. Even with Stoney knowing more about her mother than she was telling her friend, the occasions they shared together filled some alone time for Stoney.

With Mercy living in a house that was attached to the back of her parents' home, the time had finally come for Stoney to meet the parents of her new best friend. Stoney put on a façade in order to cover her emotions from the double whammy she received at Brother Mike's. Mercy marched Stoney through the back of her parents' home for their greeting.

"Mom, I'd like you to meet someone," Mercy presented her new friend to her mom. "Mom, this is Stoney Hart. And, Stoney this is my mother, Mrs. Kendra. All my friends call her that."

Wiping her hands on her apron, Kendra turned to face her only child. "Hey, honey." In a quick gesture, she lent her face to Mercy. "Nice to meet you . . . Stoney?" Kendra questioned, making sure she heard the name correctly.

"Yes, ma'am," Stoney verified. "Nice to meet you too." The two shook hands.

"Did you all go to school together?" Kendra questioned Stoney with her eyebrows. Staring deep into Stoney's face, Kendra rushed her mind to place where she'd seen Stoney before.

When Stoney shook her head, Kendra's mind was still running. "You look so familiar. Excuse me for staring. Hmm."

"We met at the drugstore," Mercy chimed in.

Listening to her daughter, Kendra turned her eyes back to Stoney. "Oh, you work at the drugstore as well?"

"No, Mom. I met her from coming in as a customer." Giving her mother the big eyes behind Stoney's back, Kendra knew not to question anymore.

"Oh. Well. Nice to meet you anyway, Stoney. Are you two hungry? Excuse me, you three?" Kendra had finally waved the white flag, letting her daughter know that she was coming around to the idea of becoming a grandmother.

When Mercy walked back toward her mother, the embrace shared between the two sent shivers down Stoney's spine.

"I. Ah. I'll meet you outside," Stoney muttered, and almost ran out of the kitchen.

Pulling back from her mother, Mercy felt bad. "Dang it. What was I thinking?" she questioned herself, and placed a hand on her forehead.

"What's the matter?" Kendra asked, and touched her adult daughter's hair, looking past the doorframe where Stoney had been standing.

Slouching, Mercy tried her best to give the condensed version of her short friendship with Stoney. "She wasn't raised by her mother or father. She doesn't even know who they are." Mercy purposely left out the part about how she was trying to help her new friend locate the missing links.

"Was she adopted?" Kendra asked with a serious expression. "Because you know you can share with her how—"

Mercy cut her mother off. "Nope. Her grandmother raised her, but never told her anything about her parents," she said. "I don't know what the deal is. She seems depressed by a lot of things. Kinda weird, but you know."

"Yep, I know *you*, Mercy. The stranger, the better your mission is. Wow. Well . . ." Kendra didn't know what to say because she had become accustomed to Mercy being there for people regardless of their situations. "Be careful, baby. You may be having a baby"—she rubbed her child's stomach—"but you're still my baby. Where are you all headed, anyway?"

With a smile, Mercy said, "I will. We're actually going to her church. They are having a youth rally and then we're going to meet up and eat dinner with some of her friends."

With a mother's beam, Kendra said, "Oh, that's good. Sounds like fun."

"Yeah, I'm excited." With a small hug, Mercy turned and walked toward the kitchen exit, almost bumping into her godmother, Gracie.

"Whoa, li'l miss. How's it going?" Gracie greeted Mercy, who was in a hurry to exit the kitchen and go check on her friend.

With a kiss landing on the cheek of her godmother, who was more like a second mother, Mercy gave a few moments to allow Gracie to bask in her glow.

"Looks as though you are hurrying along the process, huh?" she asked Mercy while rubbing her belly. "Don't be letting everyone rub on your belly, either." Gracie looked in Kendra's direction. "What?" They laughed. "I'm the girl's godmother; you know I can do this!"

"Baby, go on." Kendra brushed her daughter away with her hand. "Auntie Gracie is liable to keep you from your plans."

"Hush, Kendra. Oh, your friend is outside waiting for you. Yep, you better get going." She finally released the love grip on Mercy. "I think the young lady was crying, if I'm not mistaken. I passed by and just spoke, and her eyes were bloodshot."

When Kendra and Mercy looked at each other, Mercy shared, "Yep, I'd better go see if I can talk to her. I'll see you all later." She rounded the corner and left the kitchen, headed to the outside.

"She surely looks familiar. Whose daughter is that?" Gracie asked Kendra, believing she had seen Stoney at church before.

Shrugging, Kendra couldn't confirm anything for Gracie. "Mercy said we don't know her. Said she met her at work. Dunno."

"Oh. I surely thought she was from the church. Wow. A grandmother? I think I'm a tad bit jealous, Ken." Gracie sighed as she took a seat on a kitchen barstool, resting her aged but well-manicured hands in her lap.

Cutting her eyes at Gracie, Kendra said, "Oh, you can have them both. How about that? The mother and the baby." They shared a seasoned laugh. "Your time is coming, though. When the time is right, that is. Shoot, it wasn't even my time, but we're here now." She leaned against the kitchen sink.

"Girl, those twins, excuse me, men of mine, aren't even trying to hear that. Gregory is adamant about me not bringing up the marriage conversation to him at all, and Geoffrey said when he's out of his twenties he *may* think about it. That gives me three more years to even think about being a mother-in-law first." Gracie shifted uneasily in her seat. "Maybe he'll be so lucky as to make me a grandmother on his honeymoon like me and Marcus did with my parents."

"Poor boys. I'll have to keep you busy so that you can stop meddling in their business. Are they coming home for the holidays this year?" Kendra asked about Thanksgiving and Christmas.

Shooing her friend, Gracie pouted. "Geoffrey said he may, but Gregory said he's working through Thanksgiving. And you know if Gregory doesn't come . . ." Gracie claimed.

"Then Geoffrey's not coming without him," Kendra ended, knowing her friend's sons all too well.

"Right. Some new building design that Gregory is over; he said he has to get the finished sketches complete before Christmas. Anyway, I can't tear them boys from Atlanta. Oh." Gracie snapped her fingers. "I forgot to tell Mercy they said they wanted her to call them." She looked over her shoulder as if Mercy would still be standing there.

"Sounds like they have some stuff they want to share with her." Kendra's eyebrows raised the roof.

Taking an orange from a bowl on the counter that was full of fruit, Gracie said, "Well, you know they are a bit disappointed about the situation she's put herself in."

"Yep, can't say that I don't understand though," Kendra agreed. "Imagine how I feel. I'm the mother."

Feeling Kendra's disappointed heart, Gracie wanted to lift her friend's spirits. The years between the two had seen some complex situations that only God could have delivered them through. No longer wavering in their Christianity and their walk with Christ, Kendra and Gracie, in the end, had been each other's backbone.

"Can you believe it though? You're about to be Granny Kendra." Gracie snickered when Kendra laid into her with the evil eye.

Reaching for her cleaning rag, Kendra again commenced the cleaning she had started before Gracie's visit. "Don't even go there, Gracie. Shoot, I'm still trying to decide if I'm going to allow my salt to peep through my pepper. A baby, my foot." Kendra couldn't help but laugh at herself.

"But for real though. We've been through some thangs, Kendra."

"And we're still standing. That's because God is good like that."

"And you better believe it," Gracie guaranteed.

Having taken history in athletics during her college years, and later on being part owner at Full of Grace gyms and spas, which Gracie owned, Kendra held strong to her belief in staying physically fit. Years ago, when she made choices for herself that had led to her acquiring a disease that would break anyone's spirits, Kendra had to fight for her life: emotionally, mentally, and physically.

Her first husband, now deceased, was a world-class champion in body building, and the two shared the deadly disease. Dillian and Kendra persevered through their illness and tried to live as normal a life together as they could. After a heart attack, which led to Dillian's death, Kendra's hopes and dreams disappeared on the day he passed. No longer caring if she lived or breathed her last breath, Kendra slacked on her medication along with taking care of her body. As far as she knew, no one would care about her being gone. But her mantra held true: but God.

She couldn't even believe God's grace at times. When she looked back over her life and saw all the wonderful things He'd done just for her, joy rang out loud and clear. Especially after all the pain she'd caused in so many others. What she did know was that hurt people hurt people. Her pain from her own childhood had catapulted from her then present life and leeched on to those around her. One of those persons was Gracie.

Gracie had been her first real friend, meeting Kendra in college and connecting from day one. But with Kendra forever being guarded, she only allowed Gracie to see who she wanted her to see. Instead of telling Gracie what she needed in a friend, Kendra had allowed Gracie to be a superficial friend. All the while she really needed someone who wouldn't be afraid to go through the trenches with her. For that, their friendship suffered dearly.

Promiscuous wasn't even the word for back when Kendra lived her life on the edge. Having a boyfriend who she had premarital sex with, yet still allowing herself free rein with any man of her choosing, Kendra was labeled a modern-day harlot. No one was off limits to her . . . not even her best friend's fiancé, Dillian.

"Who would have thought?" Kendra asked.

"Not me." Gracie continued to peel her orange, which she planned on sharing with Kendra.

"And to think, you are still putting up with me. Have I told you lately how much I appreciate you? How I love you?" It was often enough that Kendra told Gracie how much she loved her. For the hurt she'd passed on to Gracie, which she was sure she'd done on more than one occasion, Gracie still genuinely showed Kendra grace and mercy that God allowed. Not many women, if any, were willing to do such a thing.

"Gracie, you've been so good to me as a friend and sister." Kendra now leaned in, resting on the island that sat in the middle of the kitchen; it was the only item keeping the two ladies from each other.

"Actually you have. But have I told you how thankful I am for you, Kendra? Years ago when you came out of that coma and became a mother overnight, and built a relationship with God, you helped me get through all the mess that I had put my own family through. And let's not even talk about when that ol'—"

"Watch it, sister." Kendra giggled. "This *is* the bishop's house."

"What? I was just going to say heffa!" Gracie joked. "But seriously, girl. It took me a good minute to get over the fact that my husband had cheated on me and could've been the father to that Michelle girl's baby. You were there."

"But God." Kendra pointed upward.

"But God," Gracie followed suit. "And if it weren't for your mama, girl! Whew." Knowing it was God and God all by Himself, Gracie still had to give Mrs. Herlene credit for how she allowed God to work through her.

"Honey, she reminded me daily to look ahead, toward the mark. She said, 'Look to Jesus because He is the only answer.' You know that lady can share a word." Gracie readied her hand for the high five she knew Kendra would give her.

"She can give a word, can't she?" Kendra raised her hand to slam her high five into Gracie's awaiting palm. "But let's not count out Mr. and Mrs. Gregory. Your parents . . ."

"God rest their souls." Gracie's eyes bore a happy glimmer. "They prayed with me and covered me with the blood of Jesus. I know you went through your thing with Dillian, but when I'd gone through *my own* ordeal with Dillian, and God spared *my* life, when I lost my baby boy and thought I'd lose my mind . . ." Gracie reminisced about a pregnancy she'd planned years ago without yoking her prayers with those of her husband, Marcus. "But God . . ."

"But God," Kendra agreed.

"Sho'nuff!" Gracie smacked hands with her girlfriend again. "Where is Mrs. Herlene anyway?"

Finally finished tidying up the kitchen, Kendra sat and took a piece of orange that Gracie offered. "You know Kenya's running a revival up north. Mama and James went with her."

"Look at God, would you. Miss Kenya is walking in her gifted anointing. Evangelist Kenya. Wonderful."

"It really is. I'm so proud of my sister. She may be twenty years younger than me, but she can give me a word any day," Kendra proudly declared.

"Now, wait a minute. You're not too shabby yourself, Missionary. What you and Bishop have going ain't nothing to play with. I'm still on a spiritual high from the tag-team message you all brought some weeks ago," Gracie affirmed.

"Thank you, girl." Kendra blushed. "I'm blessed and I have to tell it. Girl, I just have to." Kendra flipped her wrist upward, feeling the spirit jump on her.

Gracie sat, thankful how God had worked in her and her best friend's lives. Gracie may have started the salvation race before her girlfriend, but from where they were now standing, God had placed Kendra as a spiritual guide in Gracie's life.

When people still questioned her being friends with Kendra, and sometimes gave her a stare or shook their heads in wonder, she held true to what she always told them. "He's just good like that." And no doubt she meant it.

She had no clue herself how she could still be yoked with Kendra. If she dealt with flesh, she wouldn't even know how she could allow herself to breathe the same air Kendra breathed. All she knew was that God was sho'nuff, sho'nuff good like that.

Not only did Kendra use her body to come between Gracie and Dillian, Gracie's then fiancé, but Kendra exposed Dillian to the deadly disease of HIV/AIDS. Where God intervened, yet again, was sparing Gracie from any inch of the disease. No scare, no scars. And on top of all that, God had blessed her with a loving husband.

"Tell it, sister," Gracie coerced.

"For God to keep me, when people die daily from HIV/AIDS complications, is nothing short of miracles and blessings. And *then*,"—she punched her pointer finger against the cabinet—"for a man of God to come into *my* life and love me in spite of

all my impurities, a man after God's own heart . . ."
Just thinking about being married to a bishop, a
holy man of God, Kendra was in awe of how God
had turned her life around. With tears welling up
in her eyes, Kendra knew her praise was for real.

"For God to send me someone who not only
cares about me, but my child. Gracie, *hallelujah!*"
Kendra took a quick praise break. "Now you know
I have something to praise God about."

"The Word says that when you are in Christ,
you are a new creature," Gracie versed.

"Old things have passed away, and behold all
things have become new," Kendra finished. "God
raised me from a coma, gave me a new walk,"
Kendra said as she walked a few steps in a small
circle, "a new way to talk; blessed me to have my
mother back in my life. Without condemnation.
Hallelujah. He blessed me with forgiveness
from my friend." She waved her hands in the air.
Kendra praised the Lord right in the middle of
her kitchen. "I *got* to praise Him, Gracie."

"Praise Him, honey. Ain't nothing like knowing who you are in Christ," Gracie agreed, and
helped her sister in Christ extol their God together.

Breaking out in her gift of tongues right in the
midst of her kitchen, Kendra allowed her mind
to linger on her deliverance.

"I'm a product of what God can do if we allow Him to turn those things around. I let my past set me back for far too long. But when I found out about the goodness of Jesus and His mercies, I didn't allow molestation to keep me down. Rape, being promiscuous, *hallelujah,* I didn't allow jealousy, envy, or strife to rule me. My, my, my!" Kendra couldn't cease her praise. "I'm not ashamed of what the good Lord has done for me. I had a baby in the midst of being in a coma while infected with HIV. And my baby came through unharmed. You can't tell me what God can't do."

Full of tears, as she was anytime that her best friend and first lady spoke over the congregation or the many conferences that sought her, Gracie sat, full of God's grandeur.

"God, you are awesome," Gracie added without taking from Kendra's praise. Fixed on her own thankfulness, Gracie was overjoyed.

"He is. He is, Gracie." Kendra finally took her seat. "I know the Word says separate yourself from unbelievers, especially so you won't be pulled into the trenches. But thanks be to God you didn't let go of our friendship. I'm thankful for you."

Shaking her head, never taking credit for God's goodness, Gracie knew God had it all under control. "Unbeknownst to me, Kendra, it was the God in me. It was He who nudged me right back to you every time the devil tried to keep intervening."

"Well, thank you, God, for your goodness."

The two lifelong friends held hands as Gracie said, "Thank you, God, for Jesus, the best teacher anyone could have."

CHAPTER 15

Stoney

It wasn't as if she'd never seen it before. She'd seen mothers and daughters embracing all the time: at church, at the store, on television. But the closeness, within feet of her, had gotten to her psyche. Instead of standing and staring with want in her eyes, Stoney let herself out of the house.

The tears that had become commonplace in her eyes lately had once again made an entrance as she made it out to Mercy's car. Sitting and waiting for her friend to make her way out of the house, Stoney busied herself by checking her e-mail on her upgraded phone.

She still couldn't believe the actions she had taken. The day at the restaurant when she held Keithe's business card and his wife's picture in her hand, Stoney had scanned his information and locked it in her memory. The e-mail was all she needed. With her blood boiling over by the day, Stoney took a chance and e-mailed Keithe.

The first day she took a chance e-mailing Keithe, she thought she'd just write and thank him for being so kind. And maybe apologize for leaving in haste as she had, but when her thinking was reeled in to the idea that Keithe could possibly be married to her mother, Stoney jumped to a whole other level. She figured she'd try to get more information on this Michelle lady.

Now noticing a reply to her last message, Stoney allowed her heart to flutter.

Hey Stoney. I thought you had forgotten about me that quickly. All is well on this end. Houston's weather is what it is and a "real" vacation is needed for these old bones to get back into the groove of things. Talk to you later.

A broad smile had crept across Stoney's face after having read the e-mail and held its place. Stoney couldn't wait to click "reply" in order to respond. She'd been playing with the idea of getting more information through Keithe about the lady who she was certain was her mother. The only way she could do it was by getting closer to him. Any woman can tell when a man has an inkling of a feeling for her, and Keithe hadn't been any exception.

Of course I can't forget you! Old. Who? You? Please. LOL. I know a vacation is usually made up of beaches and sand, but if you take time out from work again, come this way.

Hoping he'd buy into her ploy, Stoney flipped her phone shut and thought about the possibility of letting her secret out to someone who could literally get her through her mother's door. She didn't know how, but Stoney definitely planned on getting Keithe on her side.

As soon as Mercy had made it out to the car, the tears that had plagued Stoney's eyes dried up.

"You okay, Stoney?" Mercy questioned before she was fully situated behind her steering wheel. At three months pregnant, going on four, she was already learning how to make her stomach a priority. Viewing her newly rounded face in the visor's mirror, Mercy pulled her shades over her eyes.

"Uh-huh. I'm good. I just had a moment, that's all."

"I'm sorry. I should have thought about bringing you around my family. We're a touchy-feely family. No doubt you still need to come around more often. Maybe when I come back for my first weekend back you can hang out more with me and my family." Mercy cranked the car.

"That sounds like a plan. Your mother seems really nice." Stoney wished she could have stayed a bit longer.

Mercy agreed with a dip of her head. "She is. I really can't complain. My mom has been through a lot. And I don't mean the average. But God has truly blessed her."

"Maybe she can give me some pointers on how to survive, then," Stoney suggested, half joking, really needing a mother figure even if it couldn't be her own mother. "I really don't feel like going to my church now," Stoney confessed. Not wanting to let on that she hadn't been as involved as she used to be, Stoney wasn't prepared for everyone to crowd her with questions about where she'd been. Especially not in front of Mercy.

"Uh," Mercy said, easing off of the brakes before they left the hidden gated subdivision. "Why didn't you say something sooner? I thought you wanted to take a break from the search and do something fun since this is my last full week here."

With a slight turn, Stoney pulled her left knee into the passenger's seat and faced Mercy. "I know, I know. But I think we're doing so good on the search and we are getting closer. I can feel it."

With Mercy's help, Stoney had gotten to know that it wasn't just Houston in which Michelle lived, but the suburbs. But which suburb she and her husband resided in was still up in the air.

"If you say so," Mercy responded. "It's hard finding this woman. I just wish you would have told me much sooner that her name *used* to be MaeShell." Mercy playfully rolled her eyes at Stoney. "I guess it doesn't matter since it's still hard to break into her private world. I don't see how the paparazzi do it."

With the first real laugh making its way from the pit of her belly, minus the doses of drugs she was used to taking, Stoney felt relaxed around Mercy.

"Let's go back to your place and see what else we can come up with," Stoney suggested.

"But what about your friends, uh, Vicky and Mike?" Mercy really wanted to know more about Stoney, but knew she could only do so by being around people who knew her.

Stretching her body back straight, Stoney had an answer for that. "I'll just text them and let them know that something came up." She wished she never would have told Mercy about the youth choir's annual day. Getting fired from the doctor's office would only help Stoney dodge Vicky even better. Not really knowing what had transpired with Stoney, Mercy figured she'd just go along for the ride. For the past few weeks, her friend had been on the verge of what seemed to be a depressed breakdown. Knowing prayer would only help heal Stoney's heart, Mercy was willing to be the friend Stoney needed at all costs. Unfortunately, Mercy had no idea what it would truly cost her in the long run.

CHAPTER 16

Michelle

Michelle couldn't believe it. As far as she was concerned, she wasn't going to believe it, either. Whoever had enough time to play games hadn't thought her plan all the way through. Michelle was the queen of making someone's world cave in around her. And whoever this was e-mailing her husband had some nerve.

> Hey, Keithe. It was good meeting you and hanging with you. Thanks for all the pep talks and encouragement. Thanks again for dinner. Please forgive me for cutting our dinner short. Oh, and of course I'll be praying for you and your wife as well. I hope all gets better.

It had been a while since Michelle had participated in the "Seek and Find" game that nosey and untrusting spouses played. As far as she was concerned, there was no time like the present. With months having passed since she last checked her husband's account, Michelle scolded herself for not keeping better tabs on her husband.

"She just buried herself," Michelle whispered through clenched teeth.

Knowing that her husband randomly checked his personal e-mail, Michelle went in and re-routed all of the e-mails from Stoney to her own personal account. It didn't matter that the e-mail was friendly as all get out. Who cared?

After her duty was done, Michelle logged out of her laptop and shut it down. It had been some months since he'd been back home from his little Dallas hiatus and Keithe had yet to have a real conversation worth anything with her. Now she knew why.

"Whoever this Stoney is, he must still have her on his mind," she announced matter-of-factly. With a hard stand, Michelle just stood, waiting for Keithe to make his exit from their bath quarters. "Should have checked this stupid account weeks ago." Michelle paced the floor.

Initially, the night Keithe made it home from Dallas, Michelle was so very careful not to show any annoyance about her husband jumping ship. Instead, she started her conversation by asking if he'd had a good getaway.

When he responded, "Sure," Michelle kept her cool.

"Well, the sheets are fresh if you want to call it a night." Making herself busy with continuous paperwork, the night that could have been full of hell for both of them wasn't. Michelle was glad she'd kept it cool. But now, realizing what had transpired during his time away, Michelle reached back and grabbed from the "all the devil's hell is about to break loose" stored energy.

When the bathroom doorknob twisted, Michelle clenched her fist and was ready to make a scene. It wasn't until her husband came through the door that she realized she was on the verge of telling on herself. Easing the anger out of her face, Michelle took things slowly.

"So, have you decided where you'd like to go for dinner, Keithe?" Michelle stood in a spot as if she'd planted herself, waiting for her husband to come out of hiding.

Dabbing his face with a hand towel, warding off the sting of his freshly shaved face, Keithe stopped before progressing further into their master suite.

"Uh." He gave a quick glance at Michelle's stance. "I'm not really hungry." His demeanor showed his desire for Michelle to continue doing her own thing, just as she had been doing for years prior.

Not giving him time to rethink anything, Michelle took one step forward, wanting to lunge at her husband for the simple fact that some woman had e-mailed him. And not only that, but he'd e-mailed her back. "You've been loafing around here for months, Keithe. It's a beautiful Friday, and you mean to tell me you don't want to go to dinner with your wife?"

Telling her inner man that she wouldn't break her silence about what she thought she knew, Michelle had to hold her breath and count to ten before she opened her mouth once again. Fist rolled tight, she followed her husband toward the closet. When she started again with, "It's Friday night, Keithe. I haven't eaten and neither have you," he interrupted her.

"I ate earlier. I'm good, Michelle."

As she looked at him, she realized that the man she had found and picked to marry wasn't going to budge. Michelle went like a casino's gaming machine when the jackpot was won: she went off.

"Oh, so you good? What was so good in Dallas, Keithe? Who did you stay with anyway?" She moved to the side of her towering husband. Not letting on that she had taken her own personal interval with a new steady fling during the time he was away in Dallas, Michelle kept her energy up for the rounds she was about to go. "I'm listening. You leave Houston, go to Dallas, only to do God knows what, and then you can't even have a meal with me?" Right as she nudged him in his side and landed a punch to his arm, Keithe shut her down.

"Enough. This is enough. I left Houston to get away from this," he said, referencing her hollering and laying hateful hands on him. "You're speaking and hitting on me like I'm some child, Michelle. If you must know," he said as he stared her in the eyes, "I was at Mike's. It's not like you didn't know it. You left several messages on his voice mail." He started his stride once more.

Still hard on her husband's heels, Michelle wasn't ready to let go. Pulling the tail of his shirt, Michelle held on until Keithe was almost dragging her. She shouted, "Where are you going now, Keithe?"

After he roughly withdrew his body from her grasp, Keithe only stopped for a short amount of time in their room to slide his feet into his tennis shoes. "Friday night service at church, Michelle. Do you think that would be justified?" He finished tying his Nikes. Standing and readying his walk out of the room, Keithe stopped when Michelle charged in front of the door.

After a beat, Keithe said, "What? Did you want to go?" He knew the answer before she even tried to lie. "I didn't think so. I'm sure you already have plans with one of your god brothers, play brothers, or somebody's brother." He tried again to continue his stride toward the staircase, while Michelle kept forcing her weight against his to no avail.

"Will you please stop, Michelle? Please," Keithe begged, thinking his wife would cease the circus act. The traveling UniverSoul Circus didn't have anything on his active and very energized wife.

As Michelle inched closer to her husband with what looked like tears in her eyes, Keithe stood, scratching at his beard, which had filled out within the past weeks. Even with the emotions she tried to pour out, Keithe didn't think twice about what he wanted to say.

"You know, back in the day I was upset about not having kids, but I'm glad I didn't have children with you, Michelle. Would you have beaten them like you're doing to me?" He jumped back as his beautifully aged wife soared in his direction. When her open hand landed across his full and permanently lined lips, all Keithe had energy left to do was close his eyes. The answer must have been yes.

"That . . . That is exactly what I'm talking about." He started his tread once he opened his eyes and saw Michelle soften her stance by the door. Covering his mouth with a loose hand, Keithe offered, "And for a moment I was sad when Stoney asked why we didn't have any children." He bit his lip and finished. "I'm through. I'm so through," he yelled with hands held high and blood trickling down his mouth. He'd only been waiting for time: time to make a move out of the marriage. But there was only so much he could take.

"Stoney?" Michelle's face showed anger creeping back into place, not caring a bit for her husband's injured mouth. Removing her bangs from her eyes, Michelle couldn't believe her husband had the audacity to actually say the floozy's name.

"Who is that, your woman?" She didn't want him to know she knew the name of the woman he'd spent time with while he was in Dallas. "Your floozy? How dare you share your floozy's name with me, Keithe?" She followed her husband through the door and down the stairs. Not forgetting the remark he'd made about them rearing no children together, the sting of her past wallowed in her shallow heart.

Waving off her accusations, Keithe figured telling his wife who Stoney was wouldn't do any good, but hoped the threats wouldn't start again. "She's Mike's friend," he said, knowing Michelle would never believe it, especially knowing just how serious she felt about Mike's social life.

"Yeah, right. That—"

"Then why did you ask, Michelle? We are through." Keithe abruptly stopped on the stairs just as she was about to follow him, but shortly started again once he realized that his declaration of the end of their marriage had made Michelle jolt. "Just stupid. How could I be so stupid to think this woman was going to change just out of the blue," Keithe chastised himself when he thought about the smoothness of his return home. "I should have known better." He blew out a breath before jogging down the remainder of the steps.

When Michelle saw he wasn't going to stop this time, she did what only she knew to do. In her heart of hearts, she didn't want to lose Keithe. She knew she loved her husband and really didn't want to be without him. Releasing a short breath, Michelle knew she'd stooped low . . . again.

Sleeping with another man because of her own insecurities was one awful thing. Having a relationship on the side right out of the box was downright devious. No matter what, Michelle was sinning in a major way, first against God and then herself. Her husband had been caught up in her own corrupted world.

Michelle couldn't hide behind the excuse of being insecure because of her age. Michelle knew her problem with cheating on her husband was because of a past with no security. With all the power she held, Michelle used it to her own advantage.

"Okay, okay. We can go to church together, Keithe," Michelle blurted out while holding on to the staircase with either foot on different steps. With eyes squinted and mouth held tight, Michelle let her head drop as hard as she could, trying to hide the fact that her face held no emotion. The Bobbi Brown powder attached to her face was still untouched by tears. Making a noise that resembled that of a whiny cat, Michelle almost forgot how to cry.

"I don't want you to go. *Hmm*." She tried to imitate a cry once again. "I'll go to church with you, honey. But . . ." She looked up quickly. "Well, tonight you can go ahead and go and I'll just go with you on Sunday. Okay? I'll see you when you get back."

Looking back, Keithe didn't give a gesture in any direction; rather, he kept his distance and traveled toward the exit of their home. The only thing he could think was what was next for Michelle and her schemes? Being as sincere as she'd just tried to sound, he knew she was up to something.

Making it a bad habit, Keithe had bypassed doctor's orders yet again. He had been driving steadily since he'd come back from Dallas. With the way Michelle had just flown off of her handle, there was no way he'd stop now. With no intention of even beckoning his driver, Keithe had no need to wait for someone to rid him of evil.

As soon as he'd gotten into the driver's side of his Range Rover, Keithe's cell phone rang. Once the screen displayed Mike's number, there was no pondering whether he'd answer.

"'Sup, dude?" Keithe started off.

"Hey, bruh. What's the deal? How's it going, man?" Mike dove in.

With a click of a button, Keithe accessed his cell phone's speaker.

"I'm good." With a slight roll of his eyes and shake of his head, Keithe retracted his response. "I'm lying, man. This lady is killing me. Literally killing me."

Mike wished there was more he could do, but knew nothing was up to him. No matter what, he knew all relationships were different, but seeing his best friend going through the same old same old was getting old. Seeking advice for himself, Mike quickly realized nothing would get solved with one phone call. His purpose in calling his best friend was to be counselled on his own personal affairs, but that would be something he'd deal with later.

"Aw, man. What's going on now? I haven't heard much from you. I thought it was all gravy in H-Town."

"Yep, me too. That is, until I just got popped in the mouth."

"Ouch." Mike grimaced on his end of the line and didn't dare ask for details.

"Exactly. But what's up with you?" Keithe maneuvered through the subdivision, headed to church service. Licking his lip like a wounded cat, Keithe glanced at his rearview mirror then back at the road in front of him.

With a deep breath, Mike blew out some steam and decided on sharing another time. "It's nothing. I was just going to ask for advice on some dating stuff, but . . ."

"Mike. Now you know better." Keithe added his brotherly tone to his voice. "Nothing has changed as far as talking to you about stuff like that. I thought I let that be known years ago. Your dating life is your dating life. I don't want any part of that."

Rolling his eyes, Mike did his best to calm his friend down.

"Chill, man. Geez. I know this." Mike referred to his knowing better than to share his lifestyle with Keithe. "But it's nothing like that. It's not like that anymore."

"Oh?" Keithe questioned, waiting for the assurance from his friend.

"Yes. I meant to talk to you about it when you were down here, but hey, you have a lot going on right now. I'll just hit you back later in the week." Mike lost his gusto.

"Look, Mike. I'm sorry, man. I'm just all worked up right now with Michelle and all. If you want to talk, I can pull over and we can talk. I'm here for you."

"I know, I know. But I'll let you get to where you're going," Mike said.

"Well. Okay. Should I be worried about something?" Keithe was sincere with his question.

With a slight chuckle, Mike reassured his friend. "Actually, it's something I'm sure you and my mama have been praying about. I'll catch you later," Mike answered, and disconnected the call.

CHAPTER 17

Keithe

Keithe arrived at church right on time. Everyone in attendance was in the midst of prayer. Falling in line with the others, Deacon Keithe, a title he'd earned at church and what the congregation lovingly called him, made his way to the altar.

"Yes, Lord," his voice added to the others calling out to the Lord in a tuned praise. "Yes, Lord."

The senior pastor of the congregation started off in prayer. "With our repenting hearts, Lord, we come to you and ask that you come in, Lord. Come into this sanctuary and have your way. Clear out the weeded path that crowded our week. That crowded our homes, Lord. For the mind that has been clouded by deception, come in, Lord, and take the pain away."

"Come on in, Lord," Keithe backed the prayer up. Knowing prayer never did anybody any harm, Keithe asked God to remove him so that the Lord could get the total praise. "Lord, come into my heart and my mind, Lord, for the understanding," he whispered.

On his knees in prayer, Keithe swayed from side to side as the tears began to run down his face. When he felt the pastor lay his hands on his head and the liquid feel of the blessed oil running down his forehead, Keithe yearned even more for the power of God to come in.

"Help me, Lord. Help me," he requested. It had been rough before. It was sad to even have to count, but he'd been through three other cheating episodes. With each time Michelle promising it would be the last, Keithe wanted the pain to officially be over.

There was only so much he could take and his heart had just about run its course. On his trip back from Dallas, Keithe had made up his mind to just leave. Or so he thought. It was just like Michelle to throw some loveless, superficial affection in the middle of the problem. Almost trapping him at the front door on his return home, he could tell Michelle had rehearsed all she would do while probably wanting to do nothing.

He tried. When he made his way back home, he tried to get his feelings off of his chest and let

Michelle know that he couldn't do it again. "No more," was just about all he could get out before she kept shushing him.

"Michelle, no. I—" She had interjected again. That's when he just silenced himself and listened to her recycled garbage.

On and on she went about making a mistake and knowing how she'd taken him for granted. Again. How she really, really, really loved him and didn't want anyone else. Again. When she rehearsed what seemed to be made-up lines about having no love or peace growing up and having no one to love her in her childhood, Keithe just shrugged and walked past her. And there he was, again, stuck.

Before he'd left the house for prayer service Michelle wanted so badly to get him back under her wing, under her spell, by promising a visit to church. In his heart Keithe wanted to believe her, especially since she had never been one to bring up the subject of church in the first place. He didn't know if he should even hold his breath on the whole idea, or just let it go.

"Lord, I need you like never before," he added to his plea. "I can't make this decision without you. I can't figure this out on my own," he prayed, wanting God to release him from the marriage. With divorce on his mind, Keithe wanted, needed an answer from God before making any sudden moves.

"You say it's better to marry than to burn, Lord. I married, Lord. I married for better or worse, Lord, but the worse is killing me. I don't want to give up on you, God, because I know you have never given up on me. Speak, Lord. Speak, Lord."

Crying out to the Lord had never been a problem for Keithe. Being reared in a family where God was the beginning, middle, and ending of their being, Keithe loved to praise God. With admission, Keithe knew he had found his wife while still straddling the fence himself, and knew he should have been more than up front about his love for God and his backsliding condition at the time. But it was only after they'd married that Keithe found his way back to God like the prodigal son.

For years he had felt himself going through the motions, in a revolving door with Michelle. On days like today, he felt that if God didn't move on his behalf, he'd lose it. Keithe was on the verge of breaking. The last time he had broken down was years ago when Michelle had pushed him to the limit. He had found his open hand gliding across her face, and because he didn't want history repeating itself, he knew the only way out was to pull on the hem of Jesus' garment.

"Excuse me, Deacon Keithe." His pastor tapped him on his shoulder. "Can you come with me? Follow me." His pastor didn't wait, but walked away through the long sanctuary and down the hall until he arrived at his office doors.

With a somber face, Keithe asked no questions, not even when he walked through the double doors and sat in the chair in front of his pastor's desk.

"How are you doing, Deacon Keithe?" Pastor Meeks asked.

On the verge of releasing the remainder of tears he held, Keithe silently thanked the Lord for intervention.

"I'm holding up. But I don't know for how much longer." Keithe no longer tried to keep the mannerisms of what the world classified as manly. He wept. "This hurts. It hurts really bad, Pastor. I can't even believe it's me sitting here crying about my wife cheating on me. And the bad part is I can just leave. I can just walk away from it," he said, gesturing with flinging hands. "But then again, I can't. It's like there's a hold."

Never a revolving-door member, throwing all of his life's woes on the senior pastor of his church over and over again, Keithe had long ago shared his marriage dilemmas with Pastor Meeks.

"Deacon Keithe, you know I'm all for keeping the family together." He wanted to assure his dedicated parishioner as he always did whenever they were in each other's presence. "But it takes a toll on me as well to see you so downtrodden. Believe that. What can I do to help you?" Pastor Meeks wanted to leave the healing process for Keithe, but definitely wanted him to know he was there for him.

Knowing he could give his own opinion, Pastor Meeks was no novice when it came to counseling, and knew all steps would have to be taken from whomever was seated across from him. Today it happened to be a long-time member and worker in the church.

With a slight shake of his head, Keithe knew better. "It starts with me. I know. I . . . I just can't seem to get my thoughts to stick in one direction. I mean, Michelle is constantly avoiding our marriage with outside affairs."

"Hmm." Pastor Meeks listened.

"How can I compete with whomever she allows into our marriage? How can I get this woman to see that what she is doing is wrong? I mean, it's just wrong." His voice went up an octave.

"Go on."

Fidgeting with his finger, Keithe crossed one leg over the other, and tapped his size-fourteen Nike. Figuring he should just release the pain, Keithe continued.

"I don't want to compete. I want a wife who allows me to love God and follow Him. I want her beside me, praying with me, praising God with me. I don't want to walk this walk alone." As if he thought he knew what Pastor Meeks was going to say, Keithe said, "I know God is there walking me through this trial, but I'm married. Why shouldn't my helpmate be there? Michelle's not there, emotionally or mentally."

"And when you ask Michelle to become one with you, on this journey, what is her reply?"

Keithe explained, "In more ways than one she suggests I get out of her face. As a matter of fact, she tried to throw a dog a bone before I came out to prayer tonight, saying she'd start coming to church with me . . . but, of course, not tonight."

Pastor Meeks sat up straight, confident that the Lord had placed a word in him to pass to Keithe. "Take her up on her offer. She may think she has one up on you, but show the enemy that you mean business. You want your wife, and you want your marriage to work. Bring her on in and allow the Word to work its course in her life."

"You think, Pastor? I haven't seen Michelle pray since the early years of our marriage. And I'm sure she did so then only because I did so."

"Oh, I know so. The Word is powerful. Some people come to church and make it out to be a country club affair, or come because that's what they know to do. If they stay long enough, the Word can become embedded in their hearing."

Nodding, Keithe understood what the pastor was speaking of. For him it had happened the same way. He had slacked in his walk himself once he left his parents' home. By the mere fact that he continued to make his way to the house of the Lord, and taking with him what he'd learned, Keithe eventually gained his rightful relationship back with God.

"I tell you what, in a couple weeks, Bishop Perry will be coming for a three-day revival," Pastor Meeks announced.

"Oh, okay. That's wonderful. I always enjoy hearing him speak a word," Keithe shared while feeling his joy return with the talk he and Pastor Meeks were having.

"Yes. Bring her then. You know, so she won't think she's being picked on, or pointed out. No visitor's card or visitors standing those nights. That Sunday morning he'll be presiding, and Monday through Tuesday as well."

"Definitely sounds like a plan."

"A plan from above." Pastor Meeks pointed upward.

Upon leaving his pastor's office and the church, Keithe drove around parts of the city until he settled on going to his office. Nothing interested him out in the world. Everything he had wanted was at home, but everything at home didn't seem to want him. Just as he closed his eyes to rest at a red light, a vibrating jerk hit his hip. Detaching his iPhone, Keithe wasn't at all surprised.

Chasity, his wife's court reporter, had been in heavy rotation with her advances since she'd seen him back at the shindig that was a bust. Keithe wouldn't have thought twice about how she retrieved his work's cell phone number, since he was plastered all around town on billboards, offering his law expertise. But since she had texted his personal line, Keithe gave a thought on her contact.

Just that quickly, Keithe's mind jolted in his thinking. The prayers that had still been lingering were in a downward spiral once he laid eyes on all the explicit details Chasity drove his way. Just that fast, he lagged in his thinking, and considered actually taking her up on her offer.

For all Michelle had done to their relationship, Keithe tried to hold on and not join the mess in which she put them. The one time he did stare too long at a woman in a courtroom, his wife made sure she walked right past him, landing her high-heeled footwear on the tip of his Crockett & Jones. Still, wasn't he deserving of a mess up? Especially with all he'd taken for the sake of being honorable to his wife?

The vivacious, mid-twenties, and full-of-night-life Chasity laid it on thick, explaining how good of a woman she was and how deserving a man he seemed to be. To add to the cause, she made sure she let him in on how Michelle was a philandering and disrespectful wife. Not able to argue with any of it, Keithe raised an eyebrow, took his foot off the brake, and placed it on the gas.

It was just that easy. Affairs happened all the time, and one of the reasons was because people thought they could do anything they wanted to. No foundation, no godly conscience, no thought of the next day or what consequences affairs bring.

The way Chasity displayed her no-holds-barred attitude for that which she wanted, Keithe wondered if it was as easy for Michelle to dip and dive as much as she did. With a person filling someone's head to the max with what they could do, to replace what someone wasn't doing, Keithe could see how it would be a struggle to stay righteous if one was not rooted in God's Word. Even if one was rooted in God's Word, for that matter.

While at the next red light, right as his payback thought was about to take over in his thinking, Keithe replied to Chasity's text before he deleted it:

Please don't text me anymore. Not interested. Never have been and never will be.

Just for a heavenly reminder, he added, What would Jesus do? and chuckled as he thought about what her reaction would be.

At this point, he knew that just as it was possible to slip up and begin an affair, it was also possible to remain as he had: steadfast, unmovable, and always abounding in the Word of God. All he knew to do was to keep his prayers going up and Jesus would work it out.

"Jesus, take the wheel." He declared his new catchphrase as he continued his drive.

CHAPTER 18

Stoney

Mercy and Stoney had gotten even closer over the weeks. It was to the point where Vicky and Mike couldn't get in contact with Stoney. She spent so much time with her new friend, and if they could get in contact with her, they couldn't stay in contact with her. And it was all fine by Stoney. The more she busied herself in Mercy's presence, along with e-mailing Keithe, she felt it was another step closer to being near her mother.

Mercy sat in front of the computer, plugging in the information as Stoney gave it out. They had been going strong for months, trying to locate Stoney's birth mom and everything that had to do with her. Granted, Stoney seemed to eat, breathe, and sleep the search, but Mercy just figured all the nervous ticks were because it seemed they were getting closer. Stoney still hadn't shared with her the deep, dark secrets of her past.

To break the monotony of the task, Stoney paced the floor, admiring Mercy's small home, which actually was the pool house her parents had converted for her a year prior. It was like something right out of the sitcom *The Fresh Prince of Bel-Air*.

"I still can't believe your parents handled your entire pregnancy with ease." Stoney kept walking around the petite home setting.

"Oh, no," Mercy interjected, making eye contact with her friend. "Don't let my mother fool you." She adjusted the small pillow behind her back. "My parents literally tore into me. I mean, really. A bishop's daughter? You know my dad laid it on thick."

Turning back to the screen, Mercy continued. "But they know I'm not perfect. That's not an excuse though. Don't get me wrong." She stopped typing again. "Because I really did screw up. Just stupid." Mercy stepped into sadness.

"You're not stupid, that's for sure." Stoney came to her friend's rescue. "You just made a mistake is all." Stoney thought about her own mistakes, even to the point of pushing Vicky and Mike away.

"Yep. And my parents know that I'm going to do everything I can to be the best mom. I'm still going to finish school. It's not easy, but I'm doing it." Mercy had already started off her first year of pharmacy school in Houston and made the trip back home to Dallas as often as her pregnant body would allow. Sometimes she'd fly in for a quick getaway since she didn't have class on Fridays. Other times she would carpool or drive alone.

"You're right. Wish I had that same support system." Tears welled in Stoney's eyes.

"I'm here, Stoney." Mercy rose from her seat and walked to give her friend a hug. With a wobble, Mercy embraced Stoney. When she felt the bones pushing through Stoney's back, Mercy allowed worry to cross her face, but decided to ease her concern toward her friend.

"You know what, Stoney? You can't allow this to get to you." Mercy didn't want to keep drilling it in her friend's head how important it was to keep living in the midst of her storm, but knew no one else was there to remind Stoney otherwise.

Easing from their embrace, Stoney said, "I know. But you—"

Mercy didn't let her finish. "But me, what? I'm no different than you." Letting out a breath, Mercy hoped her truth would help Stoney.

"My dad was mad about my pregnancy, Stoney, but he has a kind heart, an understanding heart at that." Then, with the roll of her eyes, she added, "I'm not even going to let you know just how hard my mother laid into me." She shook her head, wanting Stoney to believe there was truth in what she said. Mercy knew Stoney thought highly of her mother and that she was a sweetheart. Not yet meeting Mercy's father due to his traveling and his ministry keeping him occupied, Stoney couldn't even make herself believe that he would be any different.

"Look, my mom was married before, even to the point of her having a baby by her deceased husband, my *real* father. My daddy, Bishop, didn't come into my life and take the role of being my father until I was three years old."

Wanting to reclaim her seat for the sake of her aching feet, Mercy thought enough of Stoney to share what she knew her mother didn't mind. "My mom had a hard life growing up. Some of her problems weren't even hers to own. Other people brought their problems and dumped them on her, and the rest she did to herself. It got to the point of my mom being promiscuous and acquiring HIV before it was all said and done," Mercy eased from her lips, not knowing how Stoney would take the news.

When Stoney's eye drooped and dragged her mouth along for the ride, Mercy knew exactly what her friend would have said had she not been in shock.

"So when my parents initially got together, they didn't even try for their own children. They were advised not to. My dad doesn't have any biological children. So for me, having a baby, a grandbaby for them, he's charmed underneath the pain. He told me so." Mercy was glad Stoney allowed a smile to creep across her face and joyous tears to touch her eyes. "So see, you don't know someone's hurt behind their story. You can't just look at our glory and think it's all gravy, baby." Mercy made a whimpering Stoney cackle. With another quick embrace, Mercy sat back down.

"I haven't even met your dad yet and he sounds cool," Stoney said. "I mean, not even having a biological child and loving your mother enough to call you his?" Her thoughts rested on Keithe, wondering how he would react to her being his stepdaughter even if her mother didn't want her. Besides wanting to get closer to him in order to get information on her mother, Stoney wanted him to be nothing more than a father to her; the father she never had.

Studying the screen, Mercy absentmindedly said, "Well, years ago, before he came into our lives, he *did* think he was the father of a lady's baby," she shared. "Girl, yes, my mom said there was some drama going on with my dad and Uncle Marcus. What was that lady's name?" She processed her thoughts while tapping on the keyboard's keys.

Stoney looked over her friend's shoulder at the screen as Mercy still pondered her dad's ex-girlfriend's name.

"I can't think of it right now. Oh well. It'll come to me, I'm sure," Mercy said.

"Where is your dad now anyway? I never get to see him." Stoney broke up their research time.

Without looking back at her friend or stopping her typing, Mercy said, "Traveling to some church, of course. I think he's in Houston now. When I was coming into town, he was leaving."

Clicking on her YouTube icon on her computer's desktop, Mercy went to her "favorites" link and selected James Fortune & Fiya, "I Trust You."

The words, "I'll trust you/I need to know you're here," rained throughout the atmosphere.

"I will/trust you." Each word was sung in rotation with deep meaning. It crept into Mercy's own thinking and heart. Stoney closed her eyes as her mind finally listened to the words.

Backing away from Mercy and no longer wondering what was on the computer, Stoney walked over to the sofa. Seeing the song working a positive response in her friend, Mercy turned the volume up. Knowing that music could minister to a soul, Mercy started singing along with the words that blared through the speakers. The vocal ability her grandmother had passed down to her mother had also been passed down to her. Able to transition a song into her own, Mercy was able to share her gift from God.

By the time Mr. Fortune added his own vocal and started ministering in word, Mercy stood from her seat and walked to her friend.

"Dear God, please come into Stoney's heart. Allow her peace, God. The peace that only you can give her. Let her know that there is purpose in her despite what it looks like." She sat with Stoney and hugged her. "Let her know that you died so that she can live. You are her mother, You are her father, Lord. Fill her void, God. Help her, Lord, as only you can. Let her know, dear God, that in your Word, Psalm 27:10, when it says 'when my father and my mother forsake me, then the Lord will take me up,' let her know that you are the Lord of Lords, the King of Kings. You are the strong tower that she needs."

Stoney dug her head into Mercy's shoulder as the worship song screamed in unison all of what God could do.

"God will make a way."

As the song slowed, Mercy knew she had to continue ministering as God had led. Knowing He could use who He wanted to use, and when He wanted to use them, even a pregnant, unmarried young lady who had tripped up her own walk, Mercy wanted to be that person Stoney needed.

"Stoney. The Lord is the keeper of your soul. You cannot fight the battles of this world on your own." Mercy lifted Stoney's head. "Don't hinder your walk, or your praise, because of this, Stoney."

"I . . . I don't know how to." Stoney let out a breath. "This is driving me crazy. I mean"—she sniffled—"why me? Why me, Mercy? Why am I in the world by myself?" She jabbed at her chest, which covered her aching heart. "Do you know what I went though growing up?" She asked the question knowing that Mercy hadn't a clue.

Resting her own head in her lap, Stoney rocked and released. "I had to take care of a grandmother who didn't know how to take care of herself. When I was younger I just thought she was mean and hateful. But she was sick. And . . ." She hated to recall her past. "And I hate to think that my mother knew it and still left me there. Why would she leave me there to suffer like that?"

Slightly shaking her head, Mercy just wanted to listen.

"It was torture. My grandma hit me, called the police on me, and cursed me. The abuse wasn't her fault." She wanted to let Mercy know she knew the difference. "But still, for a young girl to go through that, it was way too much.

"She would think I was my mom and forget about me all together. I didn't really exist in her life after I hit junior high." Now sitting with her knees pulled together on the sofa, Stoney finally felt like sharing more of what she'd gone through.

"She even thought I was her own mother at times." Stoney replayed the times when Grandma Susie's mental problems, not leaving out depression all together, were intertwined and worked against the young girl.

"What was her illness?" Mercy thought to ask.

Stoney pointed to her left temple. "Her mind. Schizophrenia." With the look of understanding on Mercy's face, Stoney felt like someone finally got her. "The doctors had told me Grandma Susie didn't want to believe she needed the medicine and other help they offered. She just . . . she just did what she wanted to."

She didn't want to scare Stoney into hiding, but Mercy couldn't pretend with her friend anymore.

"The medicine that you used to pick up?" Mercy dared to ask, but needed her friend to verbalize what was really going on in her world.

A nod was all Stoney was giving. She wanted to go on and share with her how she had started taking her grandmother's medication at a young age, but didn't want the questions or the help in that way. There was no doubt Mercy wanted to and probably could help her move in a positive direction, if she allowed her to. She wasn't ready.

The prescriptions were the only things that were keeping her going, and with the feeling as though Jesus had put her on back burner, and certainly didn't come through with a nice reunion with her mother, Stoney only wanted to dwell in her own world. And for the time being, someone else's medication seemed to be her way out.

On his slow days, Mike had no meetings or choir rehearsals. He just had time to do whatever he needed to do. During that time the only thing Mike was required to do was to spend time alone with the Lord. Even with his surround sound blasting the latest *WOW* compact disc, while he cleaned his home, Mike was certain he heard his home phone ringing.

With his thumb still on the down button of his Bose remote control, Mike answered, "Hello, you've reached Brother Mike's residence." His announcement rang clear through the cordless receiver.

More than happy that Brother Mike couldn't see her expression, Vicky rolled her eyes and gripped her felt-tip pen firmly in her tiny hand. "Uh, yes. Brother Mike? This is Sister Vicky." It took all of her energy to carry on a bit of conversation with him. If it hadn't been for Stoney not showing up at work the last week or so, eventually getting herself fired, or dodging her calls, Vicky's silence to the guy she had gone on one date with would have been continued even longer.

Wondering why Vicky would be calling, Mike sat during the silence and considered if the woman he still had a crush on was actually calling to rekindle a friendship. "Vicky? Hey, how's it going?"

Noticing that Brother Mike left off the usual signature church title that made her everyone's sister, Vicky rerouted the friendly feel of the conversation and went right into her motive for calling.

"Stoney was released from her position here for constantly not showing up. Now I really can't get in contact with her. Is she with you, or do you have any idea where she is?"

With a "go figure" attitude, Mike allowed his response to register with what Vicky had affirmed. "She's not here. I haven't spoken to her in a couple of weeks. Have you tried her cell phone?"

"I did." Vicky allowed her worry about Stoney to take precedence over any ill feelings she held for Mike. "It's so unlike her for her to not even have her phone on. I . . . I just don't know what to think."

"For sure." Mike finally set the remote down and followed suit himself. "Well. Hmm. Hold on. I'm going to click over and try to call for myself." After Mike followed through, with the result being the same, he clicked the line back to Vicky and confirmed her worries.

"Yep. No answer for me as well," he said. "It's going right to voice mail."

"Exactly what I thought." Concern lodged itself into Vicky's voice. Drumming her manicured nails on her desk, Vicky didn't know what else to say or do.

Knowing how strong willed Vicky was, an independent woman of sorts, Mike, hearing hesitation, knew Vicky wouldn't ask anything more of him.

"I'm glad you called, and let me know. I think I'll just take a ride by her apartment and see if everything is all right. I mean, I don't know of any family Stoney has. I mean, you know her grandmother passed on even before Stoney started coming to the church."

"Right. I . . . I . . ." Vicky didn't want to lose her nerve. If it weren't for the love she had for Stoney, Vicky wouldn't have even suggested it. But before she knew it she said, "I should have known something was wrong. Stoney's been acting crazy. She went part-time at the doctor's office awhile back when her car was acting up. Then the doctor, he—" Vicky stopped short.

"He what?" Mike prompted.

"Well," she whispered, figuring she could share with Mike since both of them seemed to be all Stoney had. "They've suspected she's been taking medication from the sample closet."

"Wow," was all he could say. He was ashamed for not following through when his gut feeling tugged at him to intervene and ask Stoney more about her taking prescription drugs. He just hadn't gotten around to it. "Well. Uh. I know where she lives. I'll just call Pastor and let him know what's going on, before just popping up."

"Okay. Well. It's almost my lunch break anyway. Do you think you can call me back and let me know if you find out anything? Or can I meet you somewhere?"

"I can do better than that. How about I come through and pick you up? Are you still at Medical City on Forest Lane?" When Vicky let him know she was still in the same spot, Mike answered, "Cool, I'll be there in a few," while trying to keep in mind it wasn't about him, but all about Stoney.

CHAPTER 19

Stoney

It was too much time to spend alone for some-one who believed her world was caving in around her. But she had no choice. Being caught taking pharmaceutical drugs from the office supply quickly dismissed her from her job, leaving her all alone since college classes were in full swing. Not even bothering to sign up for fall classes, and with no friendship other than the one she chose with Mercy, Stoney sat in her apartment, literally looking at the four walls closing in.

She tried to settle on the words Mercy had spoken over her life, the prayers her friend had called out on her behalf, but couldn't let them sink in. If God had been listening, wouldn't He have let her life finally iron out? Why did she have to keep going through storms the average twenty-one-year-old didn't have to go through?

Not able to make sense of her life and how she'd been dropped off and raised with a grandmother who should have been watched by someone herself, Stoney only had energy to reminisce. Thinking back always made her ponder if things could have been different: could she have done something opposite of what had been done? Could her grandmother have made her mother take her? Could her grandmother have looked for her mother and given the information to Stoney before she had gotten as bad in the mind as she had? Deep down Stoney knew her grandmother had been barely able to find herself.

By the time she had finished grade school and advanced to junior high, Stoney's world was all but steady. There were days when she'd have to feed herself, dress herself, and get herself ready for school. Those were the days when Grandma Susie was plagued by her spells, the same spells the doctor labeled as schizophrenic.

From time to time, neighbors would come and check on Stoney, but didn't make it known to social services because they knew the girl would be taken away. Stoney didn't know if this was at all beneficial for her or for her grandmother. At times she wished someone with common sense would have intervened. It would have saved her years of what she called torture, and it could have possibly rewarded her with a real family.

"You know Susie Gene love you, girl. Just like she did your mother," her grandmother's good friend, Mrs. Inez, would share with her. "She can't help that her mind done up and left her, Stoney. When your grandfather was killed in that car accident years ago, your grandmother held on as long as she could. But she didn't have no know-how." Stoney would look up with her big eyes. "She couldn't read or write. No one would help her. She couldn't pay her bills, and raising MaeShell the best she could obviously wasn't good enough for that girl." Inez would hold a scowl on her face anytime MaeShell's name would leave her lips.

After she would hear all she could for the day, a young Stoney would jump off of Mrs. Inez's porch and head across the street to check on her grandmother.

In the middle stages of Grandma Susie's illness, the pills, the strict diet, and hardly any sleeping all caught up with her. Stress, carried over from the years, pounded her life. From what she could tell, when MaeShell had abandoned her mother, it threw Grandma Susie over the edge.

The lifestyle changes that needed to be made in order for her to remain balanced were all the things Grandma Susie didn't know how to control. Being young and having no real understanding about her grandmother's illness, Stoney didn't know when too much of anything was too much, so she just went along for the ride.

The struggle the years brought added more confusion and doubt about life, and distorted Stoney's direction. When her grandmother's way worsened to her thinking everyone was against her, even her grandchild, Stoney, kept praying, kept going to church, and finally found out how to keep herself together: by taking the pills her grandmother refused.

The more her grandmother's mind became that of someone else's, the more Stoney just played along, hoping sometime soon someone would come and rescue her. No one ever did.

"Mama," Grandma Susie would call out to Stoney as if she were a child herself. "Mama, I'm hungry too. Can I have some?" she'd ask Stoney, who could barely stand taller than the gas stove, but had no choice but to try to prepare breakfast. It was either that or starve.

After years of the entire "baby scene," as Stoney called it, she caught on and learned to just ride the wave when Grandma Susie's mental side broke through.

"Yes, chile. I'm going to feed you," she would announce to her grandmother, who would sit patiently at the kitchen table with only her underwear on.

Pills that Grandma Susie's doctor had started giving her to calm her down had seemed to take effect and allow her to relax. The prescribed medicine made her walk upbeat, and Grandma Susie was even nice to be around during those times. That only lasted so long. Once Stoney reached high school, not even the pills seemed to work.

Over time Stoney's grandmother forgot more things, people, and the way of life. She held attitudes longer and talked to invisible people and eventually declined all together the medication Stoney tried to administer. That's when Stoney became nervous, sad and found herself using the same medication for her own relaxation purposes. To Stoney, the pills were the only means to keep herself intact for any mood her grandmother would be in.

"It's just not fair." Stoney wallowed and rolled to the other side of her bed. For the majority of her unproductive day, Stoney lay around and thought about what all she had endured in her life with Grandma Susie. Thinking deeply on the conversations she and Grandma Susie had had over the years, and knowing her grandmother had never really been in her right mind, Stoney wondered how much she really should have retained from their one-on-ones.

With her hands folded, Stoney laid her head on the backs of her hands. Right as she felt the rough patch of skin on the inner part on her wrist, Stoney's mind took her back to one of the days in her past, which had pushed her to the edge.

"Did you do what I told you to do, girl?" Grandma Susie questioned Stoney right as she walked through the doors from her day at school.

"Huh?" Stoney retorted.

Halfway running toward her granddaughter, Susie raised her hand just to let it land as hard as she could across Stoney's face.

"Ugh," Stoney yelled out, and grabbed her face. "What are you doing?" she asked.

Not backing off, Grandma Susie asked, "Where is she? Where is my baby? Where is MaeShell?"

"I . . . I don't know. I don't know," a young Stoney answered, and tried to run from her grandmother's grip.

Able to sprint past her ailing and only grandparent, Stoney then locked herself in the restroom and planned to end it all. Yelling through the thin, wood-framed bathroom door, Stoney swore she would end it all if her grandmother didn't back away from her.

Staring in the mirror was always her way of coaching herself through the bad times she'd have to endure with Grandma Susie. The tears, the anger, the pain, and loneliness, the hurt, distrust, confusion and doubt all crowded her thoughts on the day she fought to end it all. Just as she had made a ragged incision on her wrist and small drops of blood began to leave her body, shouts on the other side of the door were heard from the neighbors Grandma Susie had run to get help from.

Today was no exception. The air was thick. The thought of defeat plagued Stoney's mind so heavily. Being that she didn't converse with any neighbors, Stoney figured if she did away with her life, no one would come looking for her.

With Mercy out of town, and Vicky and Mike going on with their lives, Stoney rocked from side to side in her bed, trying to decide if she wanted to continue breathing or if she wanted to give it up.

Hearing a knock at the door, Stoney became still, thinking someone had the wrong door. Not expecting company, especially since Mercy always called before she came over, when the knocking continued, Stoney got out of bed and did a sneaky walk toward her front door. With her phone ringing simultaneously, she almost lost balance and fell.

Stopping short and picking up her cell phone on the way, Stoney saw Vicky's number. Peeping through the peephole, she saw Mike. When Vicky became visible through the peephole, Stoney couldn't believe it.

"What are they . . ." Stoney whispered as she saw her friends.

"Stoney, we know you're in there. Who does she think she's fooling?" Vicky seemed upset.

Stoney didn't know whether to be glad that someone actually cared enough to come looking for her, or mad because she wanted to be alone. As soon as a smile spread across her face, her hurtful anger wiped it away.

Seeing her friend shrug, it seemed to Stoney that Vicky was at a loss for words. "Dunno. I really do appreciate you answering my call. Since she was let go from the doctor's office, no one has been in contact with her."

"And with her not coming to church for the last few weeks, I don't know what to think." Mike hadn't put his guilt away. "I should have been a better friend. I don't know what I was thinking."

When Stoney saw the two finally make their departure from her door, down the stairs, and out into the parking lot, the breath she'd been holding was let go. Trying her best not to give God credit, Stoney still knew He'd shown up and stopped her from doing the unthinkable.

***

"So what's up with you?" Mike chanced a new conversation with Vicky as they made their way from Stoney's apartment.

With a roll of her eyes, Vicky slowly exhaled. "What are you talking about?"

Having picked her up from her job, when Mike spotted Vicky standing at the doors of the hospital entrance, he tried to steady his heartbeat. No matter how many times she rolled her eyes in his direction, he still got jittery in her presence.

"Well. We did date once," he wanted to remind her.

"We went out on a date, Mike." Vicky glanced in his direction, making sure to correct him.

"Went out to eat, a movie, coffee. Whatever. I never heard from you again. Was it that bad a date? I thought we had fun."

"We did. You were just that bad a liar." When she viewed him out of the corner of her eye, Vicky was ready to spill her guts. She'd been holding in her suspicions for far too long. "I had to hear through the grapevine that I was a guinea pig." She wanted to know if he would admit to what she was talking about. "You didn't tell me you were *trying* to date women again. I had no idea and I think it was very unfair."

Now with the understanding of how things had changed, Mike steadied the steering wheel and eased off the gas. When Vicky raised her hand to express herself in conversation, Mike closed his eyes, thinking she would lay a good one on him. When he didn't feel any pain burn his face, he opened one eye at a time.

It had been told to him that being up front was his pathway to living a straight life. And that was just one of the things he wanted and needed to talk to Keithe about. With his friend having his own life crisis, Mike winged it the best way he could.

Thinking he could start over without telling others about his former lifestyle was obviously the wrong way. "I see," he released slowly. "I didn't know how to say it. How to tell you."

"How about, I'm gay, or I was living a homosexual lifestyle?" She waited. "I had to find out through Facebook. A friend of a friend of a friend let me know they knew you."

"But that's just it. *They* don't know me, because if they did, they'd know I'm not rolling like that anymore." Mike defended himself as he drove on.

"'Anymore' is the key word, Mike."

"You're right." Wanting so badly to compliment Vicky on her outward beauty, especially when she was angry, Mike knew how much of a groupie he'd look like since Vicky had on scrubs and a lab jacket. "But I haven't for a while, either. And I don't plan on it ever again." Adding sound to his car's speakers, Mike drove, allowing the silence between the mutual friends to flow in the midst of their own thoughts.

The short ride back toward the hospital was nearing an end and Mike didn't want to leave their silence the way it was. "I'm really truly sorry." Mike pulled into a parking space. "I just don't want to be associated with that lifestyle anymore." He looked up at her, seeing her concern. "Not that I want to pick it up at another time either, Vicky."

"Well, from now on, Mike, you're going to have to be honest with women you date. You can't make the choice for me—I mean, them. You can't just think they're going to be fine with anything and everything in your past. I was up front with you about me having a child out of wedlock. I mean, seriously, I can't judge you, but I have to be able to make those types of decisions for myself. Any woman will have to."

"You're absolutely correct. I really hope you can forgive me. More than that, I really hope you can believe me." He wanted so badly to ask her for another chance.

Not able to deny his handsomeness and his ability to make her smile, Vicky's stomach tugged. "I can only believe what you give me to believe," she said.

Getting geared up for the deep conversation, Mike was willing to try his hand. "See, that's where you are wrong. I didn't treat you just any kind of way. Or come off like I was holding on to my past when we went out, did I?"

Giving it a quick thought, Vicky said, "Um. No. Actually, you really didn't."

"So?" he sang.

"So . . . what?" she asked.

"How about I take you out on an 'I'm sorry' date. Can I do that, please?" When she didn't give an answer right away, Mike asked again. "Please?"

"Hmm. Sure. We can be friends again. Not promising anything else." She laid the foundation.

"And that is all I'm asking. A second chance is a first chance. Thank you."

CHAPTER 20

Michelle

By the time church service was over and Keithe had dragged her across the church to meet the guest bishop, Michelle wished she had gone with her first mind and exited to the lady's room. The entire church service Michelle had dozed into a midday nap. Behind her big hat and big shades that were not needed with the cloudy September's day, the only thing that woke her was Keithe's elbow nudge.

"Bishop Perry." Keithe approached the man who had called on the heavens on behalf of the church's congregation. The way he had preached, anyone present could tell the knock had been granted. With hands flying high and feet beating the floor at a rapid pace, the Holy Spirit rested in their midst.

Approaching the man of the cloth as he was in a leisure conversation with his armor bearer,

Keithe waited patiently as the man turned toward his opened hand. "Good to see you once again." Keithe smiled, having met the bishop on previous visits.

"Likewise, Deacon Keithe," Bishop Ky Perry remarked, laying his eyes on Michelle and losing his voice at the same time. Shocked from seeing the woman he hadn't laid eyes on for over twenty years, Bishop Perry almost lost his grip.

Not taking note, Keithe continued with his reason for the short interruption. "Your sermon was more than right on time. Me and my wife . . ." He reached for a stiff and stunned Michelle as he continued. When he didn't feel Michelle's palm greet his, Keithe turned with furrowed eyebrows. "Honey." Keithe sought her by walking two steps and guiding her with his hand on the small of her back.

It wasn't until she felt Keithe's hand squeeze and nudge her forward that Michelle caught her breath. *What in the world?* was all she could think. Instead of the questionable words she would have used if not in the house of the Lord, Michelle blinked and held her eyes shut long enough to utter from her heart, *Help me, Lord*.

"As I was saying, Bishop, the sermon hit home for me and my wife this morning. We'd been praying—" Keithe said before being interrupted.

"Your wife?" Bishop Perry questioned with the drop of his head, in a tone suggesting that Michelle could be anything but Keithe's wife. Having acquainted himself with the young deacon a few years back with his visits to the Houston-based church, Bishop Perry couldn't recall seeing Keithe with a wife, nor ever mentioning a wife. Looking down at Michelle's ring finger verified the union.

Still not picking up on the subtle hints that were on display between the bishop and Michelle, Keithe, about to continue his praises, was interrupted as Michelle braved the waters. With her hand in a stiff stance out in front of her, she broke the ice.

"Bishop Perry. How do you do?" she greeted him.

"Grateful as the day before," Bishop Perry muttered and inched close, about to make the fact of their acquaintance more real by asking Michelle how she'd been over the two-plus decades since he'd last seen her. But when she responded, "It's great to meet you," he held his tongue.

Nodding, the bishop, Ky, doubted himself. As the woman in her mid-fifties retreated behind her husband and busied herself on her Black-Berry, he had the chance to view the ring on her right hand that he'd given her all those years ago.

"Hmm. Didn't know you were married, Deacon. Newlyweds?" he asked, keeping his voice to a low range, under the other fellowship going on in the sanctuary.

"No. Not at all. We've been going at it strong for fifteen years. And I do mean every bit of that," Keithe said with a sad smirk. "But your message, it hit home. Just what we needed to keep our marriage alive. Just what Jesus ordered."

During Bishop Perry's message on the roles of men and their love for Christ, and showing the women an example of how to love them, as they themselves love the church, Keithe received confirmation in his spirit that he had loved his wife in the right manner.

Dismissing Michelle's game of not knowing him, Bishop Perry could only imagine what she had taken the poor deacon through. He could only believe, by her actions, that Michelle's past hadn't been a part of their courting sessions, nor their marriage counseling. If he were a betting man, he'd have figured that she didn't plan on discussing her past in order to heal their future.

"Glad God could use me in a way befitting for you," he said, sealing the short conversation with a handshake. "I won't keep you from your wife. I know how a wife and children are ready to feast after Sunday service." The bishop looked over his shoulder to see his own wife and her best friend inch closer. A quick thought raced back of him being in the delivery room with Michelle as she delivered a heavy, bouncing baby girl. As he looked back in Keithe's direction, no doubt he noticed Michelle slipping farther away from her husband.

"Right," Keithe continued, with no clue of what was possibly brewing. "Except we don't have any children." He let the thought sit for a minute. "It was nice seeing you once more. Have a safe trip back to Dallas, Bishop." As he turned to beckon Michelle to his side for their dismissal, Keithe noticed his always-stiletto-card-carrying-member of a wife had beaten him by a great distance on their departure.

Biting his tongue as hard as he could, Bishop Perry let the notion go to question about the baby he had held, kissed, and pledged to be the best father to . . . all before the results came back and let him know he wasn't the father at all.

"Oh," Bishop Perry yelled toward Keithe. "Deacon, I want you to meet my associate pastor."

By the time Marcus Jeffries made it to the side of his best friend and senior pastor, looking past Keithe, Marcus was able to glimpse at Michelle as she made her way out of the sanctuary doors.

While still holding on to Keithe's hand, not yet responding to his greeting, Marcus looked quickly over his left shoulder to his friend. For the moment he put Bishop Perry's title to the side. Not laying down his cloth himself, Bishop Ky Perry simply nodded in response to Marcus's impending question.

"Ni . . . nice to meet you, Deacon. I've heard wonderful things about you from my bishop here, from his visits to your city." Marcus finally accounted for holding on to Keithe's hand.

"Thank you, and likewise. I'm glad to have finally made your acquaintance. Next time I hope we all can get together for dinner," Keithe replied. "Once again, be safe on your journeys, and good seeing you again."

With a lot of nodding going on, both Bishop and Marcus couldn't wait for the scene to clear with Keithe's presence. Just as Bishop Perry was about to expound on the entire ordeal, Gracie and Kendra walked up to their husbands: Grace to Marcus and Kendra to the bishop.

"Honey, Kendra and I are . . ." Right before Michelle was about to clear the corner, Gracie's eye landed on the woman who more than once played a part in plaguing her life.

"What were you saying, honey?" Marcus asked his wife, hoping she hadn't seen who he and his bishop had seen.

"Wait a minute," Grace eased from her lips, releasing more of a suspicious tone than any anger she'd allowed to subside years ago. "Was that?" she asked more silently than aloud, not waiting for the answer from her husband or the bishop.

Taking her eyes off the exit of the sanctuary, Gracie pulled Kendra in close to her, wanting to get her friend's attention.

"Sister Gracie?" It was evident to Bishop Perry what his best friend's wife had taken note of.

"Ah." Gracie tried to pull her gaze back into their circle. Not knowing the two men had had an up-close encounter with her old nemesis, Gracie tried to play her secret reflection low-key. "Yes, Bishop, I was just saying the sermon was excellent. The power of the Holy Spirit ruled up in here this morning."

Still unaware of what was actually happening, Kendra reinforced Gracie's statement.

"Honey, Sister Gracie is correct." She leaned in for a pleasant hug with her husband. "But don't worry. I won't tell our congregation back home that you showed out this morning." The two middle-aged women nudged each other with a laugh.

Cutting the conversation short, Gracie said, "We'll meet you guys in the car." Grabbing at Kendra, Gracie started up the aisle, walking in the direction Michelle had disappeared to.

Thinking it to be a great idea for the two of them to trek behind Gracie and Kendra, Bishop Perry and Marcus were held up once the senior pastor of the church came over to make conversation with the two.

"Tell me what's the deal, and don't act as if I didn't see you, either," Kendra asked Gracie as she trotted behind her through-thick-and-thin best friend.

"Girl," Gracie said through gritted veneered teeth. "You will not believe who I just saw up in here. Come on." Gracie almost dragged her best friend along. "She went this way."

"Who? Girl . . ." Kendra's words trailed off when her eyes were drawn to the missing piece of the puzzle.

With Michelle standing outside of the church's glass door, obviously waiting for her husband to pull up with the car, Kendra saw her. The woman who had once tried to destroy her was less than fifty feet away.

Gracie stopped, turned, and drove her eyes into Kendra's surprised eyes.

Then it was Kendra who grabbed Gracie's hand and made a beeline toward Michelle.

"Girl, now that was weird," Kendra said about their three-way encounter with a dodging Michelle. Walking back toward their awaiting Town

Car, the women conversed about Michelle: not a friend, but an archenemy who never meant either one of them any good. "Just about as weird as that young girl Mercy brought over to the house some weeks ago. I tell you the truth. Something must be in the air."

"If that's the case, that means we must have let it drag in with us." They shared a laugh. "She fidgeted, blinked, and stuttered, acting as though this was twenty-plus years ago and we're still fighting her over our men. I'm not stuttin that woman," Gracie confirmed. "She couldn't even get a 'hi' out her mouth."

Kendra giggled, looked down at her girlfriend's tightly fisted grip, and understood Michelle's quandary when it came to seeing the two ladies.

"Well, I see why, Gracie," a swayed Kendra pointed. "The way you're holding that gold-plated clutch would have made me rush off too."

Holding her mischievous grin, Gracie led the ladies out to the parking lot, being respectful and speaking to the parishioners along the way. As they made it to their awaiting car, Gracie picked up the deserted conversation.

"So who has Mercy rescued this time?"

Shutting the door behind her, Kendra rested her pocketbook on the empty space between her and Gracie.

"Chile, you know the young girl you saw that day at the house. She was waiting in Mercy's car out front of the house. Mercy said she's been a customer at the drugstore for the past year. I tell you what, I'll be glad when the fall season rolls on a little deeper and she stays in Houston more. Bringing that girl around . . . She's strange." Kendra added a scared-straight look to her face. "That girl thinks she can save the world," she said about Mercy.

"What do you expect, Ken?" Gracie reached out and touched her best friend's hand. "I mean, I know now that God has sustained you, but you have a testimony that Mercy has lived through *with* you. She probably only wants to help others out, just like people have helped you."

"I know. She's my mercy all right, and you're definitely my grace. I wouldn't have it any other way." Reminiscing to herself, Kendra knew she could count it all joy when it came to her daughter.

Landing in a waterless pool of depression after Dillian's death, not taking her medications and giving up on life, Kendra wanted to resign from living. But God.

Finding herself locked in a body surrounded by darkness, Kendra was afflicted by a coma she had slipped into and remained in for almost a year. What no one knew, not even she, was that

God had allowed greatness to take place even in the midst of her storm.

The last in vitro procedure she and Dillian had committed to, unbeknownst to her, had paid off. Kendra was blessed to come out of the coma and be greeted with the news of being with child, along with being reunited with a mother she had learned to hate.

Miracles and blessings being dashed from above, Kendra turned her life over to the Lord, and her future gained momentum.

"I remember where I came from, girl. That's why I just take it in stride when it comes to Mercy. Nonetheless, the friend of hers seems to really need some prayer. I'm going to keep my eye on her," she confirmed as they made it to the car with the driver standing outside.

"And it looks as though I better send some prayers up for Mrs. Michelle, also," Gracie added.

"Oh, see there. You done said a word." Kendra gave her girlfriend their signature high five. Allowing her mind to reel in to her daughter's friend, Kendra made a note to have a talk with Mercy when she returned home.

CHAPTER 21

Ky and Marcus

"Now *that* was a flashback," Marcus threw out at Bishop Perry as they walked toward the back chambers of the church. Holding the door open for his friend and bishop, Marcus held a garment bag for Bishop's change of clothing.

"You're telling me." Ky wiped his forehead with his cloth he'd used while giving his sermon in the pulpit. "I just can't wait to see what the ladies have to say."

"Now *that* I can live without. That woman was almost the death of my marriage, man." Marcus scratched lightly at his slightly tainted salt-and-pepper goatee as he shut the door behind him. "I know Gracie saw her. That woman don't miss a beat."

"You think so?" Bishop yelled out behind the walls of the changing room. "I don't know if they caught a glimpse or not, Marcus."

Taking a look at his aged image in the mirror on the wall, Marcus cut his primping short after admiring the physique he had been able to uphold.

"Are you serious? Man, Gracie is not that slick. I know that woman and she ain't pulling no wool over nobody's eyes. I saw the way her eyes almost bucked out of her head. And she can't blame it on that thyroid stuff, either." Marcus laughed at the thought of his wife, and Bishop Perry laughed because he knew his friend was telling every bit of the truth.

Coming out of his hiding place, dressed in fresh slacks and a clean and crisp white button-down, Bishop Ky Perry faced his friend with the shake of his head.

"If anyone should be upset with her presence today, it should be me." He raised his eyebrows. "She had me fooled." He stood with hands in his pockets. "I thought . . . I thought she actually was having my baby."

He didn't want to get caught up with history, but Marcus had once dated Michelle himself before wedding Gracie. A mid-marriage encounter with Michelle left him asking God and his wife for forgiveness for the affair he'd thought he wanted.

Around the same time, Bishop Perry, having met Michelle on his own, dated Michelle to the point of believing he was a prime candidate for being her child's father. It wasn't until they were in the delivery room that the features of the child confirmed in his heart that he was still childless. It wasn't until weeks later that the DNA test authenticated his heartbreak.

"Well, bud," the bishop said, walking closer to Marcus, "looks like we will have to face the jury soon enough."

"You can say that again. A jury filled with my wife and Kendra is filled to capacity. Shall you say a quick prayer for us, please?" Marcus half joked.

"I thought you'd never ask," Bishop Ky Perry agreed.

CHAPTER 22

Stoney

Stoney didn't know what she was doing, but she knew being out of control was getting way out of hand. Another week had passed by and she took a look around her small apartment and saw clothes budding from the drawers, trash running out of the can, and the floor crowded with stuff.

Standing in front of one of the two mirrors present in her studio apartment, Stoney was hoping she could find herself. She'd become so obsessed with Michelle, trying to find a way to get into her life, so fixated with breaking through to her mother's world, it had drained her. She no longer cared about giving her cares over to her savior and leaving her burdens there.

Casting all of her cares hadn't been the closest thing to her thinking. At the very moment she couldn't get a handle on anything if it didn't have something to do with what she wanted. Keithe was the exception.

It didn't matter if it was a smiley face or just a hello for the day. The one thing Stoney was consistent at was e-mailing Keithe. It had gotten to the point where she wanted to have steady contact with him, just in case she got up the nerves to blurt out the pain his wife had left her.

She still had not shared with Mercy all that had transpired, because she didn't want Mercy to think she was a liar and stop helping her. Now that Mercy was in Houston and had only been home twice since, Stoney's mania about Michelle was doing more damage to her psyche than ever before.

She'd been let go by the doctor's office and, in turn, she had decided to let school go completely. Still living off of Grandma Susie's burial money, rent was not a problem. Most days she just stayed in her apartment and wallowed.

"Stoney, what are you trying to do?" she asked herself while pulling her skin tight on her face. Not being able to get her hands on any medications since the day she had been fired, eight weeks prior, Stoney lost all sense of get up and go. Stooping to means she never thought she would, Stoney believed there was only one more way for her to get part of what she wanted.

Picking up her telephone, Stoney dialed the doctor's office, asking to speak to Dr. Connor. Holding on the line, she tried to prepare for her lie she was willing to tell. "Ah, uh, hello," Stoney responded to Dr. Connor's voice on the other end.

"Stoney? Is that you? How are you?" Dr. Connor's surprised voice sounded through the mouthpiece of the telephone.

"F . . . fine. I'm good, thanks." She didn't know if she should be short and sweet or if it was all right to show how sorry she was for abandoning the doctor's office.

"Good. That's good to hear. How can I help you?"

"Well, I wanted to know when it would be best for me to come and pick up my last check, instead of waiting for it through the mail?" Thinking she could buy some time while there and get some sample drugs, Stoney wanted to get there as soon as possible.

"Hmm," Dr. Connor oozed. With no hard feelings thrown toward Stoney, he pondered his own desire. "How about I drop it by your place?" He purred like a cat, not really giving her an option.

Standing and pacing her apartment floor, which was covered with shoes and anything else that had its own home other than the floor, Stoney wasn't too keen on the response.

"Well, I don't want to put you out of your way, Dr. Connor. I can come up. It's no problem—"

He cut her off. "Stoney," he whispered through the line. "Look, I know what it is you want." He lent a pause to see if she'd try to deny it. When she didn't, he continued. "Let's just say I can bring you what you need if I can get what I want when I get there."

With an internal gasp and external tears rolling down her face, Stoney lingered as long as she could. "But. I . . . I . . . Uh." She knew she was stuck between a rock and a hard place, but only because she wanted to be. "All right," was what she said before she let herself change her mind.

Rattling off her address and directions, when she hung up the phone, Stoney fell to a heap on the floor. She hadn't been to church in weeks, and probably even longer had she stayed away from praying.

"I can't do this." She shook her head, ashamed of even trying to get a prayer across. Being a virgin, she had no idea what she was getting herself into. Her desire to be relaxed medically outweighed her desire to stay pure.

"What is it now, girl? Go on and let that man bring them there pills fo' ya. You making a big deal out of it. If ya God didn't want you to have it, He wouldn't make a way, don'cha think?"

"I don't want to do this. I can't do it. But I don't know any other way," Stoney yelled out. When her mind wandered to the previous week when Mike and Vicky showed up at her doorstep, Stoney knew she had been making excuses. Even when she thought about Mercy, Stoney knew if she had spilled her guts to her, she would try to help. But because she chose to stay secluded and chose to fight the battle on her own, Stoney backed herself up into a dark corner and waited until the doctor made his way over to her place.

It had been hours since the knock on the door. After it was all said and done, she didn't even bother getting up to lock the door behind him. Rolling over and getting the bag full of prescription samples Dr. Connor had brought was all she had enough energy to do.

Never diagnosed with any illness of her own, Stoney thought herself to be crazy for giving herself to a man who wanted nothing more than what he felt she could offer. No longer a virgin, and with the pain in her heart and body boiling over, Stoney cried for what she had done.

When she had energy to get up, Stoney walked slowly toward the bathroom inside of her bedroom and placed her head under the faucet. She gulped just enough water in order to swallow the handful of pills.

"If you play the game right, I can bring you anything you need. Just let me know when you're out and I'll make another trip this way," Dr. Connor had eased from his lips as he zipped his pants. "I won't tell anyone . . . and if you want your job back, just let me know."

Stoney had said nothing. There was nothing for her to say, knowing that with the handful of samples he brought, she'd certainly call him back in a day or two.

CHAPTER 23

Keithe

Keithe had been sitting and thinking. Every evening after work he'd found himself locked in his office. The little corresponding he'd done with Stoney always left him chipper. The only way he made himself feel okay about the entire conversing situation was to psyche himself to believe that he was replacing Stoney with the daughter he could have had, had Michelle not been so selfish. Wanting to believe he had replaced the void of a child with Stoney, Keithe happily replied to her messages when they hit his inbox.

So when are you coming back down? Mike has been busy with Vicky and now I feel like both my friends have abandoned me. And with my new friend living all the way in Houston, the boredom is killing me. Hey, I wonder, if I make a trip up that way, could I see you?

Confused about the abandoned part and doubly confused about the seeing each other part, Keithe wanted to question her, but thought differently. From what he had heard, it had been the other way around. Yes, Mike and Vicky had become close, but that was due to Stoney's cutting her communication with both of them. Knowing how coy Stoney had been around him, Keithe thought better than to ask about the situation.

"Well, I guess I'm due for a quick trip to D-Town soon." Keithe voiced his response as he typed on his engraved Hewlett-Packard laptop. "I'll see what I can come up with." Waiting a few moments, Keithe wondered if Stoney had been signed on and was able to respond quickly. When he saw *Great, don't let the others know. It'll be a surprise and I'll put it all together,* Keithe wondered why all the secrecy.

With furrowed eyebrows, Keithe wanted to question why it had to be such a surprise to begin with, but didn't. When he felt his heart flutter, he knew he was excited about seeing Stoney, and knew it wasn't because she was filling a childless empty space. Knowing he should cease all communication all together, he couldn't.

"I'll let you know when my schedule clears. Can't wait to see you." Not believing he'd added the last line, Keithe closed his laptop without shutting it down.

With his bowed head, Keithe spoke directly to the Lord about the way he was feeling.

"I hope I'm not overstepping my boundaries. Cleanse my heart, Lord. If there are any impurities, Lord, help me to purge them. If this friendship is not your will, Lord, please say so. Speak to my heart, Lord." Just as he finished his plea, his office phone rang.

"Keithe speaking," he answered, not worried about formalities due to anyone having his office line being in his inner circle.

"Deacon? How's it going? It's Bishop Perry here."

With the jerk of his shoulders, Keithe sat up straight in his chair. Thrown for a loop, Keithe gathered his surprise.

"How's it going, Bishop? I'm good, and thank you for asking. What a nice surprise."

"Good to hear, Deacon. That's good to hear. Hey, do you happen to have a moment? I'd like to speak to you for just a second."

"Go right ahead. I'm in no hurry. How can I help you?"

"Well," Bishop started with hesitation in his voice. "Just to let you know, I have spoken to your pastor, who gave me permission along with your contact information, in order to speak with you. I had actually e-mailed you previously."

Not knowing in what direction to take the tone of the Bishop, Keithe was ready to progress nonetheless. Clicking the tab to raise his laptop screen, Keithe rushed to sign back on to see if he had overlooked this information. Logging into his e-mail account, Keithe started to scan.

"I hadn't a clue, Bishop. I haven't seen nor do I see any correspondence in my account. That's weird," Keithe said. Taking a look at his junk file, Keithe saw where the e-mails had disappeared to. "I just found them. They went into my junk folder."

"Well, that's fine. I have you on the line now, so that's the only thing that really matters." Clearing his throat, Bishop stated, "I have to be up front with you. And I want you to hear me out." He cleared his throat again.

"I'm all ears. Please, go on." Keithe sat tentatively.

"Well. Since a few weeks ago when we were down for service, you've been on my mind. For one because you were really sincere with thanking me for the sermon and shortly sharing the problems you and your wife have been going through."

"Oh. Yeah. Thanks. I need all the assurance I can get when it comes to my marriage, Bishop," Keithe stated.

"That's what I wanted to speak with you about, Deacon." Not knowing any other way to break the ice about knowing Keithe's wife, Bishop Ky Perry released what had been in his heart since the day he'd laid eyes on Michelle. "Deacon Keithe. I've prayed long and hard about what I'm about to tell you because I didn't really know if it was my business. But what gave was the way you looked. And then something was triggered by what you said."

"And what was that?" Keithe genuinely asked.

Not doubting what he was doing, the Bishop was adamant about sharing what he'd gone through with Michelle. "You said you and your wife didn't have any children, and I know outright, it's not my business."

"Go on," Keithe said.

"Well, again, I know it's none of my business, but unless she has a twin, your wife was once my fiancée."

Not really knowing how to respond to the news Bishop had just shared with him, Keithe just said, "Okay."

"I know that this may not seem like real plausible information, but when Michelle and I were together . . . she was pregnant."

"Whoa," Keithe said, pulling at the brakes. Outright he couldn't deny that Bishop Perry had the wrong woman; especially since they had met face-to-face. But for the man in him, he had to try. "Bishop. I'm now thinking you have the wrong woman."

As if he didn't make a thoughtful suggestion, Bishop continued. "And that would be okay if she didn't have on the same engagement ring I gave her over twenty years ago. Except it is on her right hand."

Now standing in front of his desk, Keithe rubbed his bald head, realizing that his hand that was holding the office phone was trembling uncontrollably.

"We don't have any children, Bishop. My wife has never been pregnant. She didn't even want children. Look," Keithe said, wanting to get as far away from the conversation as he could, "I wish I could understand your entire motive, but I can't. You have the wrong woman."

Without a reason, Keithe's mind flashed to the early years of his and Michelle's wedded beginning. Their intimate moments often led to him praising Michelle for a body that was heavenly made. Even down to the scar she had just below her navel and above her pubic area. When he'd asked about it all those years ago, he had no reason not to believe what she'd told him, that she'd cut herself severely while jumping over a fence when she was younger. It wasn't as if he never thought of it before, but at the present time he couldn't help but wonder if a cesarean birth had made the scar.

"I know I've laid some stuff on you that is pretty heavy, Deacon, but the reason for it is because when I was with Michelle, there was a lot of confusion. I had thought myself to be the father of the child. My associate pastor you met, Minister Marcus, she had also dated him. He also thought himself to be her child's father. Truth be told," he said, raising his eyebrows to a distant Keithe, "there was never any recollection of who the child's father was." He continued. "I don't even want to get into how she had my wife, Kendra, almost beaten to death," he thought to share. "That was before me, but still."

"Whoa. Okay. Hold up, Bishop. You've said quite a bit and I . . . I just don't know how to digest it. I don't even know why you're telling me all of this."

"Because if you've seen what I've seen when I look at your face, you'd figure that hell was your best friend these days. God doesn't want you to suffer and continue to go through in the manner that you are."

There was no response Keithe could offer.

"You have my number on your caller ID, Deacon. Please feel free to call me once you've thought over some things I've shared with you. Night or day, Deacon."

"Right," was all Keithe could respond with before he laid his phone back into its cradle.

His thoughts were so heavy, Keithe didn't even know where to begin. Should he confront Michelle? Should he just believe the Bishop? Would Michelle even tell the truth? Why would the Bishop have to lie?

Keithe couldn't do anything but will himself to walk over to the empty leather sofa in his office. Whatever plan he'd had for the remainder of the day had just been dismissed. With the ache between his brows increasing immensely, the only thing Keithe knew to do was to allow the billow of tears loose.

"What have I allowed?" was all he could say as he closed his eyes.

CHAPTER 24

Mercy

Another weekend had brought Mercy back into the city. Desiring to continue to be the help her friend needed, Mercy invited Stoney to spend the weekend with her. Mercy didn't know when Stoney would put any of their findings into action, but it didn't matter too much to her. The last few months had allowed Mercy to be there for Stoney one way or the other, hoping to minister to her heart.

"Hi, Daddy." Mercy greeted her dad when she opened the door to her quaint, apartment-styled home. Leaning forward, Mercy offered her father her forehead; it was the same spot he'd kissed since she was a little girl. "Come in."

"Thanks, darling. How are you doing? How's the baby?" He walked over the threshold and turned slightly to face his adult daughter.

Once he had married Kendra, with Mercy still being under the age of five, he knew his role of stepfather would be an important one. At all costs, he never wanted her to feel as if she didn't belong to him.

With her hand pressed on her protruding stomach, Mercy answered with a smile. "We're good, Daddy."

After their short embrace, Mercy's dad walked farther into the house.

"Oh. I'm sorry. I didn't know Mercy had company. How are you, young lady?" Bishop reached his hand to greet Stoney.

"I'm fine," she said timidly.

"Dad, this is Stoney, a friend of mine. Stoney, this is my dad, Bishop Ky Perry," Mercy introduced them.

"It's nice to finally meet you, Bishop." Stoney darted her eyes everywhere but to the Bishop. Once an avid worker in the church, Stoney felt that any real person of God could burrow into her soul and see that she had strayed.

"Do you belong to the church?" he questioned the young lady, who appeared to be his daughter's age.

"No, sir. I don't."

Not removing his eyes from Stoney, Bishop said, "Well, make it a point to visit, you hear?"

He pointed his forehead in her direction. "You look really familiar? I don't mean to stare. Does your family attend?"

"No, Daddy." Mercy spoke for her friend, knowing that Stoney's little tidbits of instability had been showing up more. With her appearance being on the borderline of a homeless person, Mercy didn't know what to think nor do to help her friend. But she knew that she needed to be there for her.

"Oh, okay. Well. I will leave you two alone. I just wanted to come back and check on you and the baby."

"Thanks, Dad," Mercy responded.

"No problem. Nice to meet you, Stoney."

Making his exit, Mercy's dad waved good-bye to Stoney. "Again, nice to meet you, young lady." Bishop kept his wave going to Stoney, who was consumed with her cell phone.

With a half wave, Stoney posted a fake smile on her lips, hoping the bishop would accept her greeting. Quickly turning her fingers and eyes back to the embedded keyboard of her mobile device, Stoney checked to see if Dr. Connor had texted her back as to the time they were to meet.

CHAPTER 25

Michelle

As soon as Keithe left the house on his way to work, Michelle turned and ran back up the two steps she'd traveled down and headed into their room. Picking up the phone that was sitting on the nightstand, Michelle took a quick seat.

With her knuckles, Michelle saved the damage to her manicured nails and punched in the telephone number she held in memory. Waiting for the line to connect, Michelle pushed her bangs to the side and waited.

For weeks she had tried to get Keithe to open up and get their marriage on track. But when she saw that even her attending church with him wasn't breaking him, she slid right back into her wicked ways. The day she laid eyes on Bishop Perry, Marcus, and the heffas who had stolen both men from her, Michelle knew going back to that church would spoil everything she'd worked for so hard.

With a nosey stretch of her neck to make sure the housekeeper wasn't making her upstairs rounds, Michelle said, "Hello? Brad." Before she could utter another word, she was cut off when Brad's voice mail used his voice, begging for a message to be left.

"Hey, sweetie, it's me, Michelle. I think I better take a rain check. Keithe was on edge before leaving, and I want to be here when he returns this evening. So no date night for us." She tried her best to sound wounded. "We'll just have to meet at the condo some other time. Kisses."

Her reach to place the phone back in its holding place wasn't complete before she heard the door squeak. Jolted by Keithe's stance against their bedroom door, Michelle thought her bowels would release right where she sat. Grabbing the lower part of her silk-covered stomach, Michelle inched back until she was squared up in her husband's direction.

"Did you leave something?" she asked nervously, not knowing just how much of her private conversation her husband had heard.

Not yet moving a muscle, Keithe leaned against the frame of the door and stared. "I surely did," he announced as he finally picked up his right foot and started his stride away from the door.

"Your briefcase? But you had it with you." Michelle uneasily rose to her feet, making her way around the bedposts. "Honey, what do you need?"

"My suitcase," Keithe yelled. Not caring if the housekeeper heard his pain or not, Keithe was on a mission. "I don't even know why I came back to this raggedy relationship," he spoke to himself.

Two weeks hadn't passed since the day Bishop Perry had called with his own assumption of just who Michelle was. Ever since then, Keithe had been holding a grudge against her in secret. Now with the proof that Michelle wouldn't or couldn't stop her evil ways, he felt everything was for a reason.

"It's one thing for me to get the phone call from Dr. Philips saying that the burning that has intensified is from gonorrhea you've given me," he said, which was the news he was coming back into the house to share. "Naw, that's not enough. Today I had to walk in and hear you on the phone with your *man.*" Not stopping his intended mission of packing, Keithe continued. "But it's okay, Michelle. Now you can have all the men you want, all the men you need, and all the diseases that come along with them. Where's my suitcase?" he yelled.

With pep in her step, Michelle waltzed right past Keithe and stood in the entrance of their double-door closet. Her arms and legs spread–eagle, Michelle's body stood to compare with the letter X.

"Your suitcase? Where are you going, Keithe? What just happened? I thought you left for work. What, man?" She wanted to continue to play Keithe for dumb.

Shaking his head, grasping the fact that Michelle didn't get it, Keithe roared even louder. "Is that why you were on the phone with Brad? Because you thought I was gone to work? Huh?" Prying her hands away from the rims of the door, Keithe got agitated on every try. "Move," he said forcefully.

"No. Not until you hear me out. There was a reason I was talking to Brad," she rambled as she tossed her own body to and fro, trying to keep her husband from getting close to his bags. "Are you going to listen?"

"No. No, I'm not going to listen. What can you possibly tell me, Michelle?" Keithe finally stood still and placed his hands in his slacks. "What?" he asked again with hunched shoulders. "Are you going to tell me how you told your boyfriend that you couldn't make the room date because I looked like a lonely pup? Pah-lease. Or better yet"—he gained momentum—"were you actually going to break it off with him? Better yet, were you going to ask him to give you some medicine to give to me in my drink, because I presume this is the same Dr. Brad Stevens who belongs to the country club. Right?"

"It's not like that, Keithe." Michelle was getting angrier by the minute. Sure she was guilty. Caught red-handed with her hand in the cookie jar. No matter what, she still needed him to listen to her. "You're not talking to me. You're not hugging or holding me." She finally found her voice.

"What am I suppose to do? Hug you and hold you and thank you for burning me? Huh? You want to know why I came back into the house? Because my doctor just called to tell me that gonorrhea is my new best friend, Michelle."

"What does that have to do with me?"

"Are you serious?" he asked. "Who else would give it to me, Michelle? I'm not the cheater, you are. And to think I'm taking up for you, thinking Bishop Perry has you mistaken with some other woman."

"What . . . what are you talking about?" Michelle was shocked.

"Oh, please. It probably is true. You have a scar that you don't even like to talk about. I thought I knew you. I don't know half of you, Michelle."

Wham! Michelle laid her hand across his face. "I don't know what you're talking about. You and your bishop friend are lying fools."

Michelle could see that the mere sound of her voice made Keithe choke. A hard jerk on her arm freed the opening to the closet. The freedom Keithe looked for came with a price once Michelle kicked him from behind, right in the spot God meant for reproduction.

"All I want you to do is to listen, Keithe." She had sorrow on her face just as soon as her foot hit the floor.

Keeled over in pain, Keithe couldn't do anything but moan. Panting for air to reach his brain because his mind wasn't working, fury became his only hope. With one swoop, Keithe removed his hands from his groin area and pushed himself up as straight as possible.

"Now are you ready to listen?" Michelle had the nerve to ask as if she had the upper hand. "I just want—" Before she could state her claim, Keithe's large hands were around her neck. Trying his best to choke every lie, every vow, every curse word, every breath out of Michelle's body, Keithe just held on without a word.

For every word anyone had ever told him about his wife, even down to Bishop Perry, Keithe wasn't going to let go until he could make Michelle regret ever lying to him.

Not able to vocalize any regret, or any apology to Keithe, Michelle grabbed the rounds of his elbows, trying her best to wiggle out of the death grip. Moving her body in every direction, as soon as she spotted the nightstand, Michelle lifted her foot and began to try to kick the lamp. Keithe, not knowing what she was up to, had nothing but pain, betrayal, and marred hope in his eyes. Not even the love he still had for her was enough for him to let go.

Moving her lips as fast or slow as she could, mouthing for Keithe to let go of her, Michelle moved her grip to her husband's hands that were around her neck, and pulled. With an extra-tight hold, Michelle found the reach in her leg and was able to kick the gold-plated lamp to the floor. The crash of their bedroom ensemble didn't help earn her the right to breathe.

The only thing Keithe was focused on was taking her breath away. He wasn't listening for her moans for him to stop. He rambled about a baby, Bishop Perry, her lying, and how her cheating was way too much.

Tears wrestling for space in his eyes, Michelle could see how much she had hurt her husband and, for once, stopped fighting. Her own tears made an appearance just as she closed her eyes and lost her gaze on her husband. The only vision left was that of Keithe with tears in his eyes.

CHAPTER 26

Keithe

Keithe didn't know where he was. All he could remember was the fight with Michelle. Reeling his mind backward, Keithe recalled walking in on his wife talking to her lover while his own cell phone still burned in his hand from the call from his doctor, which led to him receiving a fax in his home's office.

On his way to work and before he could even pull out of the driveway, his doctor's office called to give him results he had no idea he would get. The call from the doctor confirming his latest burning sensation down below was a quick flash, ending with his hands around her neck.

"Michelle!" He jumped to his feet, losing his balance with no known direction to run in. "Whoa. Where am I?" He squinted his eyes. "Oh God, I killed my wife. I killed her." He sat back down without looking where his seat would land.

"Keithe." He heard a raspy voice come from behind him.

"Stoney?" He looked over. "What are you doing here? Ouch!" He grabbed for his head, which he realized, too late, had a bandage on it. "Where am I? Oh God." It all came back to him now.

The scene replayed slowly in his head. "I'm in Dallas," he half asked, half stated. "Oh, wait," he rose to his feet and charged again. "I ran over somebody." Keithe ran to the door that was only a few feet away.

"Keithe, Keithe," Stoney yelled out, hoping to stop him from going past the threshold. Seeing what kind of state he was in scared Stoney. "You didn't run over anyone, remember?" She finally walked over to him, grabbing his hand. "Think, Keithe. Just think." He touched the bandages on the left side of his head.

It had rained. No, it had poured. And he had traveled in all the wetness the entire drive. His promising day had turned into a nightmare from a simple phone call. The one phone call marinated his thoughts all the way to Dallas from Houston, and left him hitting something, someone.

Stopping in his tracks, Keithe allowed his mind to replay where his thoughts had left off. When he remembered the rain greeting him on his ride into Dallas, his thoughts took him to driving toward Stoney's apartment complex, then . . .

"You only thought you ran over someone, Keithe. It was a kid's bicycle you ran over. Remember now?" Stoney whispered with her eyes heavy from lack of sleep. She stopped short, not wanting her own recounting of her miserable night.

Keithe thought about it. Stoney was right. In the midst of his rage against Michelle the only thing that helped was the chiming of his cell phone from a text Stoney had sent. She had been on the brink of giving up, letting go, and doing away with her own life, he'd read. Without a plan, Keithe only thought to drive out of the city and into Dallas.

With the look of relief brought to his face, Keithe then recalled the details. He did run over something, and he'd even hit his head on his steering wheel. He even tried to pull whatever it was from under his vehicle, only to find a bicycle and helmet minus a child. They had lodged themselves under his car's frame. Now he remembered.

He sighed. "What a night." He then looked down sideways at Stoney. Holding in his comments about her shrinking appearance, Keithe thought about Michelle. "I've got to call my wife." He felt around in his empty pockets for his cell phone. Recalling the conclusion of their drama, Keithe recalled choking Michelle until she was close to passing out. When she came to, she had brought vengeance.

"It's over on the table." Stoney pointed.

For whatever it was worth, Keithe had to hear Michelle's voice. No one had to tell him it was over. Michelle had crossed lines and took him with her this time. His anger had peaked to the point of wanting to strangle the life out of her.

It all hit him at once. He had thought about her never mentioning a baby, acting as if she didn't have a clue who Bishop Perry was with her nonchalant attitude. It all took him over the edge and brought his anger to a whole other level, to the point of him crossing the boundaries from a nice man to a madman.

Watching Keithe try his best to get in contact with Michelle, Stoney psyched herself to believe she had been on Keithe's agenda. The real truth of the matter was that he was the angel Stoney had reluctantly asked God to send, even if she was the one who made the phone call.

Her world had closed in. It was a definite: no mother, no friends, and no drugs. She couldn't think of anything else to live for. Two hours before she'd made the call to Keithe, Stoney had let her world, the one she had created, crowd her.

She had stooped to an all-time low. Ever since she had given her body to Dr. Connor for limited gratification of sample medication, her mind had been speeding with guilt intertwined.

Standing, watching Keithe make the call to his wife, Stoney wondered what was next. Stoney gazed at Keithe standing in the middle of her studio apartment, deep in thought. She wondered if she should end the self-torture right then and there by letting him in on her hurtful secret.

"Well, would you like to grab a bite before I go? I have to head right back out. Michelle's not answering and I need to know how she is." Keithe pointed to nothing in particular with his thumb. His world had been completely turned upside down by Michelle, yet he couldn't stop caring. No one in his right mind would do the things he had found himself doing: fighting and driving all over Texas just to get away from what was embedded in his heart.

"Sure." Stoney decided to keep her secret to herself. Having slept most of his visit away, Stoney didn't bother trying to start a whole new conversation. Especially since it was Michelle who crowded both of their thinking.

Trying her best to let her quick and growing anger subside, Stoney could not help but think that Keithe was like all the rest: Michelle, Dr. Connor, and now him. Not even mentioning or asking how she was doing, Stoney's feelings were more than hurt. No one cared enough about her in order to help figure out her problem. No one thought to really care if she needed anything. No one but Mercy, but she wasn't available. So the next best thing Stoney knew to do was to follow suit.

When Keithe reached for the doorknob and gave Stoney's appearance another double take, Stoney knew just what he was thinking. She was ashamed at herself for how she had just let herself go since the last time he'd seen her, which had been more than four months earlier. When he didn't share any comments, turning the door handle to go ahead of Stoney, she was relieved.

After an almost twenty-four-hour stay, they took a quick lunch break at the Olive Garden; Keithe's main goal was to fill his hunger and to supply food for his mind. No doubt, his life had taken a jerk in the wrong direction, but he knew without uncertainty it was time to really remove himself from Michelle.

"So what really happened? You were going on and on about how you hurt your wife," Stoney whispered, not wanting anyone to hear about a man hurting a woman in any fashion.

"We had a fight. A fight that has really made a decision for me." When it looked as though she'd ask for details, Keithe said, "Don't ask."

"So you are going back home?" Stoney wanted to bare her heart and soul to Keithe, knowing he could possibly play some sort of role in helping heal her heart. Of course, he was going through his own bout with Michelle. Maybe if she finally let him in on what had been plaguing her for some time, they could help each other.

"I'm heading back as soon as I leave here. Maybe stop by Mike's, but I'm heading back. I have way too much to take care of." Just as he rested his fork for a moment, Keithe thought to ask Stoney about herself and what issues were obviously plaguing her. Before he could rest his back against the restaurant chair, Stoney's own thoughts reached lightning speed and she excused herself.

"I'll be right back . . . Ladies' room." With her cell phone in tow, Stoney scurried to make sure Mercy was available.

Waiting for her return, Keithe sat eating the last remnants of his meal.

"Deacon Keithe?" Keithe heard the familiar voice. "It is you. How are you, son?" Keithe looked over his shoulder to see who had confirmed his knowledge of him.

"Bishop Perry. Well, I'm . . . I'm making it," Keithe lied, and quickly recalled their last conversation via the telephone.

"You sure?" Bishop Perry pointed to the bandage that still lingered on Keithe's face. "You look as though you've seen better days. Michelle?" Bishop Perry asked without asking a full question.

"You don't even want to know," Keithe offered.

"I'm sure I already know if it concerns Michelle," the bishop countered.

Leaning his back against his chair once again, Keithe could not fight his bravery any longer. "I finally brought you up, and of course there was no confirmation either way." He spoke in circles about Michelle possibly knowing Bishop, and her pregnancy.

"She swore up and down she didn't know you." Keithe pondered. "Then she had the nerve to throw it back on me. Play a mind game." Forgetting he was actually talking to the bishop, Keithe thought aloud. "Cussed me like I was two-bit scum when I asked about a baby." He finally looked toward Bishop Perry. "Oh, and when I asked about the scar, I guessed it was maybe a

C-section scar, she didn't even flinch in the truth direction." Keithe shook his head.

"I swear, Keithe! I swear. If you ask me one more time about a baby who doesn't exist, I will shut you up!" Michelle had put a threat with her promise, gripping the vase that seemed to always be out of place as far as she was concerned.

"Well, what is it then?" Keithe nagged. "What, Michelle? What else could the scar be from? Why else would a man of God just put himself on the line like that for me? Just come clean about it, Michelle."

With a lift of the vase, Michelle didn't give it a second glance as she drew back her arm to gain momentum for the throw and release.

"I'm sorry to hear that," Bishop stated, bringing Keithe's thoughts back to the present.

"It's okay." Keithe lied again.

"I really hope you don't mind me praying for you. I really feel it's my duty . . . and it may just be my fault, coming at you with the information I did."

"I can't even let you take the blame. I wouldn't dare do that." He let a beat pass. "I'm actually headed back home shortly. I'm through."

Bishop Ky Perry took a vacant seat closest to Keithe. "Counseling. Have you all truly tried it?"

Shaking his head, Keithe let out a chuckle. "We got married so quickly, no counseling was thought of. Throughout the years, she has declined counseling so many times because of her profession. She wouldn't be caught seen or known of getting any kind of help. Heck, Michelle doesn't believe she needs any help to begin with. It's just time for us to part ways."

With understanding, Bishop Perry shook his head, not wanting to validate Keithe's divorce. "Well, you know I'm just a phone call away, and I know your pastor is willing and very able to help you through this trial." Bishop, for the first time, looked toward Stoney's plate. "I'm sorry, I hadn't even noticed. You have a guest," he stated.

Nodding, Keithe exhaled. "Yes. She's like a . . ." He didn't want to lie and say she was like a daughter when he didn't truly know what his intentions were. "I don't know. I met her through a mutual friend." He drew his lips in, shook his head, and hunched his shoulders.

"Two wrongs don't make a right, Deacon. You know that, I take it?" Bishop Perry raised his eyebrows.

"Yes, sir. You're right. I do know that," Keithe agreed.

One hand on his knee, Bishop pushed himself up and walked a step toward Keithe. "Place your petition before the Lord. Fasting and praying is the only way, Deacon. You have to be ready when God tells you in what direction *He* wants you to go."

A continued slight nod was all Keithe had strength for as Bishop Perry walked away.

Stoney stayed back long enough to allow Mercy's dad to leave the premises. Once she had removed herself from the ladies' room, Stoney halted once she saw him placed at their table.

"How in the world . . . ?" she'd asked herself about Bishop and Keithe knowing each other. *It can't be just a coincidence,* she thought. Whatever the case, she didn't want to make herself known for fear of having to explain how she knew either one of them.

She just waited. The longer she stayed out of sight, the more time she'd gain anyway. Having left the table in order to contact Mercy once Keithe let her know that he would be going back home later that day, her mind raced for an excuse to get to Houston. Mercy was that excuse. As soon as she got to the restroom, her phone was already dialing Mercy's number.

"Hey, Mercy," Stoney had greeted her friend via the phone she placed to her ear while behind closed doors.

"Stoney? Hi there. I've been calling you ever since I've been in town. I'm leaving in a bit. Sorry we couldn't catch up this time."

"Great," Stoney returned with a "just what I want" tone.

"Huh?" Mercy hoped she hadn't heard her friend correctly. Knowing Stoney had been stand-offish, not answering calls or e-mails over the last couple of days, Mercy really wished she knew how to be the help Stoney really needed. Helping her find her mother was one thing. Helping her find herself was another.

Hiding behind a stall and whispering into the phone, Stoney had shaken her head and let out a goofy laugh. "No, what I meant was that I'm glad I caught you before you left. I want to go to Houston with you."

"You want to go to Houston?" Mercy did a double take when she realized she had raised her voice and piqued her mother's interest. "Uh. Well, I'm actually just going to take two tests. You know, midterms. What about you? Don't you have to do the same?"

"I finished early," she lied, not sharing with Mercy how she had dumped school along with a lot of other things in her life. "Maybe I can drive you so you don't have to worry about that bulging baby belly being in the way." She laughed again.

Mercy looked down at her growing abdomen and agreed it had grown quite a bit over the past five months, but not to the point where she couldn't drive herself. Feeling that her friend would not let up, Mercy agreed to let a persistent Stoney drive her to Houston. Figuring they would only be there for three days, Mercy really didn't see any harm.

Now, as Stoney waited and watched Bishop Perry maneuver away from their table and pass through the exit doors, Stoney's thoughts were only on getting away from Keithe and meeting up with Mercy. As long as she knew he'd be over at Brother Mike's before he left town, Stoney knew how to pick up on his trail.

"Who was that?" she asked Keithe, trying her best to cover up the fact that she knew who the Bishop was.

"Oh, you made it back?" Keithe slightly rose to his feet, not forgetting the manners his mother had taught him. "That was a bishop who visits my church in Houston several times a year. He had noticed me sitting here and came over." He didn't know if he should share the conversation he had had with Bishop Perry.

With gathered brows, Stoney said, "Wow. He picked you out of the crowd, eh? I thought you went to a pretty big congregational church."

"It's more personal than that." He pressed a laugh from his abdomen. "I recently found out he used to date my wife . . . even more than that." He didn't share how the bishop had shared the possibility of being his wife's baby's father. A baby he had no clue about and a baby Michelle denied. "Way too complicated to share."

It was as if a ton of bricks had fallen on her head. Stoney replayed what Keithe had just shared. Bishop dated Michelle. *Bishop dated my mother*. She tried to unscramble the lingering thought.

"Are you okay, Stoney?" Keithe asked.

"Yeah, yeah. I'm fine. Just drifted off. Daydreaming, you know." She shifted nervously in her seat.

"Well." He crossed his knife and fork over one another. "I mean, period; are you okay? You look worn out. Tired. Is it the semester?" He gave her an excuse.

"Yep. Yes. It's school. Work and school have me beat. But . . ." She thought of more to add on. "I'm finished up for the rest of the semester, so I'll get to rest. Look," she said, sitting up straight, wiggling, showing how restless she was, "not trying to rush, but if we're finished, can we go?"

"No problem," he said. "I need to stop by Mike's before I head out anyway. Want to ride over?"

"No!" Stoney tensed up as she stood up and pushed her seat under the table. "I mean, no. I have plans with my friend later on."

"Right." Keithe remembered that Stoney was keeping her distance from Mike. "Uh, Stoney?"

With her neck stretched, Stoney used her gesture to warrant her waiting for a question Keithe had for her.

"Is everything all right with you? I mean, you seem as if some things are bothering you."

"Fine. I'm fine, Keithe. Thanks for asking. But seriously, I'm good. Can we go now?"

"Sure," was all Keithe responded with when he saw the eagerness in Stoney's display.

CHAPTER 27

Keithe

When he arrived at Mike's front door, Keithe knew once again that his friend wouldn't say anything harsh. He didn't have to. This time Keithe knew it was time to pour out his soul to someone. Since it couldn't be his wife, because she had now become his ultimate nemesis, his best friend would have to do.

It was as if he were becoming a permanent traveler instead of a lawyer. That's something he would have to get straight also.

"A leave of absence," he idly voiced. "Maybe even a change in scenery will do the trick," he thought aloud. Whatever his decision was, Keithe knew his plans would no longer surround Michelle after their divorce.

Instantly, his chest warmed underneath his shirt as he thought about Stoney. He didn't know why he was thinking about the young girl who could have easily been his own child's age, had he reproduced. But he hadn't. So thinking of Stoney as far as he was concerned was just fine. At least that was what he really wanted to believe.

"So you're calling it quits, huh?" Mike asked a long-faced Keithe.

Nodding his response, Keithe knew it was very overdue and knew his friend thought the same. "Michelle ain't trying to be nobody different. She likes being the person she's become."

"Don't you mean who she's always been?" Mike said sternly, while his friend gave him a dumbfounded stare. "But for real, Keithe. You need to wake up. Michelle has been as evil as she was since the day I met her. And I met her two days after you did."

When he saw he wasn't getting his friend's understanding, Mike took it a step further. Rising from the sofa, Mike walked toward the house phone and said, "Oh, I still have the messages she left when you were here last time. If you want, I can play them for you." He waited.

"Not necessary," was all Keithe said. Resting his eyes and his head against his friend's sofa, Keithe knew it would be fine if he took a siesta before his road trip back home.

"No longer Keithe and Michelle," he let slip from his lips, and added, "never was," before closing his eyes to drift off to sleep.

CHAPTER 28

Ky and Keithe

Bishop didn't know what to do. He was almost in denial, but he knew his daughter wouldn't play any practical jokes in this manner. Receiving a text from his only daughter, he took his responsibility of being a father seriously.

> Daddy. Can you say a prayer for me and Stoney? She offered to drive me back to Houston, but she's acting weird

Was how she started off her messages. Several messages later, Mercy had spilled the beans on how she had been helping Stoney locate her mother. By the time Mercy informed her dad how her friend seemed to be on a mission for Houston, feeling no real threat in the situation, Bishop Perry didn't think to call, but to only stop and pray for the girls.

Later that afternoon, walking from the back door of their home, Ky wandered toward Mercy's secluded home on their premises. Using the key, he entered with a mind for prayer over his daughter's home and surroundings.

"Dear Lord. I don't know if I should worry, but I'm coming on behalf of my daughter and her friend, Lord. If Mercy is feeling uneasy and there is no need for her to be, dear God, please bring her comfort." He went around the house with his anointing oil, leaving invisible crosses.

When Mercy's computer made a humming sound, Bishop Perry looked in its direction and walked over. With a click of a single key, the screen appeared. Obviously Mercy had forgotten to shut it down before she left. With information displayed on the screen, he sat down to take a closer look.

A document was open on the screen. A paid search engine was open as well. There was one name listed over one hundred times from the state of Texas.

"Oh my Lord," he said aloud. "Michelle Morgan," he read on the search engine's page. On the document that had been saved to the computer's hard drive, Bishop Perry read, "MaeShell H. Morgan, now known as Michelle Morgan. Married to Keithe Morgan . . ." Taking a moment to try to comprehend what he was seeing, Ky searched more on the file titled, "Find Stoney's Mother."

Having an inkling that his daughter did not know to what extent she'd gotten involved, Bishop Perry knew that if Michelle Hart had to be involved, he had to get involved.

Keithe's ride, once again, back to Houston was a long, treacherous one. The only difference this time was that he was going back to pack and move forward with his life, away from Michelle.

The last straw had come and gone. It wasn't as if he hadn't been down the road with Michelle plenty of times before. The only difference this time was that he'd heard it for himself. He didn't have to hear it through the grapevine, or receive hints from people in his office. A disease had to make its way through his bloodstream. The doctor's call, along with Michelle's conversation to her beau, had told him everything he needed to know.

Finally pulling into his distinguished and well-constructed driveway, Keithe clicked his car's garage door opener, thrust his car into park, and waited for the door to rise. Just as he was about to switch his car into drive, his cell phone rang while in its holster.

"Keithe Morgan speaking," he answered, not knowing what information lay on the other end of the phone. Instead of turning off his engine, Keithe jerked his car in reverse and sped away from his home.

"Now what?" He wanted—no, he needed—to make sure he had heard Bishop Perry correctly. Driving toward his downtown office building, Keithe adhered to what Bishop Perry suggested: to not go home. He didn't think it necessary to tell the Bishop he had already touched ground in front of his home and then drove off. Instead, he continued with the conversation, although his body was tired and his eyes were heavy. Traveling without any preparations, Keithe hadn't taken any medication for the day, and hoped the whole situation wouldn't keep him away from home too long.

Bishop Perry cleared his throat and cloudlessly eased into his approach with Keithe. "Since last seeing and speaking to you, ah, earlier, a lot has transpired in my family life." He left room to just dwell on his thoughts. "And not all for the good, Deacon," the bishop shared as he and his wife, Kendra, were being driven to Houston in order to get Stoney as far away from Mercy as possible. The phone calls he had been making to his daughter, on her cell phone, had gone unanswered, only adding to their worries. With her text messages being sporadic, their only focus was to make it to Houston.

"Oh wow, Bishop. I'm sorry to hear that. Is there something I can help you with? I mean, I doubt Michelle is at home. I could have spoken with you there." Keithe hadn't a clue that the Bishop's heartbreak included him.

"There is. Deacon I'm asking for your help because, well, it's your wife." Bishop didn't know how to break the news to Keithe any other way. He was sorry for having to continuously dump hard information on Keithe about his wife, but he had no choice. "I'm on my way to Houston now, Deacon. I know you are a saved and Holy Ghost–filled man of God. This is personal."

"I'm listening, Bishop." Keithe agreed to be and do whatever it was that Bishop Perry needed, even before he had completed his thoughts.

For the next fifteen minutes, Bishop explained how his daughter had befriended a girl who turned out to not have good intentions. With no mention of the friend's name, Keithe held on to the story, hoping he could actually help the Bishop.

Bishop Perry went on to inform Keithe how the young girl had been looking for her mother for some years. Per the notes he'd seen and what Mercy had texted him, since she and Mercy had become friends, Mercy had been helping her as well. He finished his rundown by reading off the text messages he had received from his daughter.

"They are headed to Houston if not there already," Bishop stated, having no idea that Stoney had driven as close as she could to Keithe the entire trip. "I need someone to find this girl. My daughter is frightened for some reason, and Mercy is a strong enough individual to know when something is out of whack. I have the police involved from this end, but being that you are there and—"

"And what, Bishop?" All Keithe needed was the name. The story was too familiar, and though he felt as if he were in the midst of a *Twilight Zone* episode, Keithe knew what was coming next.

"The girl is no doubt coming to look for her mother, Deacon." Bishop looked over all the information he had taken from Mercy's apartment. There was no easy way to break the news but to just do it. "She's coming to your home, Deacon. Your wife is her mother. Michelle is Stoney Hart's mother."

When he finally heard Bishop Perry release the information, there was nothing that could help Keithe hold his peace. Keithe, knowing the information would activate stress, clutched his chest when his breathing was thrown off course. Gasping for big gulps of breath, Keithe couldn't pull over quickly enough before his mind started to cloud and the feeling he'd so often felt before crowded his body. The onset of his seizure had already begun, leading his vehicle off the road.

CHAPTER 29

Michelle

She woke from what should have been a good sleep; instead, she was stiff as a board. All of the hoopla she had caused when Keithe had retraced his steps, finding her on the phone with Brad, had paid off in the wrong way. There was no way she would be traveling too far away from her house today.

Only one missed phone call came from Keithe, and though she felt sorry about the entire ordeal, Michelle knew it was over. She also knew he was in Dallas. Not caring to return his call, Michelle had other things on her mind.

The tracking system she and her husband had agreed to install for their vehicles made it easy to pull up their account on the Internet. While busying herself watching her husband's whereabouts, she logged into Keithe's e-mail account as well.

Finding another e-mail from Stoney, Michelle wasn't thrilled. Especially when he'd just tried to choke the life out of her about a man in her life. "And he has the nerve to question me about my past and his mess is all up in my face." Michelle rested her elbows on the computer desk. With her hair all over her head, Michelle grabbed a fistful and pulled until she felt the tug that released her nagging headache.

No matter how long she tried to continue to put the blame in Keithe's lap, it was inevitable: it was all hers. Michelle was the cause and the effect of their failed marriage.

Logging in to his cell phone account, Michelle couldn't help but pull up his list of text messages from the last twenty-four hours. "Stoney." There she was again, winning her husband's affection. And from the looks of it, Keithe had headed right into Stoney's arms.

It had appeared that Stoney had text messaged Keithe her address. When realizing what it was, Michelle bore tears as she went down the list of hot spots her husband's vehicle had traveled. Besides his office, one of the last resting spots was Stoney's place. When Michelle noticed the time frame of his vehicle in one place, her heart grew heavy.

"Oh my goodness." Michelle felt the pain. No doubt, it was the same pain Keithe had dealt with for almost the entire length of time they'd been married.

"Okay. Okay. You win," she said in the smallest voice, not realizing she had even surrendered. She could definitely dish it out, but couldn't take it. When she didn't feel any immediate response, she decided to express what was beating up on her heart. "I said you win. You! You, God. You hear me! You win."

Getting up from her seat in front of the computer, Michelle felt the sting in her heart. Another woman had captured her husband's heart. Thinking her outburst granted her serenity and a clean start with God, when she didn't feel any different and the pain still throbbed and the tears were still coming, Michelle became angry.

"Michelle, wait a minute. Wait. You're stronger than that. Ju . . . just call up Brad and . . ." She reached for the phone, not caring if her home number appeared on his caller ID.

After two rings, Brad answered, "Hello?"

"Brad, it's me." Michelle put on her perfect persona and sniffed her tears back.

With disgust reeling in his voice, Brad asked, "How can I help you, Michelle?"

Not understanding, nor liking, the cold, calloused, and what seemed like calculated response, Michelle tried her best to look past his greeting.

"Oh, Brad." Michelle held tears in her eyes. She knew in her heart that Brad was nothing more than a scapegoat, like all the other men in her life. Just something to do. Michelle hated the truth, but she had an image to uphold. "No more pain for me" was her motto. "I just wanted to know if you'd like to get together at the condo."

When a chuckle left his throat, Michelle had borrowed confusion plastered on her taut face. "What's that all about?" she questioned.

"Michelle, what were the rules, sweetheart? What was our agreement?" He didn't allow her to finish. "I told you about the games. You want your husband, fine. But the other men were out. Totally," he barked at her, belittling her as if she wasn't worth the time she had given him over the past year.

"Wh . . . what are you speaking of, Brad?"

"Don't insult my intelligence. I am not your husband. Maybe that's the problem. Did you actually think I'd let you play me?" Brad asked with a threatening tone. "Did you actually think I wouldn't find out about some of the lowlifes you mess with?"

Wishing she knew from which direction he'd all of a sudden acquired his information, Michelle just sat and wished the one-way conversation to be over with.

"Michelle. It's a shame how you waste your beauty on being stupid," the pot called the kettle black. "You're so lucky it's just a case of gonorrhea that you passed on to me. But don't take me for granted. You better make sure you get to my condo and get your things. And leave my key. I don't care if the door stays wide open. Leave my key." He slammed down the phone.

With the dial tone beating up the side of her face, Michelle stood numb. "What?" was all she could come up with.

Sliding the phone's receiver back into its cradle, Michelle made her way into the bathroom at a slow pace. Just as she crossed the threshold, the programmed gospel station of Keithe's liking blasted an inspirational song:

"The stone that the builders refused,/has become the head corner./The stone rejected by men . . ."

Michelle stopped and realized she knew the song. Turning up the volume, Michelle's heart melted as she leaned against her vanity, admiring the voice and admiring the words.

Back in the day when she had tried the whole God thing, the whole church thing, one of the women at church she attended with Bishop Perry had actually sung the inspirational song as a solo. From then on, Michelle was in love with the song. At one point, Michelle became so infatuated with the words that she made the song her first gospel purchase. Unfortunately, it was also her last.

"Who was that singer?" Michelle snapped her fingers, hoping to jog her memory. Without thinking twice, Michelle backtracked and ran to her nightstand in search of the CD. When she didn't find it in there, she pushed tears to the side and ran to her closet, pulling, pushing, and moving things to the side until she found what she was looking for.

Walking back into her bedroom and opening the case, Ky sprang to Michelle's mind as she finally laid her hands on the CD. Thinking back to the days when she listened to the Vanessa Bell Armstrong CD repeatedly, it was then, within her relationship with Ky, that she had attempted to know more about God and see if He could really help her from her demons. It was being with Ky, hearing him go on and on about how God was a healer, a burden bearer, that finally made Michelle realize she had been carrying a heavy load. Unfortunately, as their relationship dwindled, so did her search for God.

Pushing play on her flat-front CD player, Michelle stood in the middle of her bedroom and listened. Michelle listened to the song in its entirety. By the time the last word hummed, Michelle had a somber feeling on the inside. Recognizing the sensation of God warming her spirit, a tug-of-war grew in her and all Michelle could do was take a seat on the bed. From a new standpoint, on the brink of being a divorcée, no longer someone's mistress, childless, and motherless, Michelle freely let her tears fall.

Only able to mumble her pain, her disappointment within herself, Michelle crawled her way to the top of her bed and lay back on her pillow. "It's not fair. I don't know. Ugh," was all she wanted to say. She knew to say more, and that she had her ability to call on Jesus, but her anger made her blame Him for all of her disappointments.

All of her plans, education, and moving as far away as she could from Greenville, Texas, still didn't get her the happiness she had longed for. Michelle couldn't fix what was broken on the inside. Believing that a desired lifestyle she was granted, along with being away from her mental mother, was fulfillment, the life she was running from caught up to her.

Until she had cried herself to sleep, Michelle repeatedly argued with herself about being alone, having no one, hating her life, and blaming God for the decisions He had allowed her to make.

CHAPTER 30

Stoney

The whole while she and Mercy had made their way from Dallas into Houston, Mercy was more than begging Stoney to tell her what was going on.

"My campus isn't this way, Stoney. Why aren't you listening to me? Where are we going?" Mercy looked from the roads ahead back to Stoney, who seemed to be overly focused on the same. "Slow down."

"I can't," she said in a daze. "I'll lose him," Stoney said, licking her lips as if she were one of the drivers in a NASCAR race.

"Who? Who is he, Stoney?" Mercy worryingly asked, afraid of the answer.

"Keithe. I'm going to lose him if I don't stay close," Stoney muttered.

Thinking as hard as she could, Mercy couldn't figure where she'd heard the name Keithe before.

"Stoney. Who is Kei—" It hit her. Their last bit of research concluded with a Keithe as next of kin for Michelle, Stoney's mother.

"Huh?" Stoney took her eyes off the crowded expressway for a moment. "He's my mom's husband."

Tears already began to make their home on Mercy's lap, and her worst nightmare was coming true right before her. Recalling the file the two had started on Stoney's mother, a Keithe Morgan had been linked to Michelle by marriage. Grabbing her pregnant belly, Mercy said a word of prayer. "Lord. Help us right now, dear God. We need you. Stoney needs you to comfort her pain right this minute, Lord. Come in, God, and take control of this situation. Dear God, show us the way . . . your way, Lord."

"Would you shut up, Mercy?" Stoney shouted, then retracted with an, "I'm sorry, but He ain't listening to you. He don't hear you. God is not interested in helping me out, so keep your prayers, Mercy."

"That is just not true, Stoney. It's not true. Jesus cares about you; you have to allow Him to care about you. Walk in His love." Trying her best to calm down Stoney, Mercy's hidden texts to her dad were the only things that kept her hope alive.

"You walk in His love. I'm going to find my mother." She looked through dilated eyes toward Mercy. Drugged up on prescription drugs and running off of no sleep, Stoney was too wired for Mercy to talk her down.

When Mercy went for her phone, and showed signs of more texting, Stoney took one hand off of the steering wheel and snatched Mercy's phone away.

"Stoney!"

"You will not hinder me. Everyone has hindered me! No more." She threw Mercy's cell phone over her head and into the back window, sending pieces flying.

At that very moment, all Stoney could remember was the look of being terrified that was placed on Mercy's face. At the point when she followed Keithe into one of Houston's suburbs, Mercy was in full panic mode, and Stoney was extra hype and almost riding his bumper.

Not worried about him identifying her because of a baseball cap and Mercy's car, Stoney stayed as close as possible.

Not able to get into the gated community after Keithe's car had accelerated past the coded lockdown, Stoney stopped the car in the middle of the street and got out. Not once did she look back.

Retrieving the files from Mercy's computer, Stoney recalled the house's address from memory and eased herself through the gate and started half jogging. Seeing Keithe's taillights, she followed him as much as she could.

Left alone in the car, Mercy tried to get her breath under control. Jumping out of the passenger's side and running around the car, Mercy sat behind the wheel and turned on her headlights. The day had turned to dusk. Reversing her Volkswagen Beetle, Mercy drove down the road until she came to the nearest convenience store.

As soon as she had made her way around the small neighborhood of winding homes, Stoney found the house owned by Keithe and Michelle. Peering behind the bushes, in the dusk of the day, Stoney was confused when she saw Keithe pulling out of the driveway from barely settling for all of a minute. When the taillights of his vehicle disappeared, Stoney looked backward, not knowing if she should go toward the direction from which she came. Knowing Mercy was long gone, Stoney became scared and then sad. All which lasted every bit of a minute.

Picking up a large stick before walking from behind the bush, Stoney walked across the street until she reached the front door. When she found it locked, she walked backward until she thought about the garage door Keithe had clicked open. Off to her left, Stoney made her way to the open entrance.

Little by little, Stoney walked through the halls and listened in her unfamiliar surroundings. Easing her body through doors until she found a closet built off the living area, Stoney stood in the dark, thinking of her next move.

The house was quiet. With no children of their own, the large house only held noises made by the settling of the foundation. Stoney had waited and waited for the perfect opportunity to finally be alone with her mother, and her plan fell right into place. With Keithe away from the house, Stoney sat in the closet, trying to come up with a plan that would allow her an opportunity she'd waited most of her life for.

Listening was what Stoney did. She waited and listened for doors to open or shut . . . something. She waited for the footsteps that would let her know her mother was in the house. Placed inside of a disclosed utility closet, Stoney waited.

Then there it was. More of a scooting sound, Stoney heard footsteps pass by the door and continued without echoing as if they'd descended from the staircase nearby. Stoney listened. Closing her teary eyes, she thought about all the questions she'd want to ask. All of the subject matter that had plagued her mind while growing up. Today was the day that her worries, her desires, her wants would be answered.

No doubt, Stoney, as a young girl, had wanted to connect with her mother. The feeling had always been on her mind, to the point it stained her heart. But within the last few months, knowing Michelle didn't care, nor let the world know that she had even existed, Stoney felt even more neglected. Even more, she felt downright cheated.

Mimicking words of Grandma Susie, Stoney's eyes were more than bucked in the darkness of the closet. "She don't want you, why you think you here with me?" she mocked. "Oh, Grandma Susie, why did you have to say that? I know, I know, it wasn't you. It was the medicine," Stoney answered in the way her grandmother had on so many occasions. With her hands shaking from nervousness, it didn't take long before Stoney's twinkling eyes took effect.

Blinking uncontrollably and feeling the cool air throughout the closet, Stoney gripped the handle of the small but thick stick she'd picked up on her way through the neighborhood. She still didn't know why she had it, or why she even picked it up. All she wanted to do was to ask her mom some questions, then she'd be on her merry way. Maybe she'd picked it up for protection? Knowing the devil liked to rear his head, Stoney made herself believe it was for her own protection. But she knew better.

She wanted Michelle to feel all of the aches and pain that her own heart had endured throughout life. Longing for the hugs and forehead kisses as only a mother can give, Stoney was betrayed by a mother who didn't want her, and a grandmother who just took her, wanting to help, but couldn't because her mind wouldn't allow her to.

Once she heard the voice of someone, Stoney held her breath. Realizing the blare was coming from a television, Stoney envisioned Michelle sitting in the grand living room in front of the set she had seen while sneaking in. With the turn of the doorknob, the creak that sounded no longer mattered to Stoney. She took her chances.

With her body on the other side of the door, having shed her shoes inside of the closet, Stoney paced her bare feet as they made contact with the cool and wooded floors. A blouse long enough to be a dress hid the shape she once had. Tears streamed down her face as she made conversation in her mind.

Stoney, now you know that God don't like ugly. You gots to get it together, go on with your future. If she don't want you, she just don't want you, her medicated soul tried to reason.

Stoney replied in a small whisper. "This lady done hurt you, left you for nothing, with nothing, all because of nothing. Uh-uh. I ain't letting it go." She put a little pep in her barefoot step.

With no shoes or socks on, Stoney eased forward until she was a good enough distance not to be sensed, but close enough to know that Michelle, her mother, was alone. When she heard the television, Stoney couldn't help but focus past the back of her mother's head and glue her eyes on the set to the person speaking.

"In your reading, 1 Peter, verses 15–16. The Word calls for us to be holy, for our God is holy. Don't look to your neighbor, but ask yourself, am I holy?"

Am I holy? Stoney silently asked herself, and then shook her head, thinking it was crazy of her to participate in a television sermon when she was on a mission.

"What does it profit a man to gain the world and lose his soul? Is your soul saved? Aren't we worth more than that?" the television blared. "Aren't we worth more than the cares of this world? The homes in which we live? Am I holy? Don't ask what someone can give you materialistically. Ask if they can show you holiness."

Stoney shrugged and felt the message wasn't for her, but then looked around the house in which she'd broken into. The finer things in life were what Michelle had obviously chosen over raising her. About to start her short journey again, Stoney halted once the preacher spoke again.

"Let me share this with you. Saints of God, we are a chosen generation. The life you were given was no mistake. The family you grew up a part of was no mistake. It may have been full of the devil's dwelling, molestation may have played its part, your parents may have provoked you, but the good news is that even though we are carnally birthed, Jesus died so that we could be born again.

"If you were the one molested or the one doing the molesting, God can change you, purify you, purge you, and set you free. If you felt you were abandoned, or the one doing the abandoning, know that God can cover you. He can be your mother. He can be your caretaker. Know He can bring your children back, and make your family whole."

The words dug deep for both Michelle and Stoney. Michelle sat up on the curved sofa and listened to the preacher speak life into her situation. Being the one who did the abandoning, Michelle squinted her eyes and just thought. Stoney who was standing no more than seven feet away from her mother plastered on a face of want. On different levels, both had felt what the evangelist had allowed to seep through his spirit.

Snuggled under a blanket with only her head appearing, Michelle sat off to Stoney's right, propped by sofa pillows. Focusing in on her mother, Stoney thought the present time would have been the perfect opportunity to get the answers she needed, the answers she wanted. With the point of the remote, Michelle was about to change the channel until a lady came on stage.

"The stone," the sung words flowed through the set, "that the builders refused,/has become the head corner." The words of the psalmist lingered.

Being a lover of gospel music herself, Stoney's mind wouldn't allow her to lose focus on the unfamiliar song that was coming forth. Stunned by the words, the melody, and the meaning, Stoney froze in her footsteps, unable to move. Stoney's boisterous attempt into getting into her mother's world was halted once her thoughts were surrounded with the lyrics. The song ministered. It was as if it had spoken directly to her.

With the song rekindling feelings in her hours before, Michelle couldn't believe in the odds of a woman now mimicking the very song. It wasn't until she heard the sniffles of someone behind her that she became coherent. Violently pushing herself from the sofa, Michelle was afraid to make a move.

Realizing she had made a noise, Stoney was shocked herself when Michelle turned around. Raising her hands, wanting, needing Michelle to recognize her tears as the pain only a child could have for her mother, Stoney lost her voice and was unable to make her announcement. Opening her arms, Stoney thought Michelle would make her way into them.

"Who are you?" Michelle screamed at the top of her lungs while jumping from the sofa. Not having time to put her slippers on, Michelle stopped in her tracks once she saw the stick in Stoney's hand. "I said who are you? Say something. I'm calling the police." Michelle started her small jog around the sofa, which brought her in close proximity with Stoney. "Oh, God," Michelle called out when she saw a stunned and still crying Stoney walking rapidly toward her.

"I . . . I . . ." was the only word Stoney managed to release. Raising her hands, longing for Michelle, Stoney forgot about the timber wood being in her grasp. Close up on her mother, Stoney tried to reach for Michelle.

"Stop it! Get away from me." Michelle fought off Stoney, who wasn't fighting at all but rather trying to embrace Michelle in the midst of crowded tear ducts. "Get your hands off me. Who are you?" Michelle demanded once more.

"Ke . . .Keithe," Stoney whispered, wanting to explain her very beginning to Michelle.

"Keithe? My husband." They both stopped the struggle.

"Stoney," was all the young girl was able to share.

Not able to catch her breath and complete a sentence, when Michelle heard "Stoney" release from the girl's mouth, she couldn't hold back.

"Are you kidding me?" Michelle pushed Stoney. "Are you my husband's girlfriend?" she yelled. "Get out! Get out!"

Confused and not understanding where Michelle was coming from, placing her as Keithe's girlfriend, Stoney became angry. She started pushing back. She thought her mother would recognize her name. When Michelle didn't, and with the stick in her hand, Stoney's frustration and anger, spun with pills, pain, and disappointment, motivated her to lift the timber wood and strike her mother over the head.

"Jesus," Michelle called out as the blood poured from the open gash. Able to push Stoney several feet away, Michelle ran toward the stairwell and climbed the stairs two at a time. Finding herself in her bedroom, Michelle placed an emergency call.

Unable to make another sound, realizing what she had done, Stoney stood in the middle of the room until the swirl of the room consumed her vision. Stoney blacked out and remained unconscious, unable to give her part of the story once the police and ambulance made it to the Morgan doorstep.

CHAPTER 31

Keithe

The news Keithe had received from the other end of his cell phone was still a blur. It had caused a sporadic seizure to come upon him. Thankfully for him a side rail was able to allow him to have just a one-man accident without any major injury.

By the time Keithe came to, Bishop Perry was standing over him, praying for his complete healing. When the paramedics found Keithe, they dialed the last number in his call log. Giving Bishop Perry the hospital's location, the bishop made his way to Keithe.

After Keithe regained his momentum in the hospital room, the bishop had shared with him all that had transpired and all the findings between Stoney and Michelle. Thrown for a complete loop, Keithe couldn't grasp that for fifteen years he'd been married to someone he didn't even know.

"MaeShell," Keithe whispered. Hearing all the details from her past from someone who had only gotten to know her for a short amount of time himself, made pain sting Keithe's heart.

"But how? I mean, when? Stoney? Michelle?" Keithe couldn't get his questions together for all of the events that had puzzled his mind. Before he could get the answers he needed from the bishop, Michelle made her way into his hospital room with a bandage on her head. When she walked in to see Ky standing close to her husband, she didn't know in which direction to run. Then, anger, instead of embarrassment, crept in.

"Deacon. I didn't mean to meddle or add harm, but . . ." Bishop Perry looked at Michelle, shook his head, and stepped closer to Keithe. "But my daughter was at stake. She's pregnant, and I just couldn't let this go by," Bishop Perry explained.

"You just couldn't go on with your happy life, huh? You want to tell so much about my life, did your wife ever tell you she had AIDS or have you been living life with blinders on yourself?"

Before Bishop Ky Perry could respond and let her know that Kendra did indeed have HIV/AIDS, but that the disease didn't have her, Keithe cut him off. "Michelle, wait a minute." Keithe tried to pull himself up from lying flat.

"No. It's all right, Deacon. My wife?" Bishop pointed to himself, wondering why he even made an effort to call Michelle and let her know about her husband's accident, especially if she was still going to possess ignorance. "My wife?" he asked Michelle again with deep security about him. "What my wife is not is a liar, a cheat, or a manipulator. You know what, Michelle? I'm not going back twenty years with you. I'm not wasting my time on you." Looking at Keithe, Bishop Perry said, "I'm happy all is well, Deacon. "

"The same for your daughter, Bishop," Keithe eased from his dry lips. "Do you know what will happen to Stoney?"

Shaking his head, he looked over to Michelle and thought she ought to be the one to tell her husband. "She," the bishop said, pointing lazily at Michelle. "Um. Michelle."

"I pressed charges. Yes, I surely did. What do you expect of me? Your mistress came after me in our home—" Michelle was cut off.

"My mistress!" Keithe yelled. "Are you kidding me?" He looked back and forth between Bishop and Michelle. "Didn't you tell her?"

"No. No, I . . . I didn't. I thought that ought to come from you."

"Tell me what?" Michelle stood up straight on both of her feet. "What, Keithe?" She took a step closer to her husband's bedside. "Well?"

Finally making up his mind to sit up in the hospital bed, Keithe was drained of all the drama that had crowded his days and nights and knew the end had finally come.

"Michelle, Stoney isn't my mistress. Yes, I met her through Mike up in Dallas, but she'd been living there for the past year or so. She's been . . ." He had to go on. "She's been searching for her mother for quite some years. She pieced together that you and I were married."

"So? And what? She came on to you; you fell for the sob story? What? What, Keithe?" Michelle asked.

"No, Michelle. Stoney is your daughter." He released the news Michelle hadn't seemed to grasp. "So that scar, Michelle"—he pointed at his wife's midsection—"wasn't for naught. I know your real name is MaeShelle."

Now it was her turn to look between the two men who had her cornered.

"Wha . . ." Michelle couldn't seem to complete her thoughts. "How . . . I mean, she must have me mistaken for someone else. I don't have any . . ." That quickly she had forgotten Bishop would know the lie she was about to tell about not having any kids.

"Michelle. There is no need to even try . . ." Before Bishop Perry could finish his sentence and before she could complete her thought, Michelle's knees must have felt what she knew. "Marcus," was the only thing she could release from her thoughts before her body made contact with the floor.

CHAPTER 32

Marcus

They had driven their comrades in Christ to Houston, not to interfere in their family affairs but to support the bishop and first lady of their church. Marcus and Gracie Jeffries stood as their friend and bishop walked into Mercy's hospital room.

"How is Deacon Keithe?" Marcus asked.

"Fine, fine." Bishop Perry couldn't look his friend in the eyes. He wanted so badly to tell Marcus about Michelle's fainting and what she'd mumbled, but knew his daughter's hospital room was not the place. There would be way too many questions, and his daughter didn't need the extra stress on herself or the baby. The news he had to share with Marcus could easily be known to break a man down, and Bishop wanted to save Marcus any discomfort.

Marcus knew something was off-kilter by the minimal use of words Bishop was using; so did his wife and daughter. "What is it, Bishop?"

"Honey," Kendra called out to her husband.

"Daddy," Mercy called out to her father.

Not feeling the need to answer his wife and daughter, Bishop only worried about his daughter's health at the moment. With her anxiety level running her blood pressure up, Bishop Perry needed to make sure his daughter and grandchild were out of harm's way.

"How are you, dear? And the baby, of course?" Bishop asked.

"I'm good, Daddy," Mercy answered, knowing they wouldn't get any more out of her father than what he was willing to share.

"We're waiting on the test results on the baby. Mercy's blood pressure was high and the doctor is worried about distress on the baby," Kendra explained.

"Right." Bishop leaned down and kissed his daughter on her forehead. Placing his hand on his daughter's pregnant belly, he prayed. "Dear God in heaven, Lord, we thank you for forgiving our hearts and we ask you this day, Dear Lord, for you to come into this baby's breathing space. Come into Mercy's womb right now, Lord, and cover this unborn child, your child, Lord. This is your child, Lord, and we ask for you to cover all, heal what needs to be healed, keep what needs to be kept. Touch this mother and child right now,

God. Keep this child in his holding place until you see fit for him to be released to our care. In Jesus' name. Amen."

"Amen," the others declared.

"Kendra, Gracie, can you two please stay here and get the results and make sure everything is okay? Marcus, can you come with me?" Bishop Perry asked.

Always there for his friend, Marcus said, "Sure."

Frat brothers since their own time spent in Houston, it was Marcus's love of college football that had led him to Dallas. After having worked for his alma mater for six years after graduation, Marcus was offered a head coaching position at a local university in Dallas. It was there that he literally ran into Gracie, his high school girlfriend.

At the chance meeting in reuniting with Gracie, Marcus had been casually dating Michelle, who took their time spent more seriously than she should have. Yet, if it hadn't been for Marcus's chance meeting with Gracie at her fitness center, he didn't know if his and Michelle's season would have ended as it had. His test came later.

More than six years after their marriage began, and their love for each other stood solid, Gracie's overbearing ways began to play on the foundation of their union. Making a decision for their family without allowing Marcus his rightful place wound up costing Gracie her pregnancy with their third child, a child not planned by either of them.

Marcus's journey to lead his family in a direction provided by God was tested in his fleshly pain. Not feeling needed, wanted, appreciated, or respected gave way to Marcus making the mistake of reminiscing too long about Michelle, who he reacquainted himself with. With their own chance encounter leading to a physical affair, Marcus's approval of his manhood was temporarily fulfilled.

"So what's really going on?" Marcus interjected as they crossed the threshold.

Bishop let his held breath loose. "Marcus." Bishop removed all formalities. "I don't even know how . . . I don't know how to tell you this, man."

"Just let it out. What is it? Mercy is okay," Marcus affirmed. "You said—"

"I was just upstairs with Deacon Keithe and Michelle." Thinking the shoe could have easily been on the other foot, Bishop wanted to get to the meat of the story. "Michelle thought Stoney was Keithe's mistress."

Bishop Perry's own history with Michelle came by chance. Meeting her at a restaurant on the same night Marcus became reacquainted with her, but at a different time, Bishop was naive when it came to Michelle. Striking up a private relationship with Michelle, not sharing anything with Marcus, he fell deeply in love over a short amount of time, seeing the potential not even Michelle saw in herself. In the beginning, she purposely used him for her own desires, but became overwhelmed with the good man he presented and held himself to be. Not knowing Michelle had cheated with Marcus during their courtship, everything changed the day Michelle let him know about her pregnancy.

"Wow. Did they get that cleared up?" Marcus asked.

Nodding, Bishop looked down at his Sperry shoes. "They did. She fainted when he told her that Stoney was her daughter."

"Is she okay?" Marcus held his hands inside of his trouser pockets and stopped rocking.

"She is. But . . ." Bishop went forward with what he needed to share. "But before she fainted, right after she realized Stoney was her daughter, Michelle blurted out your name."

It was enough for Keithe to get where Bishop Perry was going. Slapping his right hand against his own chest, Marcus took several steps backward until his back smacked against the nearest wall.

"Are you okay?" Bishop wanted to make sure his friend wasn't feeling ill at the news, at least physically.

Unable to speak, Marcus nodded vehemently. Shocked for a second, the breath he willed to take finally lodged itself in his lungs. Hurt bleed through his heart for a possible daughter he knew nothing about; thought didn't exist. Anger crept in toward Michelle from the secret she had obviously kept from him.

"You mean to tell me . . ." He didn't want to verbalize it. "Why didn't she?" he tried to ask Bishop, knowing his friend wouldn't know the answer. "Why?" Marcus's first set of tears danced around in his sockets until they fell.

Bringing comfort in the form of a hug toward his once just a mentor and friend, now brother in Christ, Bishop Perry held Marcus in a tight embrace.

"I don't know, Marcus. I don't know. She gave me the same news all those years ago, about the baby not being mine, and said the same about you. I can't explain why she did what she did." He released his friend. "Perhaps she did it for your family: Gracie, the boys."

"The boys?" Marcus thought about his adult sons and how they would now know how he had, once upon a time, been unfaithful to their mother.

"Marcus. Let us just take one step at a time. Let us get the details and the certainty from Michelle that you are Stoney's dad before you wear yourself out. Testing doesn't take long, and Gracie—"

"Gracie," Marcus bellowed. "Man. Whew. My wife, man." Marcus shed a few fresh tears in the presence of Ky. "Things are good, I can't keep anything from her. I'm just going to have to tell her where we stand right now."

"And that is your right, Marcus. Gracie is a praying woman. She forgave you and you forgave her. Just look how God has blessed you all over the years."

He did that. Marcus recaptured the past years of God's grace and mercy that He'd poured out on their union. Their marriage, their sons, and their ministry had flourished because of willing their lives back into God's will.

Initially it hadn't been as easy for Gracie to forgive Marcus for his trespasses. But with Christian counseling, and her learning that she too had trespassed against him, the two worked on their marriage and succeeded in moving forward.

Marcus wiped his tears with the embroidered cloth he kept in his pocket.

"You're right. God has blessed us." He took a breath and shook his head. "Let me go and get Gracie." He finally rose from the wall.

Not letting his friend get too far away, Bishop said, "Marcus, I got your back. Believe that. And if all else fails, you know God does."

"This I know," was all Marcus had energy enough to confirm.

CHAPTER 33

Stoney

She was strapped to a hospital bed. Stoney's eyes were swollen and her heart was destroyed. She couldn't even piece together what she had done. All she could remember was her trying to get close to her mother. If she were honest with her intentions, she didn't have any plans, good or bad. What she knew was that she wanted to get close enough to her mother. Just enough to smell her. Maybe even hold her.

A knock at the door halted her sorrow.

"Come in," Stoney said.

"Stoney," Vicky cried out as she rushed to her young friend's bedside. "Oh my goodness. Are you all right?" she asked, walking closer to a bandaged and IV-filled Stoney.

Embarrassed by her presence and the way she was sure she looked handcuffed to the bed, Stoney turned her head away from Vicky, but couldn't avoid Mike, who had also walked into the room.

"Stoney. Stoney, are you okay?" Mike asked the same question as Vicky.

No longer able to shut them out or hide away from them, Stoney released her cries in front of the two who had shown they wanted more than anything to just be her friend. She didn't even know how they were aware of the entire incident, but figured Keithe may have been behind the information given.

"We are here for you, Stoney. The nurse said you are dehydrated and malnourished. Your iron is very low." Vicky tried to hide her heartfelt cry. "I'm not going anywhere until you are better."

"But . . ." Stoney wanted to share more of herself. No doubt, she knew her friends would hear how bad of a person she was. Before then she wanted to share her real predicament, and her real purpose from the very beginning. "They are taking me to jail," she cried.

"I know." Vicky looked up at Mike. "We know everything. No matter what, we are still here. No matter what."

"Just like we were in the beginning. We should have never allowed you to get so far away from us," Mike interjected. "So far from God."

Closing her eyes, Stoney wanted and needed to get her breakthrough. She was no doubt physically weak, but she was tired of being mentally and emotionally weak as well.

"See, my . . . my grandmother raised me by herself. But most of the time it seemed as if I raised her." Stoney shook her head. "She had schizophrenia. I didn't know it at first, when I was little." She looked between her friends, wanting to know if they were taking in her shared information.

"The most I know is that my mom dropped me off. Didn't want anything to do with me. I don't know who my daddy is and I don't know what I'm going to do in this world now." Stoney hollered a weak cry, rambling all of her woes together.

"You don't have to think or talk about that right now, Stoney," Vicky said.

"Yes, I do." Stoney was too weak to raise her head from the white, covered pillow. "I do because it hurts so bad not to know. All I wanted was to talk to her, but I couldn't. When I saw her, I couldn't say anything. I wanted to hug her, but I scared her. I . . ." Stoney broke down, thinking about the opportunity she had made for herself and the way it had ended.

"It's okay, Stoney." Mike patted her on her right shoulder and rubbed her hand. Vicky held her left hand and rubbed the top of it in a circular motion. "It will work itself out."

The medication in her intravenous tube started to take effect. Wanting to struggle and plea about all that had taken place, with her eyes becoming heavy all Stoney could do was shake her head back and forth.

Mike and Vicky joined hands as Stoney's eyes appeared heavier than her will for them to remain open. Speaking life over their friend, their sister, the two went before the Lord on Stoney's behalf, asking Him to decree healing in her body, in her mind, and in her heart. Virtuous living and thinking was what they asked of the Lord. Purpose and patience for the young woman to be able to ascend into womanhood without any regret, any turmoil, and any distorted view of what the Lord had in store for her.

CHAPTER 34

Michelle

"Oh God. Oh God," Michelle yelled, not wanting to believe the child she had given birth to had been in her presence, her arms, for that matter. They may have been struggling within a fight; nevertheless, Michelle had touched her child. "What happened?" She wanted to believe it was all a dream. "What happened, Keithe? Why am I in here?" Michelle looked at the hospital surroundings.

He didn't want to just blurt it out. Rather, he wanted her to figure out her own truth.

"Michelle." He lingered with his head down, but his eyes were still on his wife.

"Is she my daughter?" Her face appeared as if she had never signed up for monthly Botox fill-ins. "Stoney is my daughter?" she asked again as she rubbed her stomach, which once held her baby. The years' worth of worry and scorn had jumped from her past and made a spot on her present.

Michelle had named her daughter Alexia. "Her name . . . my daughter's name is Alexia," she stated to Keithe, knowing he wouldn't know one way or another. No one would, maybe the nurses who delivered her, maybe Bishop would, but who would care to remember her? No one.

All those years ago, once DNA results came back and Bishop Perry was announced not to be the father, he left Michelle's world, and being that he was the only one remotely interested in her, Michelle hardened her heart. The day she dropped her baby on her mother's doorstep, Michelle drove the road back, all the way back into Dallas, from Greenville Texas, with the birth certificate on the passenger's seat. Crossing city limits back into Dallas, Michelle tore Alexia's birth certificate into the smallest of pieces. As far as she was concerned, the day was never supposed to happen. It was as if she was continually dealt a bad hand.

Her hard luck seemed to begin the day her dad passed away. It seemed as though the day her father died in the car accident was the same day her mother took her own life. No get up and go and no family support system, Susie Hart lost her way, and in the center of it all, Michelle lost her mother. Just barely in high school herself, Michelle couldn't grieve the loss of her dad due to watching the next move her mother would make.

A manic depressive, one day her mother would be up and the next she would literally be out for the count, to the point where Michelle would walk in Susie's bedroom and find her on the bare floor just lying, staring at the ceiling. For two straight years, until it was time for graduation, Michelle had to fight the demons her mother usually let win. Even with the memories, the knowledge of illness, it didn't persuade Michelle's thought of leaving her child. The life she had built for herself and the things she wanted outweighed her want to do right.

Her mother didn't have a job before her father died, and having no trade she didn't even try to find one afterward, so the county supported them. With no clothing, Michelle had to piece together what she could. It had gotten to the point where Michelle loathed her mother for giving up, for not fighting. Even the church Michelle had tried to continue to go to had given up on Susie. Seeing that for herself, Michelle gave up on the church and their so-called God in turn.

"Even youths grow tired and weary, and young men stumble and fall," Michelle rattled Isaiah 40:30 off the top of her head.

"But those who wait for the Lord will renew their strength." Keithe wanted to help his wife complete the scripture he had no idea she knew.

"I waited," Michelle yelled out with burning tears in her eyes. "I waited for the Lord, Keithe." She wanted her husband to understand her plight. "For two years I prayed and cried and waited for the Lord to pull my mother out of her depression, out of her self-induced depression. Do you think He listened to me?" She spat venom, thinking about God not showing up.

"My daddy." Michelle looked at her husband, now despising herself for never opening up to the one person who seemed to sincerely love her. "My father died, Keithe." She started on a story that she never shared before with her husband. "But she had no right, no right, to give up, leaving me alone in a world by myself." Sitting up in her hospital bed, still fully clothed, Michelle shifted her body to one side.

"My father died. Not me!" She screamed forty years worth of pain from her vocal cords. "My mother grieved so much, so long for my father. She never let him rest. I needed her, Keithe." Michelle's voice trailed off into a calm pain.

"I needed my mother to let me know everything would be all right. That life still goes on, that we could have made it together. But she gave up!"

Keithe squeezed his way into Michelle's hospital bed. "It's okay, Michelle. I'm here for you," he said, wanting her to believe it.

"But you can't fix it. You didn't do it," she snapped.

"You're right. I didn't do it, and I can't fix it. Only God can. Only God can mend your heart. Only God can allow you to be the mother you wanted in your own life." Keithe seemed to have struck a nerve.

"Oh, God. I can't. I can't do it."

"Jesus said you can do all things through Him," Keithe witnessed to his wife.

"Stop it! Stop it now! You go on and on about what God can do, and here I am, fifty-five years old, and I don't even respect you as my husband. You know why? Wanna know why, Keithe? Because I can't even respect myself for all that I've done to myself. What I did to my mother." She shed tears for leaving her needy mother. "What I did to her." She couldn't bring herself to release the truth.

She tried to break free from Keithe's hold. With her mind swarming about, with the possibilities of leaving the hospital and getting as far away as she could from Houston, Keithe prayed a declaration over her life.

"The place you think is dead is indeed alive, Michelle. God said He will bring health and healing to your life. Jeremiah says God will heal his people and let them enjoy all the peace and security they can handle. He can rebuild you, Michelle." Keithe held his grip on his wife.

"No. Let me go," she fought.

"Let Him back in, Michelle. God can cleanse you from your sin and rebellion. He will walk you into a place of joy, praise, and His glory. God has peace for you, honey. Seek Him, Michelle. Seek Him."

Tired of running, and tired of being the person she had built, her pride was broken, and Michelle released her pain by crying as if a hydrant had been unscrewed. She released tears nonstop. The wrestle she had given as a fight ceased.

"I don't know how," she whispered.

With tears all ready in their holding place, the revelation of his being in Michelle's life released them. Through his pain, he silently praised God because there was purpose. All of what he'd gone through with his wife of fifteen years was for a reason: God's reason. God's purpose for Michelle and her daughter to be reunited so that they both may heal.

"Tell God about your pain. Tell Him what you've been holding in. God placed us together for a reason. Today is that reason. Trust God. Trust us, Michelle." Keithe let go of his own tears.

"I dropped my baby off. I just left her. I just left my baby. Oh my goodness. Oh, God. Oh, God. Forgive me." She asked something of the Lord she had never asked before.

"Call out to Him, Michelle. Honey, call out to the Lord. Tell Him to renew your mind."

Groggily, Michelle obeyed the voice she heard. Though it was Keithe's physical voice speaking, the piercing in her heart let her know that God was asking her to release her cares over to Him.

Come unto me, Michelle heard the Lord speak.

"Oh, God. I . . . I need you." She closed her eyes.

What do you need of me, my child? Michelle heard the Lord say. *Speak to me so that I may speak to you. Fear not.*

"The Lord is my light," Keithe started off. "Whom shall I fear?" Michelle carried in full verse, barely taking breaths until she had completed all fourteen verses.

Astonished, but not without doubt, Keithe thanked God for Michelle's hidden knowledge of God's Word. The Word that had been hidden deep in her heart. Keithe could only marvel at what God had shown. Planting a kiss atop his wife's head, Keithe rocked Michelle in place as she mumbled prayers from her soul. Her continued conversation with the Lord showed to soothe Michelle's eternal pain, bringing peace to her heart and salvation to her soul.

CHAPTER 35

Gracie

"What?" Gracie blew out the question in a rigid breath. Running her hands through her hair, no longer caring about the present curls, Gracie couldn't believe her ears. "Wait." She placed one hand over her open mouth. "So. You . . . you may be *her* child's father?" She questioned her husband, who stood as close to her as possible. As if she could hear his heart beating through his shirt, Gracie placed an open hand on her husband's chest, over his heart.

The small and vacant conference room that was available was cold and quiet. Removing her hand, Gracie half wrapped herself with one arm.

Marcus knew he didn't have to profess his love to his wife. It had been evident taking his vows decades ago how much he adored Gracie. Not even halfway into their marriage, when he made the mistakes often made by insecure people, Marcus realized how undying love resurfaced.

"I don't know for sure. I don't even know if she knows for sure, honey." He really wanted to believe Michelle had just blurted his name just because. "Tests will have to be run."

"They were run all those years ago, Marcus," Gracie snapped, and turned her back to her husband.

"I never saw them. She told Ky that neither of us was the father."

"Humph." She gave off an attitude. "And you just took her word for it?"

"You were right there along for the ride with me, Gracie. You could have spoken up. You could have demanded, or asked about having the paper results. Right? I wasn't thinking. It never dawned on me."

Turning back around, Gracie rolled her eyes, bypassing his question all together. "But all of these years? This isn't a baby." Gracie's mind jogged back to the time when her husband had stepped out on their marriage, on their vows. The same pain that had bred inside her feelings all those years ago, Gracie felt again.

"I don't want to hurt like that again. It's bringing all the pain back." Gracie shuddered and dove into her husband's arms.

"No. No, it's not. This is just a moment. We don't have to relive that. I'm here now, and now I haven't cheated on you."

"But if this girl happens to be yours, she's a product from what you did do." She buried her head into Marcus's chest.

He couldn't deny it, nor could he keep finding ways to play around with the wording. The only thing he could do was get with Michelle and Stoney as soon as possible to see what the truth would come to.

She tried to stay strong. Marcus had just thrown her off her stationary bike, by putting wheels on their marriage. With the news he'd just shared, Gracie felt herself peddling backward to the past filled with hurt and pain. Wishing she were home in order to lock herself in her prayer closet to speak with Jesus physically, Gracie had to make do with what she had spiritually.

Marcus left the conference room before she did. Giving him a few steps in his exit before she made her own, Gracie made a detour into the lavatory that was placed at the front of the vacant area. Walking into the tight area, as soon as the door shut itself, déjà vu hit her like a ton of bricks.

Gracie's stomach felt as if a wrecking ball had made contact with her current affairs. Her knees buckled and Gracie tried to pull from her stored strength, trying not to give in to the trick of the enemy.

"Okay. Okay. If Marcus has a daughter . . ." She placed her left hand over her eyes as if she needed shade from what she was about to bring forth. "A daughter? That means he has another child by someone else. Wait a minute," Gracie tried to reason with herself, "Marcus may be the father of Michelle's baby? Lord Jesus." She allowed her reality to settle once more as if she hadn't just come to the conclusion a minute before.

"Why now, Lord?" Gracie couldn't help but ask her maker. "If this had happened when everything else happened, I could've been over it." Gracie spoke of the affair Marcus had with Michelle. Admittedly taking her husband for granted at the time, solely making decisions on her own instead of as a couple, Gracie couldn't help but to take some of the blame off of Marcus. "Now I have to go through this again. Jesus, you are going to have to give me strength . . . unmatchable strength."

Gripping the sink as tightly as the steel would allow her, Gracie wondered how one person could be so evil, so manipulative. If it were up to her, she'd set Michelle straight once and for all. But she walked God's path now, and there was no turning back. It wasn't up to her to bring damnation on Michelle, if that was needed to be done.

"Oh my goodness," Gracie bellowed when the past thought of her husband being with another woman crossed her mind again. Over twenty-two years ago she'd been in a hospital restroom, wondering in which direction her life and marriage would take off. To Gracie, life had a funny way of repeating itself. Back then, Gracie had been more than five months pregnant with the couple's third child and had no idea her husband had stepped out on their marriage. Now, over two decades later, the result of that affair was taking advantage of her heart once more.

"But God shall supply all of my needs." She stood firm, in the middle of the restroom, ready to take the storm with authority.

"Devil, you may have had this waiting in the wings for me." She rubbed her hands together and then placed another stiff grip on the steel bowl while looking in the mirror. "But you're not going to get the result I'm sure you're looking for." Gracie allowed her tears to have their own way while she went to God in prayer. "Father, I come to you with a sincere and repenting heart, asking you to hold me. Hold me, dear God, so that I don't break, so that I *cannot* break under the devil's holding.

"When it's time for the test, even before the two of them have spoken, before the test is even spoken of, I'm not going to ask you to have the DNA results speak one way or the other. I'm going to ask you, Lord, to allow us strength in whichever way the answer settles. I know you love me, Lord, and I'm thankful even now for the blessings you have for my storm.

"Peace be still." Gracie spoke to her storm as she felt the enemy try to bring on the feeling of uncertainty. "I'm not going to hate Michelle, devil. God, only you can help Michelle. Only you can finally, once and for all, break the chains that have captured this woman's heart for far too long. I don't know her story and I don't know her issues. Oh, but I know a man who sits high and looks low. Jesus, I know you to be a healer and a way maker. Ha!" Gracie broke out with a happy praise.

"I know you to be a deliverer, dear God. Show up in Michelle's life. Yes, devil, I call on my Jesus for Michelle's healing. Save her, Lord." Gracie stamped her feet and tried not to get too loud, but there was something about the name of Jesus that made her not worry about anyone else. If anything, maybe some of her prayers could seep through other hospital doors.

"Set her free, Jesus, and fill her with your precious Holy Ghost power." Gracie concluded her prayer vocally, but still gave the physical remnants of shouting for the Lord. Trying her best to quiet her praise, Gracie had no choice but to let out what was still in her. "From the crown of her head, Lord, to the soles of her feet, Jesus, set Michelle free."

CHAPTER 36

Michelle

"Judge, you have to sign in." The police guard stepped in front of the hospital door as Michelle tried to make her way around him. "Judge? Judge?" He looked back and saw Keithe follow his wife, along with their attorney. Reading between the lines, the policeman released his persistent tone.

While still in the hospital room and in her own recovery, Michelle had known what her heart wanted to do, but she still couldn't take any chances just doing as she pleased. A lot had happened over the decades, and her prestigious title of judge had made many people try their best to corner her into a lawsuit.

After spilling her feelings to Keithe and accepting God back into her life, it was as if Michelle was a very different person. Outwardly, Michelle had seemed to have a breakdown, but in actuality, she had encountered an inward release of peace she now displayed.

"I want her. I want to see my daughter," she had announced while still in her hospital room. They were the first words of release she sprang at Keithe, who had not left her side. Showing signs of being physically weak, Michelle knew she was only drowsed because of her conversation with God. Before she lost the nerve, or the enemy snuck back in to her life, Michelle spat out instructions for Keithe to contact their lawyer and start the process of seeing her daughter.

Hard on his wife's heels, Keithe made sure he was there every step of the way. Not just with the reunion between Michelle and her daughter, but with her walk with God. Inwardly proud of all that had taken place, Keithe knew a changed person when he saw one, and was proud that his wife was that person.

Michelle had been devastated and hurt, and felt she had been left to fend for herself. In reality she was, but not even her mother could be at fault. Mentally her mother had checked out of her responsibilities. In doing so, Michelle physically checked out of being her mother's help when her mother needed her most. Not healing from the pain many years ago, she repeated and passed the same wound to Stoney. But God.

On the short ride over to the hospital across town, Keithe found the opportunity to minister more to his wife about how God could restore, renew, and revive. It was right there, on the car ride over, when Michelle repeated the sinner's prayer and charged her life back over to the Lord. It was then that Keithe announced his decision to stick by her side as long as she wanted him to. No condemnation would come from him. Michelle simply nodded her agreement toward her husband of almost sixteen years. Riding the streets with one hand in Keithe's and a handkerchief in the other, Michelle showed that she was a changed woman.

Once the officer moved to the side, Michelle eased open the door and walked in. Looking back, Keithe could tell she wanted time by herself. Understanding, he planted himself by the door. Seeing Vicky and Mike down the hall, Keithe and his lawyer made their way toward the two.

Stoney, a bit dazed from medication given for anxiety, blinked uncontrollably when she focused on who had entered her room. Taking a deep breath, Stoney's chest swelled and so did her eyes, which were full of tears. Reaching for the bed's controller, she sat tall, not knowing if Michelle had come in peace or to continue what had transpired earlier. When she saw somberness placed on Michelle's face, Stoney relaxed.

That was what she had wanted. For all she'd ever dreamed of in life, the moment that had just passed was all she wanted: for her mother, Michelle, to walk into her life. And just like that, after the fighting, the pill popping, all of the searching, Michelle walked right into her daughter's life.

"I didn't know who you were," Michelle let out in a hard breath. She walked with authority until she reached Stoney's bed. "I had no clue. I thought . . ." She looked back at the door, reminding herself that Keithe was on the other side. She declined to unbury her thought of Stoney being Keithe's mistress.

With her eyes landing on Stoney's eyes, Michelle made sure she spoke from her heart. "I am sorry." She hunched her shoulders. "Until a few hours ago, I've been lost." She told herself not to be embarrassed, but to just speak from her heart. "I've been torturing myself for decades, trying to forget you, trying to forget all about my mama. You should hate me, just like everyone else probably does. Just like my mama probably does." Michelle wondered about her mother.

"I dropped you off. Ugh," she said, remembering the day vividly. "I literally dropped you off with my mother. Because . . ." She sat on a small portion of the hospital bed to regain her composure. "Because I was a coward, because I had messed up lives, and I knew in the end I'd mess up yours. But look what I've done." Michelle grabbed Stoney's free hand in her own. "I messed it up anyway."

"But you're here," was the first thing Stoney spoke since Michelle had entered into the room. "You are here, for me. And you want to be," she stated with crunched eyebrows. "I just wanted to be with you. Every day I'd wake up I wanted you. Every minute I wanted you to come back and get me, tell me you made a mistake." Michelle leaned in and Stoney moved forward for their first embrace.

Not releasing her hold, Michelle said, "I did. I made a mistake. When I drove off I knew I'd made a mistake, but I was caught up in a world that I'd made for myself," she figured she had to tell her. Sitting up, Michelle went on. "For the record, Stoney, I love you. I mean it, I mean it from the bottom of my heart."

Unable to talk, or respond in the manner she wanted, Stoney held her mother tight.

After the two calmed down from their meeting, which was long overdue, Michelle felt it necessary to keep going. "I've done a lot of wrong, Stoney." Michelle shook her head. "I had dated your dad. I . . . I thought we'd one day get married because we cared about each other. But it didn't last."

"You know who my dad is?" Stoney asked. When Michelle nonverbally answered yes, Stoney asked, "Do you know where he is?"

"I do." Shamefully, Michelle tilted her head to the side and gazed into the eyes of her daughter. Michelle could see where her daughter resembled her father. In the slight smile Stoney had finally released, Michelle could see that the small rings that widened her smile were given by her father as well.

"And you know him too, Stoney."

Confused, Stoney tilted her own head, allowing her smile to disappear. "I do? Who is he?"

EPILOGUE

The kitchen was busy. Gregory and Geoffrey finally made it their business to make their mother proud by making their way to Dallas from Atlanta. Christmas was the very next day, and in thirty minutes they would be arriving from the airport: one with a fiancée and another with a girlfriend. Gracie couldn't be more proud. What a difference a year had made.

"You want to check on the cake, Kendra? I'm going to go ahead and get these dressing rolls out of the oven." Gracie had been up all morning long, preparing a small Christmas Eve dinner for their home. She'd been over the stove since the early a.m., and when Kendra finally broke away from her grandson, she arrived just in time to help her dear friend out. Since Bishop had been away with his bishop duties, and was not scheduled to come home until later that afternoon, Kendra had been tending to her grandmotherly duties.

"Is Mercy bringing my great-godson over for dinner?" Gracie asked.

Not able to contain her giddiness anytime her grandbaby was mentioned, Kendra eased her best friend's worries. "You know she wouldn't have it any other way. They should be here any minute now."

"Don't laugh, Kendra. You know I'm just as bad as you are. I can't get enough of little Grant either." Gracie placed the two dozen dressing rolls on the pan rack to cool.

"Isn't he just a doll baby?" Kendra's eyes gazed and mouth oozed like only a grandmother's could when talking about her grandchild. Setting the cake, which was baked just right, on another cooling rack, Kendra leaned against the counter, not believing just how much she actually loved being someone's grandmother. "That boy has my heart wide open."

"Mine too," Gracie said honestly.

The doorbell sounded throughout the intercom system. Gracie threw her pan holder on the counter and went toward the front of their home. Looking through the side panel, Gracie was excited to open the door for Mercy, her boyfriend, and the baby.

Gracie beamed as if she were the actual grandparent. "Merry Christmas." Taking Grant Jr. in her arms, Gracie leant her cheek for Mercy and Grant Sr. to leave their hellos. "Your mom is in the kitchen," she directed them. "Come on, Baby Grant. I need to get my snuggle time with you."

"Aunt Gracie, did G and G-Money make it yet?" Mercy asked about her god brothers, calling them by the nicknames she had given them.

"They should be pulling up soon. Your Uncle Marcus picked the two up from the airport. It's good to see you again, Grant." She wanted the twenty-three-year-old father to feel welcomed.

"Same to you, Mrs. Jeffries," Grant Sr. replied.

The four made their way into the kitchen area, where Kendra put finishing touches on the German chocolate cake she'd made. It was Marcus's favorite.

"There is my little man. Come to Grams," Kendra cooed to the almost-year-old, bright-eyed little boy.

"Ooh, no, you don't." Gracie rocked Baby Grant in her arms. "I heard he spent the night with you last night. Let this child breath." Everyone in the kitchen laughed in unison.

"Anybody home?" Marcus's voice rang toward the kitchen area.

"Okay. Maybe for just a bit." Gracie reluctantly handed Baby Grant to his grandmother. "I need my hands for those big boys of mine." Gracie's eyes watered as she half ran to greet her sons.

"Mama," Geoffrey's voice rang out.

"Hey, Ma," the almost-thirty-year-old twins said simultaneously.

Not knowing who to hug first, Gracie wrapped her arms around both of their necks. "My boys. Oh, thank you, Lord. Oh my goodness." She kissed one and then the other. "I can't believe you all are here. Look at you."

Landing their own kisses on both of her cheeks, Gregory and Geoffrey took turns picking up their mother as if she were a rag doll. As soon as she yelled, "Put me down," and swatted one's arm, the other duplicated the love gesture.

Finally settled, Gracie thought to look around for the ladies in their lives.

"Where are Tosha and Rachel? I know you two haven't dumped them that quickly," Gracie joked with her sons, knowing they had been chick magnets in college.

"No, Ma," Gregory answered first. "They are going to tour the city. Tosha has family here. Plus, we wanted to spend some family time and make sure—"

"Uh, make sure we had everything in place for Christmas," Geoffrey cut his brother off before he continued the real reason for the two coming without their beloveds: family business needed to be taken care of. Seeing Mercy over their mother's shoulder, he was glad he interrupted his brother. Noticing a bright-eyed Mercy, the two ran to hug the young lady who grew up as if she were a little sister to them.

Marcus waited in the wings, allowing his sons time with their mother and Mercy. With Gregory's almost mishaps, he figured it was time to cut in. According to his watch, they only had another fifteen minutes before their company made it over. "Honey, do you need anything else done? I was going to go out to the garage, but if you need me to do anything, it can wait."

Glad about the change from where the conversation had almost ventured to, Gracie answered her husband. "It's all done. Kendra is in the kitchen; her, Grant, and Baby Grant. We're fine, honey. You can go ahead and busy yourself." She walked up to and placed a kiss on her husband's lips. "Ky called and he's running a little late."

The past year had been a new detour in their steady lives. The wind blew in and tested their faith, their loyalty, and their ability to keep forgiving. Their past year was a testament to God's fresh anointing.

"Cool. Is the baby here too?" Gregory had heard his mother, and wanted the confirmation from Mercy. "Come on, G. Let's go see what this cat Grant is all about." He slapped his brother on the chest with the back of his hand.

"Right," Geoffrey totally agreed.

"You two!" Mercy yelled and ran after the twins.

As Gracie was about to make her exit behind her boys, Marcus grabbed for his wife's elbow. "Honey, how is Kendra?"

"She's good, babe." Gracie added a smile to her face, and silently asked God to walk her friends and family through the tedious journey they were about to dive deeper into. "We need you, Jesus," she whispered as Marcus turned toward the door.

Stoney was finally able to kick her habit: a habit that hadn't been hers to begin with. Just a year prior, when Michelle finally claimed her, the two promised to work hard for a relationship they both needed and wanted. For Stoney, with that came the honesty of being hooked on prescription drugs. For Michelle, it was time to be honest about all the hurt and pain she'd caused herself and others.

Stoney never made it past Houston's exit sign once the relationship that never was, sparked. The day at the infirmary was the beginning of what should have been for Stoney and Michelle.

The charges that had been placed against Stoney by Michelle, before Michelle knew Stoney's identity, were dropped. Before it was all said and done, Stoney and Michelle walked out of the hospital arm in arm. With Keithe behind the duo, there hadn't been much for him to say. The mere fact that God did the impossible was enough for him.

At her mother's insistence, Stoney moved right in with Michelle and Keithe, her stepfather. The air had been cleared and a three-way discussion laid the foundation of Keithe and Stoney's meeting and communication. Whatever it was that Keithe thought he had for Stoney was settled to that of a father figure for his stepdaughter.

During their full year of recovery, a lot of time was spent between the two ladies. Michelle's title of judge had been put to the side for the time being. Vacation time, sick time, any time she had available for use was used for one-on-one time with Stoney.

Michelle started their relationship with the truth. She explained her life with her own mother and father. She tried to clarify the tragic happening that took her father when she was just a child herself, and how her mother, Grandma Susie, fell deep into depression.

"I wasn't as strong as you, Stoney," Michelle had said. "There were days when she wouldn't get out of bed, wouldn't cook, wouldn't bathe." Michelle still had a hard time making reference to Susie as her mother at first, but the more they talked, the more she missed the person who gave her life. She realized her mother didn't purposefully do her wrong, and once she did, she took responsibility for her action. "She wasn't responsive to me. I wasn't enough to pull her from the fact that my father was no longer there," she shared with Stoney.

In return, Stoney shared how, by the time she had come along, Grandma Susie's depression had gotten aggressive, and with medications involved, anger presented itself. Before long, schizophrenia somehow lodged itself into the elderly lady, making Stoney's life full of child-hood heartbreak.

A lot of crying presented itself during late-night girl talks, with Michelle usually falling asleep holding her twenty-two-year-old baby. Waking the very next morning, the entire day's scenario would sometimes repeat itself.

Stoney tapped in to who she really was and wanted to be: a God-fearing young lady. Praying together as mother and daughter had become a part of who Stoney and Michelle were. With

Stoney leading the prayers, she was able to teach her mother that it was okay to praise God even when her heart was heavy. In return, Michelle inadvertently showed Stoney how to let go and let God. Still learning about one another, the year in review had been a promising start to their new future together. Even to the point when Michelle explained to Stoney about who her father was.

"Ready, Stoney?" Keithe walked down the hall and halted in front of Stoney's door. Giving two knocks to the door like an impatient father would, Keithe said, "Your mother is already downstairs in the car. Girl, how many more bags do you need?" Not believing Michelle was actually teaching Stoney bad shopping habits already, Keithe shook his head.

"Pops. Give me one minute please and I'll be down," Stoney yelled out to her stepfather, who she was more than thankful to have.

She had tried to prepare herself for the day that had been on her calendar for months. All the time she'd spent with her mother and Keithe, Stoney had finally gotten to the point where she wanted to learn more about her other half: her real father. After the four-hour drive she would be face-to-face with him and his immediate and extended family.

"You ready?" Michelle asked Stoney as soon as she added herself to the backseat of Keithe's Range Rover. He punched in their destination to his GPS system.

With his own life settling, mind at ease and marriage traveling the path meant by God, Keithe's inability to drive without fear of stress-induced seizures had been put to ease. Given a lower dosage of his anti-seizure medication was good enough for him to add himself behind the steering wheel once again, permanently.

"I'm ready." Stoney sat back and looked at her mother with a smile of thankfulness.

On the drive toward Dallas, the new family made small conversation about movies, music, and other amenities revolving around their lives. Enrolled back in school, Stoney told them how she was enjoying being at the University of Houston.

A new adventure for Michelle, and a now permanent fixture, the conversation geared toward their church lives and how worshipping together made a difference. Michelle even apologized to Keithe about how she waited so long to be the woman God had blessed him with. He accepted, and admonished her for finding who she was in God.

"Mom, so are you going to sing with the fifty-plus women when they sing on New Year's?" Stoney snickered, knowing Michelle didn't know if she was for real or not.

"Um. Stoney?" Michelle whined, hoping her daughter wouldn't push her to do the unthinkable. Michelle and singing never did mix.

"Just kidding. I just wanted to see your face light up." Stoney and Keithe laughed.

"Very funny." Michelle was relieved. She had told herself she would try to be the mother Stoney needed, instead of what she felt a mother should be. She knew she hadn't stayed in her mother's presence long enough to get the feel of how a mother is supposed to be to her child. "But actually, I was thinking about signing up to usher."

"Shut up," Keithe and Stoney both said at the same time. All three broke out in a unified laugh.

Riding in the backseat granted Stoney time to nap. With their arrival in Dallas, Stoney woke up just in time to take a look around the metropolitan area, which had been her home for a few years. It was just a pass through for her, but the stay had taught her a lot, and lasting friendships had blossomed.

It was Mike who had invited their three-member family down for the Christmas holiday. He and Vicky had been dating for almost a year and they were becoming closer and commingling together. Bygones would have to be bygones and forgiveness would have to settle in. With Michelle and Keithe rooming under Mike's roof for the entire weekend, God's love would have to be in full effect.

This would be the first face-to-face meeting between Mike and Michelle since the hospital scene a year ago, though they had spoken several times over the phone. Mike was on her list of those to ask for forgiveness. Michelle really did mean the vow she made with the Lord the Sunday she was baptized.

"Are you going to call your father and let him know you're in town?" Keithe asked Stoney, waking Michelle from her short nap.

The downtown buildings veered off to her left from Central Expressway. Michelle pushed herself up in her seat and pulled down the mirrored visor. Sitting quietly, this was going to be one of the last apologies Michelle would have to face. Though she had spoken with Stoney's father back when she revealed to their daughter that he was indeed her dad, Michelle had only spoken to him a few other times. With all of the hurt and pain Stoney had to go through, Michelle had wished more than anything she had just told the man she once loved that he was indeed the father. Back when the DNA tests were first taken, he just took Michelle's word for it. Even if he had tried to get the information that was rightfully his, being as wicked as she was, Michelle would have countered it.

"I texted him and let him know." Looking at her watch, Stoney said, "He's probably just settling in himself. Oh, but he said he'll drop me back at Mike's later on tonight. And he said it would probably be late, because everyone always gathered and stayed extra late on Christmas Eve."

"That's good, honey." Michelle jumped into the two-way conversation. "No matter what, don't forget we will be leaving early in the morning, headed to Greenville." Michelle didn't want to miss the opportunity to sit alongside her mother's grave and give her proper recognition for all that had happened. In her heart all was well, but she wanted, needed, closure.

Another fifteen minutes and Keithe was turning off his GPS system, thanking it for its handy detail. "We're here," Keithe called out. All three looked over their shoulders to the right, and admired the house that looked to come off of the street they lived on in Houston.

"Nice," Michelle spoke.

"It is," Keithe agreed.

"Yeah. It is. But, of course, it's not prettier than ours," Stoney joked.

"Girl, hush." Michelle swatted behind her.

Stoney and Keithe got out of the truck. Keithe went to the back to retrieve her tote bag. Stoney made her way to the front door and pushed the doorbell.

The door opened and Stoney drew in a breath. During the past year, she had made two trips to Dallas in order to spend one-on-one time with her father. Other times he'd traveled to Houston to see her. Now able to spend the holiday with her family and who her father deemed extended family, Stoney was walking on eggshells when she didn't see her father's car. Having to meet her stepmother on a totally different level than before was a bit nerve-wracking for Stoney.

"Stoney," Marcus happily answered the door, wanting to show the young girl who could have easily been his daughter that he had no qualms about her joining in with him and his family.

"Hey, Mr. Jeffries," Stoney said. "Is my dad, uh, er, Kendra here? I was told to come over here."

"First off, young lady, you can call me Uncle Marcus."

"Okay," she agreed.

"And you can call me Aunt Gracie, if you'd like," Gracie said, standing beside her husband.

Feeling weird calling someone she really didn't know uncle and aunt, Stoney obliged, knowing they played a major role in her father and stepmother's lives. Hearing the sound of a horn blowing, Stoney turned just in time to see her dad, Bishop Perry, pulling behind Keithe's vehicle.

Still sitting behind the wheel of his car, it still bothered Bishop terribly to know he didn't get to play a role in raising his daughter. And just when he thought he had to be there for Marcus, it was he who turned out to be Stoney's father. With Michelle calling out Marcus's name before she fainted, for whatever reason, the incident threw them for a loop. The second round of DNA testing that he and Marcus had to take confirmed him to be the father of Michelle's baby. It was the same result the test showed all those years ago. This time he had to see them for himself. Taking Michelle's word all those years ago didn't pay off. Nevertheless, with the regret, he still rejoiced for the time he still had left to spoil Stoney.

"Hey, Daddy." Stoney didn't wait for Bishop to come closer to the house before showing her affection.

"Hey, Stoney. Hey, honey, how are you?" He didn't wait for an answer, knowing his daughter was more than okay. "Come on. Let's get you inside. Oh." He looked beyond Stoney. "How's it going?" He reached out to shake Keithe's hand, while hugging Stoney with his other arm.

"Good, good," Keithe said and looked toward the Jeffries, plus Kendra, who had added herself to the door.

Moving farther into their home, Marcus and Gracie gave the blended family time to themselves.

"How are you, Stoney?" Kendra grabbed at Stoney and held her as if she'd birth the young lady herself. Knowing how a hard childhood can play into someone's future, Kendra never for a minute blamed Stoney for anything she went through.

"I'm good, Mrs. Kendra," Stoney replied.

"That's good. We're so glad you're here," Kendra reassured her.

"I'll take the bag for you," Bishop offered to Keithe. "Would you all like to come inside?" He never acknowledged Michelle, but without a doubt knew she was in the truck. Bishop had already forgiven her, but having to remain in her presence was another thing.

"No. We have to be going," Keithe said, looking back at the truck. When he saw that Michelle was looking down, he chopped the conversation in half.

"Okay. Okay. Well. I'll bring her to where you all will be later on tonight. Don't wait up for her."

Starting his short trek to the car, Keithe hollered back, "Sounds like a plan. We'll probably be up though. Playing spades always keeps us going." He wanted Bishop Perry to read between the lines and know that he'd become an overprotective dad overnight.

"Right."

Before Keithe was able to get in the car, Stoney walked out of the house and trotted a short way to her stepfather. Michelle giving her life over to the Lord, and Stoney coming into their life, was cause enough for Keithe to put any ill feelings or wayward thoughts away about Stoney. When he realized God's plan for all of their lives, he walked the walk and talked the talk.

"Thank you, Pops. I'll see you later." She stood on her tiptoes and gave him a peck. Walking over to the passenger's side where her mother sat, Stoney opened the door.

Stunned by the door opening, Michelle gasped. "Stoney. Girl what are you doing?"

"I had to come give you a hug and a kiss. I won't see you until later on," Stoney stated.

Turning her body to the right, Michelle got out of the car, knowing it was inevitable and she would eventually have to make her presence known in not only Bishop Perry and Kendra's life, but in Marcus and Gracie's life.

"I love you, Mom. I love you very much." Stoney didn't try to whisper. She wanted to be as real to both of her parents as she possibly could.

"I love you even more, Stoney Alexia." Michelle was proud they'd been able to amend her birth certificate and give Stoney the name she'd picked for her all those years ago.

With dual kisses to seal their love until later on, Stoney turned and walked back to her dad's and Kendra's arms. Michelle stood in place. Stoney disappeared into the house and Michelle fought with herself to lift her eyes from the ground. When she did, she saw Bishop and Kendra standing in the door, arm in arm.

Before she could turn quickly and get into her seat, Michelle looked their way once more and saw the genuine smiles that had crawled onto their lips. Giving the same gesture back, tears formed in Michelle's eyes when she noticed Gracie and Marcus making their way to the door. When all four lifted their hands and waved in her direction, Michelle waved back, feeling as if a white flag presented itself between the two families

Getting back into the truck, Michelle whispered something to herself.

"Huh? What did you say, honey?" Keithe asked as he grabbed for his wife's hand.

"Oh, I said"—she looked in her husband's direction—"God really is the keeper of my soul."

Agreeing with a nod, Keithe said, "Yes, He is, dear. Yes, He truly is."

Readers' Group Guide Questions

1. Why do you think Michelle kept the DNA results from Marcus when her baby was born?
2. Do you feel Marcus should have been more specific in needing the physical evidence when it came to the results?
3. Were you shocked to know that Ky and Marcus became ministers?
4. Do you believe people like Kendra can really change their ways, as she has?
5. Knowing Kendra's background, would it be possible for you to be under her and her husband's ministry?
6. Do you believe someone should have come to Stoney's rescue in her youth?
7. Why did Stoney not want Mercy to know she had already come close to being in her mother's presence?

8. Do you think Stoney should have been up-front with Keithe in the beginning?

9. Did Keithe waste his years on being married to Michelle, who was a repeated cheater?

10. Do you think Kendra will ever be more than cordial to Michelle? Is that possible?

UC HIS GLORY BOOK CLUB!

www.uchisglorybookclub.net

UC His Glory Book Club is the spirit-inspired brainchild of Joylynn Jossel, Author and Acquisitions Editor of Urban Christian, and Kendra Norman-Bellamy, Author for Urban Christian. This is an online book club that hosts authors of Urban Christian. We welcome as members all men and women who have a passion for reading Christian-based fiction.

UC His Glory Book Club pledges our commitment to provide support, positive feedback, encouragement, and a forum whereby members can openly discuss and review the literary works of Urban Christian authors.

There is no membership fee associated with UC His Glory Book Club; however, we do ask that you support the authors through purchasing, encouraging, providing book reviews, and of course, your prayers. We also ask that you respect our beliefs and follow the guidelines of the book club. We hope to receive your valuable input, opinions, and reviews that build up, rather than tear down our authors.

What We Believe:

—We believe that Jesus is the Christ, Son of the Living God.

—We believe the Bible is the true, living Word of God.

—We believe all Urban Christian authors should use their God-given writing abilities to honor God and share the message of the written word God has given to each of them uniquely.

—We believe in supporting Urban Christian authors in their literary endeavors by reading, purchasing and sharing their titles with our online community.

—We believe that in everything we do in our literary arena should be done in a manner that will lead to God being glorified and honored.

We look forward to the online fellowship with you.

Please visit us often at:
www.uchisglorybookclub.net.

Many Blessing to You!

Shelia E. Lipsey,
President, UC His Glory Book Club

ORDER FORM
URBAN BOOKS, LLC
97 N18th Street
Wyandanch, NY 11798

Name (please print):_____

Address:_____

City/State:_____

Zip:_____

QTY	TITLES	PRICE
	Battle of Jericho	$14.95
	Be Careful What You Pray For	$14.95
	Beautiful Ugly	$14.95
	Been There Prayed That:	$14.95
	Before Redemption	$14.95
	By the Grace of God	$14.95

Shipping and handling: add $3.50 for 1st book, then $1.75 for each additional book.
Please send a check payable to:
Urban Books, LLC
Please allow 4-6 weeks for delivery

ORDER FORM
URBAN BOOKS, LLC
97 N18th Street
Wyandanch, NY 11798

Name (please print):_____

Address:_____

City/State:_____

Zip:_____

QTY	TITLES	PRICE
	3:57 A.M Timing Is Everything	$14.95
	A Man's Worth	$14.95
	A Woman's Worth	$14.95
	Abundant Rain	$14.95
	After The Feeling	$14.95
	Amaryllis	$14.95
	An Inconvenient Friend	$14.95

Shipping and handling: add $3.50 for 1st book, then $1.75 for each additional book.

Please send a check payable to:

Urban Books, LLC

Please allow 4-6 weeks for delivery